A SCALLOP SHORES NOVEL

Trapped *in* Tourist Town

JENNIFER DeCuir

author of *Wynter's Journey* and *Five of Hearts*

CRIMSON ROMANCE

F+W Media, Inc.

Published by
Crimson Romance
an imprint of F+W Media, Inc.
10151 Carver Road, Suite 200
Blue Ash, OH 45242. U.S.A.
www.crimsonromance.com

ISBN 10: 1-4405-8867-8
ISBN 13: 978-1-4405-8867-9
eISBN 10: 1-4405-8868-6
eISBN 13: 978-1-4405-8868-6

Cover art © iStockphoto.com/Squaredpixels and 123RF/Chee-Onn Leong

This book is dedicated to the town and residents of York, Maine. Growing up in such a beautiful backdrop has given me a wealth of cherished memories. Scallop Shores is my way of remaining a part of my hometown. I hope I have done it justice.

Acknowledgments

My sincere thanks to Ginger St. Clair for her amazing photos taken around York and various other areas in Maine and New Hampshire.

Thank you to Lauren at Crimson Romance, who offered some terrific suggestions to improve this book, and I only hope I did them justice.

I really want to thank my readers. You have an incredible amount of choices in reading material and I am humbled that you chose one of my books. Extra thanks to those of you who have taken the time, or will take the time to leave a review on Amazon or Barnes & Noble. You really have no idea how valuable that is to an author.

Chapter 1

"I'll tell ya what's worse than them stupid geese dressed up in people clothes—" Old Man Feeney jabbed a gnarled finger in the air, waggling it around for effect. "Those plywood cutouts Margie Nixon stuck in her yard of the ladies bent over showing off their bloomers. Downright scandalous!"

Gritting her teeth and glancing around the bakery, Cady did a quick inventory to make sure her customers didn't need an immediate refill of their coffee. She reached under the counter and withdrew an empty jar, setting it on the Formica with a thunk. That garnered a couple of bored looks from several of her elderly customers but they quickly went back to their discussion.

She rummaged through a basket under the cash register and came up with a marker and some Scotch tape. Smiling, she neatly wrote: Cady's NY Dream Fund. Taping the label to the jar, she slid the container toward her regulars sitting at the counter. "There you go, boys. Tip jar. Fill 'er up." She winked at Old Man Feeney.

"Ayuh. Good luck with that, Little Miss Fancy-Britches. I think all your tippers are already in New York City." Feeney and his cronies chortled.

Cady blew out a sigh and rolled her eyes. They were probably right. The people of Scallop Shores were stuck in their ways. They were stubborn. They didn't like change. They didn't do fancy. They cringed at exciting.

She'd been trying to get the morning regulars at Logan's Bakery to try something besides regular drip coffee for almost a year. Mr. Logan had refused to approve the expense of a new espresso machine so she'd gone out and bought one with her own money. Needless to say, it had not been the wisest investment.

Earl Duffy tossed back the last of his caffeine and held the ceramic mug out for more. Like an assembly line, empty coffee mugs were pushed out toward her side of the counter. Dutifully, Cady filled them all and then headed for the display case of pastries. They'd be asking for their second helping of morning sugar now.

"Cady, be a doll and get me another bear claw?"

"I could do with another cheese Danish while you're at it."

Down the line she went, refilling coffee and topping off bellies. It was the same thing every day. Nothing ever changed in this town. So dull. So predictable. Crouching, Cady opened a new box of sweetener packets so she could refill the containers on the counter. The tinkling of the bell over the door signaled a new customer. Deciding to have a little fun with her theory that the town was indeed predictable, Cady called out from her spot on the floor to the woman who came in at this time every morning.

"Good morning, Gladys. Be right with you. How's that hip this morning? I made your favorite today, raisin bran muffins."

The long pause was enough to wipe the smug smile from her face. The snickers from the old men lining the counter had her cringing. Then the deliciously deep voice that told her "I love raisin bran muffins" made Cady want to sink beneath the surface of the old cracked linoleum. Her cheeks hot with embarrassment, she rose on shaky legs and faced her unexpected customer.

"I'm so sorry. I thought you were someone else."

"Clearly."

Once she got a good look at the source of her mortification, she decided it had been well worth it. This man had *city* written all over him. In a room full of flannel and denim, his gray slacks, wool blazer, and perfectly crisp white shirt were a welcome sight. His neatly clipped dark hair and baby-smooth cheeks were a direct contrast to all the buzzards turned to him, their own visages long due for a trim and a shave.

"What can I get you?" Cady asked breathlessly.

"I'd like a soy latte—and one of those raisin bran muffins." He winked. Her heart skipped a beat.

"Look at that, would ya, boys? Someone who's willing to try one of my fancy coffee drinks." Cady smirked at the men who made no effort to hide their curious stares.

"Enjoy it while you can. Who knows when you'll make another?" said one of the regulars.

"Actually," the stranger interrupted, "if it's good, I'll order one every day." He spoke to the men at the counter but kept his eyes on Cady. Mesmerizing green eyes.

Shaking her head to get herself back on task, Cady rushed to fill his order. Her fingers lightly caressed the espresso machine as she poured, packed, and pushed buttons. Working this fancy coffeemaker, inhaling the heady scent of the beans, and listening to the loud whirs and chuffs as it transformed raw ingredients into a delicious hot treat made her happier than she thought possible. Would it kill the rest of the town to give something different a try? Just once in a while?

Her hand trembled slightly as she set the paper cup on the counter. She shook open a tiny paper bag, snagged a muffin out of the case with a pair of plastic tongs, and slipped it into the bag. Folding the top over, she handed it to the gentleman. He reached out, covering Cady's fingers with his own. Truth be told, she'd been expecting the touch, but not the jolt that traveled all the way up to tickle her behind the ears. He held her gaze even after he released her hand. Flustered, she broke eye contact.

"Cady's NY Dream Fund," he read aloud, gesturing toward the pathetically empty tip jar.

She nodded, irritated with the way her body was reacting as she felt her cheeks signaling a second blush-fest. *Stop acting like a ninny. He's just a man.* A gorgeous man who looked like he'd just stepped from the pages of a fashion magazine—or straight out of her fantasies.

Cady's eyes widened as he stuffed the change she'd handed him into the tip jar. He'd just bought a twenty-dollar muffin and latte! A smile crinkling the corners of his eyes, he gave her another wink and turned to go.

"Gentlemen." He called the farewell over his shoulder, the bell tinkling overhead once more.

"Them tourists sure are getting here earlier and earlier every year." Old Man Feeney slowly shook his head.

"No." Cady narrowed her eyes and tapped her finger to her lips, her gaze focused outside on the man stepping into his fancy foreign car. "This one's not a tourist. I'm not sure what his story is, but I'll find out."

• • •

The computerized voice belonging to his GPS chirped that he had arrived at his destination. Burke frowned. He wasn't a "roughing it" kind of guy. Yeah, he wrote for one of the country's leading travel magazines, but he left the sleeping-on-the-ground, no-indoor-plumbing assignments to the more adventurous writers. Give him a five-star hotel any day.

He'd been picturing a cheerfully painted little bungalow. A cute white picket fence surrounding the property. Bright contrasting shutters at the windows and immaculate landscaping. And a shoreline. Or the hint of a shoreline. Where the hell was the Atlantic Ocean?

Slumping down in his seat, Burke made no attempt to leave the comfort of his Lexus GS. He took a sip of the latte cooling in the console. So far it was the only thing the small town of Scallop Shores had working in its favor—a decent soy latte. Okay, that wasn't fair. His mind wandered to the perky townie behind the counter.

It was hard to judge her age, given that her honey-blond hair had been pulled up in a high ponytail. She wore no makeup, which had made her rosy pink blushes even more evident. A slow smile spread across Burke's face. He'd enjoyed putting that blush on her cheeks. The barista, bakery worker, whatever her title, was nothing like the women who normally caught his eye. But he doubted he was going to find sophisticated, polished women who spent hours at the salon in Scallop Shores. So, when in Rome—

Snatching up the white paper bag from Logan's, Burke pushed open the door and unfurled himself from the car. A sickening squelch had him squeezing his eyes shut and muttering a few curses. Not a paved driveway, or even a gravel one. No, his cottage-by-the-sea came with a mud driveway. Charming. Well, he could kiss his leather loafers goodbye.

The magazine was putting him up for the summer. Financially speaking, it wasn't cost effective for him to stay in a fancy hotel for months on end. If there were even such a thing as a fancy hotel in Scallop Shores. He said he'd make do with one of the numerous B&Bs. His editor told him he'd take the cottage and be grateful. Oh, the glamorous life of a travel writer.

Leaving his bags in the trunk for the time being, Burke stepped away from the Lexus and turned in a slow circle. Taking a deep breath, he filled his lungs with clean, fresh air. Pine mixed with the salty tang of the sea. It seemed an odd combination but it worked. It was so quiet out here. Surely that would change, once tourist season was in full swing. But for now, if he listened closely, he could almost hear the trees whispering for him to slow down, take it easy. He shook his head, wondering where this fancifulness came from.

He'd come to Scallop Shores as a favor to his editor. His assignments normally focused on the more metropolitan areas of the world. Meredith had promised he could go anywhere his heart desired if he'd spend tourist season in this little dot on the map she'd discovered a few years back, and had finally convinced the magazine to do a series on. Much as he adored the woman, he'd been fully prepared to hate the town.

There was one street light that he'd counted. Not a single Starbucks, Barnes & Noble, McDonalds, or any other sign of civilization. He knew that going in, having read that the town was zoned as a historical landmark and would not allow any chains to build inside city limits. The reality of it was no less of a shock to his system. If it were possible to go into withdrawal over these modern conveniences, Burke was sure he was experiencing it.

Fumbling for the key that he'd picked up from the realtor in the town-proper, he headed for the weathered front door. He paused to scrape the mud from his shoes before entering the cottage. He'd been expecting a musty, closed-in smell, so he was pleasantly relieved to see the windows cracked open and crisp curtains rippling in the slight breeze. He detected a whiff of lemon—furniture polish, perhaps.

The front door opened directly into the kitchen with a hallway to the right that led to the rest of the house. Burke's tour was over quickly, as there were only three other rooms to explore. The living room was on the other side of the hall. A quick glance out the large bay window revealed tall pines obscuring his view of his neighbor. He shrugged. This was probably a good thing.

One bedroom and a small bathroom were at the back of the cottage. Burke peered into the bedroom, ready to find fault with the tiny room. He arched a brow, nodding his approval at the sight awaiting him from this vantage point. Now, there was the ocean. Sure, it was farther away than he would have liked, but he imagined sunrises and sunsets were spectacular. There was no writing desk in the bedroom and he began to mentally calculate whether or not the beat-up table in the kitchen would fit down the hall and through the narrow doorway. This was where he wanted to write.

And as it did, more often than not of late, thinking of writing brought that niggling sensation of dissatisfaction. Burke wanted to write. He loved putting his thoughts on paper. But travel writing? Working for the magazine? It wasn't his passion. He wanted to write novels.

Not just any old novels, but horror novels. Grinning at the irony, Burke wondered if Maine was big enough for two horror authors. Hopefully his schedule would allow for a weekend sojourn to Bangor to visit the home of master storyteller Stephen King. The man was a legend. Burke would make the time.

Sparing one more glance at the inspirational view of the Atlantic, Burke headed back outside to get his things. It wasn't the Ritz-Carlton, but this was his home for the next few months. Recalling that at least one writer on the magazine's payroll would be sleeping on the cold, hard ground tonight put his own situation in perspective. Provided he could get a latte every morning, and a little time with Blondie Ponytail, it might not be so bad.

Chapter 2

"There's no way your piece of junk is going to pass inspection," Chase called from under the hood of Cady's ancient Honda Civic.

"Oh, it's going to pass. It *has* to pass. That's my only transportation."

Cady bit her lip and frowned at the expression on her brother's face when he finally reemerged. He was giving it to her straight. If Chase couldn't fix it, she was done for. She'd always been lucky enough that her father or brother was around to fix minor car needs. The less she had to fork out on car expenses, the more she could squirrel away for New York.

"My diagnosis? Junk it. Get a used car. You must have enough in savings by now to buy one outright."

"You know damned well that I can't touch that savings. It's my ticket out of here." Cady switched strategies, batting her lashes and favoring her big brother with a pleading smile. "Unless, you could *help* it pass inspection?"

"Whoa! I'm going to pretend you didn't just suggest that. You know it's a criminal offense to bribe an officer of the law?"

"Hey, I wasn't bribing you. That would involve money. And we've already established that I intend to hang on to every penny." She tried for a humbling tone. "I'm just saying it would be awfully nice of you to help out your baby sister in her time of need."

"Well, why didn't you say so? I'd be happy to take you down to the lot and help you pick out a dependable used car. I'll wear my uniform. No one will dare give you the runaround."

"Oh, you ..." Cady glared at her brother and stormed off before she said something she'd regret or hurt him—or both.

Her family was kind. She knew without a doubt that they loved her, could see it in everything they said and did. They were indulgent of her plan to move to the city. They knew it was something she'd wanted for a long time. But they didn't actually believe it would happen. Perhaps they didn't want it to happen. She chose to think it was because they loved her so much that they didn't want to lose her. So she was used to chasing this dream on her own.

Still, a little support now and then would go a long way. All she needed was a working car for a few more months, just something to get her around while she saved up a little more cash. She was so close. Then once she got to the city she could sell it. She wouldn't need a car there. But Chase wouldn't help her out. And by not helping, he was holding her back.

Cady barreled angrily through the door, stomping into the kitchen. Her expression softened when she spied Amanda, her best friend and now sister-in-law, seated at the table, a laundry basket in front of her. The very pregnant young woman was folding baby clothes. The little wisps of fabric were so tiny, so precious. Cady's sigh was weary as she slumped into a chair across from Amanda. She plucked a miniscule sock from the basket and held it in the palm of her hand.

"Bad news about the car?"

"Bad news about my life." She slid the sock across to Amanda, who held its twin. "You realize this ruins everything. I need every penny I have in savings. I can't afford a new car—not now, when I'm so close."

"It's just a setback, sweetie. You'll do this."

"Yeah, well if *your* husband could just pull some strings ..."

Amanda laughed outright at this.

"You two are so alike. When Chase is angry or annoyed with you, it's always '*your* best friend', never 'my sister.'" She fixed Cady with a sobering look. "You know you can't ask him to use his position like that. He takes his job on the force very seriously."

"Tell me about it. Do you remember when he was just a summer rent-a-cop and he slapped us with citations for jaywalking? I tried to get Mom to talk him out of it, but she insisted he was just doing his job. She always took his side." Cady knew she sounded petulant but she didn't care.

"It hurts him, you know ... that you want to leave town so badly. He takes it a little personally." Amanda pushed the laundry basket aside and leaned closer to her childhood pal.

"Would it be so awful to stay in Scallop Shores? What are you looking for that you can't find here?" She covered Cady's hand with her own. "We used to talk about living next door to each other, raising our kids together." As one they turned to focus their gazes on Amanda's swollen belly.

"I've explained this before, Amanda. What I need ... it just isn't here. I want to have adventures. I want to experience culture. I want to live!" She squeezed her shoulder blades together and tried again.

"It's not like I'm going to fall off the map. I'll be back for holidays, birthdays—any time you need me. I'm just a few hours away. Call me and I'll come home."

Cady stood up, rounding the table to kneel in front of Amanda. She wrapped her friend in a warm hug, then sat back on her haunches, a sad smile on her face.

"I know it's hard for you to understand. You've always loved it here. It's enough for you. I get that. Try to put yourself in my shoes for just a moment. There is so much world out there that we'll never experience just living our lives in Scallop Shores." She stood up and began to pace.

"No one ever does anything exciting or out of the ordinary here. Everyone has routines. Lives are patterned after the generation before, and the one before that. That's great for some people, but not for me."

"But if you fell in love? That could change your outlook, right?" Hope shined in Amanda's eyes.

"You were lucky. You've got a good guy there. I know he drives me up the wall sometimes, but Chase is a really decent person. You'll be very happy here. I want that for you. It makes me happy."

Cady had been circling the kitchen island. Now she hopped onto the countertop, drawing her legs beneath her.

"At this point in my life, it's too hard to imagine falling for a man who I'd give up everything to be with. No way. I need to get out of Scallop Shores, see what I'm missing. There is so much I want to experience before I even think about settling down."

"Promise me you won't get so caught up in your new life that you forget us?"

"Bite your tongue, sister dear. That would never happen."

•••

A twangy guitar riff coming from her ear buds muted the screeching of the seagulls and the crash of the surf to her right. Cady's sneakers pounded the packed surface of the beach as she felt the slow burn building in her muscles. At nearly six o'clock in the morning, she had this stretch of sand to herself. She did her best thinking out here.

She'd miss her morning runs along the beach. Regret tried to worm its way past the euphoria of her runner's high and Cady banished it by pushing her body to new limits. She would be sore later, but it would be worth it.

The short drive to the shore had only reinforced what Chase had told her the day before. Lucille, the old Civic she'd bought the summer she'd graduated high school, was dying. Cranking the car stereo up to mask its worrisome noises was not going to make them go away. She was putting off the inevitable, and it was to her own benefit to look for a replacement now, while she had the chance to negotiate for a lower asking price. Used-car salesmen could smell desperation on a person and that could take even more of her precious savings away.

She needed money. That tip jar at the bakery wasn't going to bring in the kind of cash that would help her move to the city. No, she needed a second job. Tourist season was just gearing up and there would be no shortage of jobs around the beach areas. The waterfront hotels would be looking for chambermaids, restaurants needed dishwashers and wait staff, and all the little souvenir shops would hire on cashiers.

This was her last summer in Scallop Shores. Surely she could come up with something more exciting than cleaning out hotel rooms, waiting tables, or putting out the latest stock of T-shirts with the state of Maine or a cartoon lobster printed on them. *Think, Cady, think.* What could she do to earn the extra money she'd need to get settled in the city?

Her feet slapped rhythmically as she quickly covered the one and a half miles of waterfront that made up Long Beach. She briefly considered taking her run up to the lighthouse, but she knew she wouldn't make it back to open Logan's in time.

Thank goodness she lived right above the bakery. The cranberry scones she made before her run would be cool enough to carry downstairs after a quick shower. It always amused her that at seven o'clock on the dot, Cady would find a cluster of regulars with their noses pressed to the glass door. If she were even a minute late, she'd hear about it.

Nearing the end of the beach, she pivoted on a heel and began to head the other way, back toward her car. A tiny figure in the distance showed her she no longer had the shoreline to herself. Concentrating on the summer cottages that dotted the opposite side of the road, she forgot the person until he was nearly on top of her.

It was City Guy! And damned if he didn't look just as good in old sweats and a Yankees tee as he did in the fancy duds she'd seen him in before. Maybe better. He slowed his pace as he approached her, stretching his arms over his head and pulling the fabric of his shirt tight across his well-toned pecs. Yeah, definitely better.

"Wearing a Yankees tee in Red Sox country could be dangerous to your health. You ought to be more careful." Cady trotted to a stop, drawing her knees up to her chest a few times to stretch them out.

"Yeah? Who's gonna jump me? You?" His challenge thrown down, he grinned like the devil.

Cady smirked as she pulled the ear buds from her ears and continued to walk to her car. Not bad.

"Yankees tee, metrosexual … everything else. You're from New York, I take it? What brings you to Scallop Shores …" She waited for him to supply his name as he raced to catch up with her.

"Burke. I'm Burke Sanders. I guess you could say I'm here to give your town its fifteen minutes of fame. Or try to make a smaller tourist destination a bigger deal. Anyway, I write for a travel magazine. And yeah, I'm from the Big Apple—born and raised."

The thrill that passed through her upon learning he was indeed from the city, she'd explore later. But for now a giggle bubbled up too quickly to be stopped and Cady let out a chortle. She gestured toward a large, flat boulder near her car and made her way over the smaller loose stones to get to it. This one she had to sit down for.

"You lose a bet?"

"Excuse me?"

"Someone else get the cushier assignment? Are you being punished? What did you do to get saddled with Scallop Shores?" She sat down, drawing her legs up and patting the rock to invite Burke to sit beside her.

"I didn't do anything wrong. I just ... wow." He shook his head. "You want out of Dodge in a bad way. I'm thinking yours is the better story here." He took a long sip from a plastic water bottle and then held it out.

The idea of drinking from his bottle suddenly seemed wildly intimate, wholly inappropriate. Her mouth got drier at the thought and she grabbed for the container before she lost her nerve. The spout was still warm from the touch of his lips. She couldn't resist darting her tongue out to search for just a little taste of him.

"My name is Cady Eaton. My family stepped off the Mayflower and kept wandering until they made it to Scallop Shores. And that is where they have stayed ... ever since." She returned the water to Burke and focused her attention on the waves rolling toward them.

"So you'll be the first Eaton to leave town for the big city?"

"No, actually. My great-aunt Cadence spent a summer there once. I've grown up on her stories of nannying for a rich family in Central Park West."

"So why didn't she stay?" He cocked his head toward her.

"I've been wondering the same thing. From what I understand, she left the love of her life to come back here."

"Because she loved her family more?"

"Because that was what was expected of her." Cady knew he was watching her, but she stared at the horizon, her jaw set.

They passed the next few moments in silence. The less said, the better. She couldn't believe she'd gone and blurted out family business to a complete stranger. He must think she was a real nutcase. Risking a quick glance, she chanced a sidelong look from beneath her lashes. Burke was studying the rolling surf.

"Yours is a unique angle," he finally spoke.

"Excuse me?"

"I'm sorry, it's just that I need to research the town, but the whole tourist trade thing has been done so many times before."

He turned to Cady, his steady emerald gaze rooting her to the spot.

"You've lived here all your life and you can't wait to see it in your rearview mirror. How would you sell Scallop Shores? What will you miss most when you're gone? What memories of this town will haunt you the most?"

Cady blinked. She had an idea. She clapped her hands and barely kept from squealing in her excitement.

"You should hire me!"

"I beg your pardon? I'm a travel writer. It's a one person job."

"I'll be your research assistant, your tour guide. I can give you all sorts of unique angles." She nearly shuddered at the heat that shot out at her from Burke's intense gaze. *Whoa, poor choice of words.* "I can even type up your notes, take pictures, whatever you need."

"I don't think it's in the budget to hire on an assistant, much as I would enjoy it." His grin was wolfish.

"Please. I need the money. You saw that pathetic tip jar. And my car is about to give up the ghost. I'm never going to get to New York unless I find another source of income."

She knew she was begging but she no longer cared. Burke was her ticket out of Scallop Shores and she would convince him that he needed her as much as she needed him.

"So then we'd have a working relationship?" He sounded disappointed.

"For now ..." Cady shocked herself with that coquettish response.

"I'm probably going to regret this, but what the hell? You're hired." He held out a hand and they shook on it. She had to tug to remove her hand after the shake went on just a tad long.

It looked like she wouldn't have to worry that her last summer in Scallop Shores would be boring. Things just got really interesting.

Chapter 3

Burke smiled and nodded at a young mother on his way to Logan's Bakery. Intent on his daily dose of caffeine, and perhaps a fresh round of blushes from the adorable Cady, he explored the few square blocks that made up downtown Scallop Shores.

He knew he shouldn't be flirting but that woman brought out the devil in him. The attraction was mutual, of that he was certain. And now he'd agreed to work with her? He'd be lucky if he could pull together one article for the magazine before the summer was up, let alone a whole series. What had he been thinking?

He couldn't help the grin that crept onto his features. Ever since he'd met the woman, he'd been looking for a way to get to know her. When she suggested a working relationship, it was perfect. And more importantly, she thought she'd come up with it all on her own. Burke chuckled to himself.

"Good morning. Beautiful day, isn't it?" An older couple passed him on the street, the man calling out in a gravelly voice as he tipped his ball cap.

Folks sure were friendly around here. That part wasn't so bad. But the nosy bit? Good grief! He hadn't watched nearly enough episodes of *The Andy Griffith Show*, whatever the heck that old '50s black-and-white show had been. He just hoped when he started asking around about their town, that the residents wouldn't balk at the way their roles had reversed.

He'd been stunned when the cashier at the grocery store asked how he liked the cottage out on Pebble Way. He'd asked the kid how he knew where he was staying. His answer had been a convoluted list of names that he understood to be a mix of relatives and acquaintances and how so-and-so worked for such-and-such. It had made his head spin.

Burke strolled down the sidewalk, browsing in shop windows as he got the lay of the land. He'd expected to bore quickly. Discontent would have him pining for the noise and bustle of the city. The crowded skyscrapers closed him in, made him feel safe. So all this wide-open space should be throwing him into a panic. Only it wasn't.

Ever since he'd stepped foot in Scallop Shores, things had been different. Burke never found himself distracted by a woman while on assignment before. He wasn't a monk. A casual fling sure beat spending an evening alone. But to find himself repeatedly thinking of one woman? And taking a vested interest in her goal to leave town? That just wasn't like him.

Burke pulled up short when he discovered the town had a bookstore. Praise God, Glory Halleluiah, and all that crap. He hurried inside and stopped to fill his lungs with the rich scent of paper and ink. Books. Walking into a bookstore was like being wrapped in a mother's arms. Warm and comfortable and you just wanted to stay there all day. Snorting, he realized that wasn't the best analogy when applying it to himself. His own mother didn't have a maternal bone in her body and he couldn't recall her ever having hugged him. Walking into a lover's arms. There, that was better.

A woman, about his age, with fiery orange hair, sat on the floor with a wiggly tot. "Hey, you must be Burke. Welcome to the Book Nook." That old *Cheers* theme song floated into his brain. *Where everybody knows your name.* He nodded, trying to keep his discomfiture from showing on his face. The speed with which small town news traveled was still creepy, but he was starting to get used to it.

She smiled and turned her attention back to the baby, who had started to lift her tummy off the floor. "This one's gonna be an early crawler. You mark my words. I'm Wynter…with a Y, by the way. Let me know if I can help you find anything." She grinned at him as she tickled the chubby babe.

Burke left the two of them alone for some cuddle time and began to explore the aisles. He studied a rack of new paperbacks, and not finding anything that appealed, he ventured deeper. For a small town, they had a sizeable horror section. This would do nicely. He scanned the backs of several books, reshelving some and hanging on to his two favorites. Then thinking about the fact that Scallop Shores had very little in the way of nightlife, he grabbed two more.

He brought them up to the counter, started to reach for the card he used for charging expenses, and had to switch it for his personal credit card. He could spin a creative expense need out of just about any receipt, but the magazine's accounting department would not buy "paperback novels" as a writing expense. Nope, this was on him.

Speaking of which, he hadn't been lying when he told Cady that he couldn't pay for an assistant. He'd turned down the assistant Meredith offered him while writing that piece in Tokyo. So asking for one in a town the size of Scallop Shores would just look ridiculous. If he paid Cady out of his own pocket, he didn't have to admit to anyone but himself that he was doing it just to spend time with her.

Anxious to get to the bakery, Burke tried to convince himself it was because he was desperate for a caffeine fix. And he was hungry. Starving. Yeah, that was it. He passed a couple of more storefronts, spying his own reflection in one window and nearly groaning at the freaking toothpaste ad that smiled back at him.

He was only in Scallop Shores as a favor to his editor. He'd already made up his mind that the boredom would probably kill him. He was supposed to be missing the city life. He should have been thinking about the next assignment. Quick! Think. Where should he go next? Paris?

Would the sidewalk cafes and boutiques have planters there that looked as charming as these half whiskey barrels full of flowers that he was passing? Gah! He was a guy, a man's man. He shouldn't be thinking of flowers or sidewalk cafes or especially the city of love. Argh! Where did that come from? No love! There was no love. There would never be love in Scallop Shores.

By now he was muttering to himself, eyes to the ground, ignoring the people who spoke to him as though he'd lived here all his life. Everyone was so welcoming. The sense of community was infectious. It made him think things he had no business thinking. Home and family. Little League and white picket fences. It was awful—horrifying.

Where was he? Burke looked up and found that he'd run out of sidewalk. Well, technically it continued on the other side of the street, once he passed the Civil War monument. He was just surprised that he'd walked so far past the bakery and hadn't realized it. Shaking the cobwebs from his brain, he turned on his heel and headed back the way he'd come.

Forget his next assignment. He ought to be focusing on a vacation. Seeing as he couldn't remember the last time he'd traveled for pleasure, he was overdue. Though to be honest, all-inclusive island resorts and European cities steeped in culture and history held less and less appeal for him. Burke's footsteps slowed. He kicked a pebble out into the empty street.

His idea of a luxury vacation now? Uninterrupted time at his laptop. Holed up in a cabin in the woods. Unbidden, his little rental cottage came to mind, that picture-perfect view of the ocean staring at him from that one tiny square window. Finally turning years' worth of jotted ideas into a real novel.

Good God, he needed his coffee now! He was starting to hallucinate. Envisioning some fanciful dream world. Rolling his eyes, he half expected the people around him to start breaking into song, birds alighting on his finger. Stupid Scallop Shores! Cady had it right. Best to get out while he could.

•••

"Hey, if it ain't Gladys." Old Man Feeney slapped the counter at his own joke.

Cady tried to pretend she wasn't paying attention, as she took someone's order in the corner.

"How's it going? It's Burke, by the way. Nice to meet you." Bold move. She watched him walk up to the old man and stick his hand out. Clearly shocked, Feeney returned the handshake out of habit, too stunned to come up with a smart-alecky reply.

Burke's eyes swept the tiny space behind the counter and she was pleased to notice he must have been looking for her. Enjoying the fact that she had the element of surprise, she stepped up behind him and tapped his shoulder.

"Boo." She grinned.

"I'm ready to order," was his curt reply.

Ouch. Ego bruised, Cady shrugged and slipped between the glass pastry case and the counter. Maybe she had read him wrong and the spark she'd sensed was completely one-sided. She'd be lying if she didn't admit to being disappointed. It could have been a very interesting summer. But since that's all it would have been, this was just as well. She mustered a smile.

"Soy latte?"

"With an extra shot. Two pumps of hazelnut. Sugar-free, if you've got it."

Cady nodded, her humor restored as she realized her peanut gallery was following their conversation. Following and not understanding a word, from the looks on their dumbfounded faces. She waggled her fingers at the men, scrunching her nose up and shooting them a smirk.

Mr. Cranky Pants wandered off to wait for his drink. He definitely wasn't in the mood to chat. Too bad. They hadn't firmed up their working relationship. She'd thought up some ideas for his magazine series and wanted to run them by him. Pouring Burke's latte into a large stoneware mug, she carried it to an empty table and waved him over.

"Where's my to-go cup?" He scowled.

"Oh, relax. It won't kill you to spend a little time with other human beings for a change." She shrugged an apology when it appeared she'd struck a nerve. "I know. I'm pulling you out of your comfort zone. Get used to it. It's what I do."

Grumbling, he yanked out a chair and sat down. Fixing her with an *"Are you happy?"* look he picked up the mug with two hands and took a long sip. If there was such a thing as a mood meter that could be read on a person's face, Cady saw the dial on Burke's change from angry red to a serene blue with just that one sip.

Satisfied that he wasn't going to bolt the second her back was turned, she grabbed the pot of plain ol' Joe and topped off the old men who had temporarily gone back to their own business. Heating up a cinnamon bun, she slipped it on a plate, grabbed herself a diet soda, and carried both to Burke's table.

"What's this?"

"Sometimes when people are cranky it's because they have low blood sugar." She leveled him with a look. Ignoring the fork she'd placed in front of him, he snatched up the sticky bun and took a giant bite.

"Better?"

"Much."

She popped the top on her can and took a few swallows before noticing his peculiar stare.

"What?" She swiped a hand across the back of her mouth. Did she have something on her face?

"You run a bakery with a fancy-ass espresso machine and regular drip coffee up the wazoo. Why the hell would you drink soda?"

"Truth?" Cady's expression was sheepish. "I hate coffee. Well, that's not true. I love the smell of it. I love brewing it and making my espresso drinks. But I have never acquired a taste for coffee. Uck!" She shuddered.

Laughter bubbled up from somewhere deep inside the man, genuine amusement. No matter that it was directed *at* her. The sound made her feel good. "That's the most ridiculous thing I've ever heard."

She shrugged. "All the more for everyone else."

Burke set his half-eaten pastry back on the plate. Cady swiped a finger through the icing and brought it to her lips. Her eyes widened at the strangled sound coming from his throat. He was staring at the finger in her mouth. He looked—hungry. She swallowed hard, suddenly finding it hard to breathe.

Time for a little redirection.

"I've been trying to come up with some outside-the-box ideas for your articles."

"No, this isn't going to work. I need to do this assignment on my own if I have any hope of getting it turned in on time." Burke pushed his plate to the center of the table, all the while shaking his head vigorously back and forth. His lips were set in a hard line.

Panicked, she reached for his hand across the table and squeezed. The quiet murmuring that had been friendly conversation just moments before was now deathly silent. Apparently theirs wasn't to be a private conversation, as the entire bakery strained to listen in. Closing her eyes, Cady pushed her temper down before she completely lost it. Taking a deep breath, she caught Burke's eye and spoke softly.

"You see why I need to get out of this town?" She raised her voice. "In the city, people mind their own business!"

She stood up, sweeping her arms out in front of her.

"Okay, gentlemen, it's time to start your days. Get a life. Find somewhere else to perch."

"Aw, but the soaps are on." Earl Duffy whined.

"And this is one of my favorite episodes," added Tony, a retired school bus driver.

"Out." Arching a brow, she sent them all a look that had them scrambling from their stools and shuffling toward the door.

"I'm telling Logan you kicked us out. He's not going to be happy," said Old Man Feeney, the biggest grouch in the bunch.

"You feel the need to tattle that strongly, you go right ahead." Cady hoped to heck he was bluffing. She didn't need any trouble with Mr. Logan when she was so close to having enough money to finally quit this job.

When the last man had left and the jangling of the bell over the door had receded, she turned to find that Burke was still sitting at the table, nursing his latte. He stared into the bottom of the mug, the corners of his mouth pulled down. He certainly was a man of mercurial mood changes. In someone else she might find that annoying. In Burke, she looked at it as a challenge.

"Ah, peace at last." She turned her chair around backwards and straddled it.

"You going to get in trouble?" He still refused to look up.

"Oh, please!" Okay, yeah, probably—but she'd deal with that when it happened.

"I meant it, Cady. I can't do this. I don't mix business and pleasure." Chagrined, he rolled his eyes toward the ceiling. "Jesus, that came out corny, but you know what I mean."

"It doesn't have to get complicated. We stick to business. Look, I've been thinking of some locations we should scout." She tugged a napkin from the dispenser on the table and pulled a stubby pencil from behind her ear. Distract him with facts. Gloss over the attraction kindling between them.

The next half hour was spent kicking around ideas. Cady tried to tamp down the pleasure that came with knowing she'd been able to put another smile on that handsome face. Yeah, they could totally do this.

"Fine. I'll consider a trial run. Meet me later this afternoon, somewhere ... public." He averted his eyes, and she watched his Adam's apple bobbing in his throat.

"How about the library? The children's section is quieter after about four thirty. We won't be disturbed there."

This time he spun his emerald gaze toward her and stared hard.

"What? We'll have a chaperone. Hello? Librarian?" Cady stood up and cleared the table before Burke could come up with an excuse to get out of their meeting.

He headed for the door, then paused.

"Thank you for the cinnamon roll."

"You're welcome."

"You are going to drive me completely insane. You know that, don't you?"

"Probably."

He shook his head slowly before turning away and leaving the bakery. She hurried to the window to admire the view. Burke might not be able to mix business with pleasure, but Cady was all for it.

Chapter 4

Her nose twitched as it always did when Cady entered the bright, antiseptic lobby of Kittredge Manor, Scallop Shores's only nursing home. Today was her day to coordinate activities in the game room. She peered down the long hallway, smiling and waving at the residents, some in wheelchairs and others leaning on walkers. Her great-aunt was not among this group. Cady ventured toward the game room, knowing Auntie liked to spend as little time in her bed as possible. Cady peeked her head around the door frame.

"Cadence Elizabeth Eaton, I hear you are getting up to no good with that new city boy. Hoping this one will sweep you away to his castle overlooking Central Park?" Cady's great-aunt and namesake patted the couch cushion beside her. Cady hurried over, drawing the old woman into a tight hug as she sat down.

If that question had come from anyone else, she would have taken offense. She knew her aunt was joking. The two women often talked about Cady's future. The image of a man coming in to sweep her off her feet was laughable. The whole point of moving to the city was to live on her own. She didn't need a man to rescue her from Scallop Shores. She just needed cash. And no, she reassured herself, Burke was not rescuing her by taking her on as his assistant. He was helping her stick to the timeline she'd set for herself. Yeah, that was it.

"News travels too damned quick around here, Auntie. Who told you? Old Man Feeney?"

"That old geezer? Please!" Aunt Cadence waved away the question as she would a hovering fly. "That pretty young nurse ... What's her name? Tina? Her mother saw you and Romeo down at the beach. Lois, one of the part-time girls at Kayla's Kut and Kurl, filled her in on who he was."

Even though she'd lived in Scallop Shores all her life, it was times like this that could really make Cady's head spin.

"That is just amazing. The poor man isn't in town a full twenty-four hours and there is a surveillance team monitoring his every move. Tell me, Auntie, how's his credit history? Any bounced checks?"

"I can think of a better question to be asking. Like, is he married?"

"Oh my gosh! Is he? What have you heard?"

"Gotcha!" Cady's aunt chortled happily, slapping her knee with a palsied hand. "Well. From the look on your face, this is one young man I want to meet. He seems to have made an impression on you. And as the men in this town have learned, that is one hard thing to do."

"Come off it. It's not as if I care. I was curious, that's all. We're going to be working together and I thought I ought to know a bit more about him."

Cady shrugged off the suggestion that she had a vested interest in Burke's marital status. She went on to explain to her aunt why he was in town. Excitedly, she filled the older woman in on the places she intended to take him. She told her about how the magazine wanted to do a whole series on Scallop Shores.

"It's going to be fun. He said he might even stay until October. He could get a feel for how the tourist season winds down. I can show him how the summer tourists differ from the 'leaf peepers.'" She bounced in place. "Ooh, maybe we could do the Haunted Hayride!"

"Sounds like you've planned out his whole summer—and then some." Cadence arched a bushy white brow.

"I told you. He's paying me. I'll save every bit of it. Then when autumn comes ..." She smiled inwardly.

"You'll ride off into the sunset together."

"No, I was going to say that when autumn comes, I'd move to the city. He may not even be there. He's a travel writer, after all. He could be on to his next assignment by then. Besides, I'll be busy settling in to the city." Didn't mean she couldn't pick his brain while she had this amazing opportunity. Cady looked forward to learning what Burke's life in the city was like.

"You're going to have such an exciting time. Some people might see the hustle and bustle as chaotic, overwhelming, but you will do just fine. I know you've got big plans inside you. I can't wait to see what you do with them."

Big plans. Like running her own coffee shop. There was plenty of time for that. She was only twenty-six, after all. She'd be happy to get a job as a barista and save the monumental dreams for later, when she'd had a few years of city life under her belt, and the confidence and experience that would surely come with it.

Cady threw her arms around her aunt and pulled her close. She closed her eyes and sighed, breathing in the scent of the lilac perfume Auntie always wore.. She loved lilacs and would always associate her favorite flower with her favorite relative. It was said that smells triggered memories and Cady would wholeheartedly agree. The smell of lilacs made her think of baking cookies in Auntie's kitchen when she was just a few years old. Her aunt had been the one to teach her to bake. She had used Auntie's morning glory muffin recipe just that morning. It had been the first flavor to sell out.

"Okay, enough chit-chat. I'm supposed to be winding you all up so you go to bed like good boys and girls tonight."

"No more Bingo! That game's for old farts." An elderly gentleman scowled at Cady from his perch in the corner.

Gerald Potter. She didn't blame him for being cranky. The man's family lived right in town and only made it over to the nursing home on Thanksgiving and Christmas. It was disgusting. Pasting on a bright smile, Cady walked up to him, crouching down so they were eye to eye.

"You any good at Texas Hold 'Em? 'Cause I'd feel just awful if I ended up taking all your money." She winked.

"Raise the stakes, Missy. Strip poker. And I ain't gonna go easy on ya. You'll be in your skivvies in no time."

"Gerald! You mind your tongue, you dirty old man," Cadence hollered from the couch. Cady nearly fell on her butt, she was laughing so hard.

Getting up, she rummaged in the roomy storage closet and took out three card tables, scattering them around the room. Gerald wheeled himself up to the closest table, telling Cady he'd save her a spot next to him. She flashed him a thumbs-up and headed out into the hall to round up some more poker players.

The afternoon passed quickly and Cady had to admit that there were some real card sharps in attendance. Gerald Potter was definitely one of them. He was such a character. She really looked forward to the time she spent volunteering at Kittredge Manor.

"Hey, Cady, you're still here? We could use some help getting everyone down to dinner if you aren't too busy." One of the nurses had bustled in to break up the poker tournament.

Wait a minute! Surely it couldn't be dinnertime already.

"What time is it?"

"Going on five thirty."

Oh, crap! She was an hour late for her meeting with Burke. Way to show what a responsible assistant she could be. Smacking herself on the forehead, she tugged her hair for good measure.

"I love you, Auntie, but I am so late. I'll see you in a few days." She gave the old woman a hug, blew a kiss to Gerald, and hoped she had a prayer of finding Burke still waiting for her at the library.

Her brother, the cop, would have thrown her in jail if he'd caught her speeding through town to get to the library. Throwing open the big glass door, Cady jogged up to the second level to the children's section. She looked around wildly. There was no sign of Burke.

"He's pissed."

Wincing, she turned to face her old friend, the head children's librarian, Bree.

"How long did he wait?" She scuffed toward Bree's desk and sat down on the corner.

"I'm not sure. Maybe an hour?"

"I am *such* a jerk! I was at the nursing home. We were having a poker tournament. I completely lost track of time."

"You and your play dates. Really, Cady, you are such a bad influence on those poor people."

She wanted to laugh but felt too guilty to manage anything more than a chuckle.

"He was so cute, too, sitting over at that little bitty table. His knees were all the way up to his chin."

Cady followed the direction of Bree's finger, visualizing Burke folded into a chair built for a preschooler. If it were possible to feel worse, now she did.

"I'll catch you later, Bree. I need to go bake up a batch of 'I'm-sorry-I'm-such-a-bonehead' brownies. And maybe some cookies."

"A pie wouldn't be a bad idea too." Bree lowered her eyes, a smile lurking at the corners of her mouth.

"A pie too, then." She started to compile a grocery list in her head as she walked to the library exit.

It was going to be a long night.

• • •

His fantastic view of the ocean went unappreciated as Burke glowered into the bottom of his third crappy cup of coffee. He'd been up since dawn. He had hoped to run off his anger on the beach, but coming back to the cottage and standing under the lukewarm shower spray, he found himself snarling under his breath.

It was just a huge reminder that Cady wasn't his type. He shouldn't be counting on a townie for anything. He was here to do a job and as soon as he finished, he'd be off to the next assignment. So what if she'd actually made him feel excited about this series for the first time since it had been handed to him? She hated Scallop Shores. She'd probably just decided there were limits to what she'd do to earn enough money to get to New York City.

Burke brought his coffee mug up to his lips and swore when nothing came out. Now he was angry with Cady, angry with his editor, angry with himself for running out of coffee. The list was getting longer as the morning went on. He shoved the cup aside and went back to constructing notes about possible town landmarks to visit.

He scratched off the last two he'd added, ripping the entire page from the notebook for good measure. Wadding it in a ball, he tossed it toward the garbage can in the corner. It bounced off the rim and landed on the floor. Of course.

A fresh page stared back at him, the promise of something new and exciting. Burke resisted the urge to lean down and take a whiff. Something about a new notebook, new writing supplies of any kind, really. He knew he'd probably been the only kid in school who looked forward to back-to-school shopping. His nanny had always taken him. His own parents couldn't be bothered with the actual raising of their son.

Burke took a cleansing breath and let his mind wander. He had loved Maria like a mother. She was old enough to have been his grandmother, looking back, but Burke hadn't been looking for a grandmother-figure. He'd needed a mom. So it was Maria he had gone to with his first juvenile stories. It was Maria who had encouraged him to write. It was Maria he'd told when he first got the job with the magazine. She'd been so proud but also a tad disappointed.

"I am happy for you, sweetheart, if you are happy. But promise me something. Do not abandon your stories. Keep writing from your heart. Someday, when the time is right, let go of your fear and just write."

He was supposed to be working on his article. His editor would be expecting the first in the series next week. But that empty notebook called out to him, enticing him to write something far more interesting. Something dark and creepy. Burke started to smell damp leaves, to feel a chill wind pass through his bones. It would take place in October. It was dark, the dead of night. The trees were newly bare but that didn't stop them from pressing in on the hero. He was lost. He knew someone or something was watching him, following him.

A loud rapping sounded on the front door. Burke pushed his rickety wooden chair back with a screech. His heart mimicked the knocking on the door, even louder if that were possible. He rubbed at his eyes with the heels of his hands. Blinking hard, he stole a look at the clock on the bedside table. It wasn't even nine a.m. Who bothered their neighbors this early?

Shaking his head to get back into the here and now, Burke plodded down the hall and into the kitchen. This had better be good. He'd been working. Well, he was supposed to have been working. He wrenched open the door harder than was necessary.

"You might want to nuke that latte for a bit. Someone took his time getting to the door." Cady winked.

She handed him a large paper cup and breezed inside, apparently seeing the open door as the only invitation she needed. Heading for the counter, she set down a large basket and immediately began to unload it. Burke threw a gaze heavenward before closing the door and folding his arms across his chest. He tried to ignore the enticing aromas that just compounded, the more items Cady withdrew from the basket.

"So most of these are desserts, because who doesn't love desserts, right?" She tossed the question over her shoulder, seeming to prefer keeping her back to him.

"And what if I told you I was diabetic?" He raised an eyebrow in challenge.

Cady whirled around, her mouth open.

"Are you? Diabetic, that is?"

She looked horrified at the idea her baking could possibly bring harm to someone. Burke felt a twinge of guilt for scaring her.

"No, I'm not diabetic. And I suppose I could be persuaded to take some of this off your hands." He stole up to the counter, spying a plate of brownies and reaching out, only to have his hand slapped. "What the hell?" He snatched it back, glaring at the infuriating woman taking up space in his kitchen.

"Those are for later. You can't eat brownies at nine o'clock in the morning."

"Hey, if it's late enough for social calls, it's late enough to eat chocolate." He tried again, only to be thwarted when she threw herself in front of him.

"You can eat all the brownies you want once I'm gone. But for now I have raisin bran muffins. You did say those were your favorite. I hope, for both our sakes, that you weren't just being nice."

"So if I eat one of your raisin bran muffins, you'll leave?" He regretted the barb the second it sailed off his tongue and hit its target, causing her to wince.

She straightened her back and finished emptying the basket of goodies. There were three different kinds of cookies, brownies, muffins, and, good grief, was that a pie? Cady had been a busy girl!

"I could go looking through your cupboards for plates and silverware, but that would be rude."

"And you certainly wouldn't want to do anything that could be construed as rude."

They stared each other down before Burke finally broke eye contact and went in search of plates and forks. He gave her points for not flinching.

Cady put a muffin on each plate and whipped a couple of paper towels from the roll on the counter. Burke took the opportunity to pop his latte in the microwave for a quick nuke. She picked up the plates and turned in a slow circle, her brow wrinkling in confusion.

"Where is your table? Where do you eat?"

"Oh, I moved it. It's in the bedroom."

And just as she had entered his little rented cottage, Whirlwind Cady blew past him and headed down the hall. She pushed aside his empty coffee cup and the notebook, index cards, and assorted pens. Placing their breakfast on the table, she rubbed her hands together and sighed happily.

"There we go."

The smile on her face faltered as she took in her surroundings. Square footage already at a premium, adding the kitchen table had only made the small room that much more cramped. Burke chose to remain in the doorway, not willing to add to the awkwardness that was slowly building.

As one, they turned their attention to the bed. Single bachelor that he was, neatening up his living space hadn't even occurred to him. The blankets were turned down, the sheets rumpled; it should have looked like a cozy retreat. But with Cady in the room, this seemingly innocent scene pulsed with an erotic charge that was impossible to ignore. She swallowed hard, wiping her palms against the soft faded denim of her jeans. The silence in the room was deafening.

"There's a suspension bridge not too far from the center of town. I thought maybe you could use that for your first article."

"Grab that notebook on the table. I'll get my camera and laptop and meet you outside." Anything to get her out of his bedroom.

He didn't breathe again until she'd brushed past him and he heard the front door close behind her. This was the worst idea in the history of ideas. He should just sleep with her already. The tension was gonna kill him.

Stuffing the supplies he'd need into an old backpack, Burke started to leave the room, doubling back for one of the muffins. Cady was already behind the wheel of an aging Civic. When she started the engine he began to have doubts that they'd even make it out of his driveway. She waved cheerily from the driver's seat, the screech of country twang rivaling the whine in the engine. Burke suspected this was intentional. He wrenched open the passenger side door and prepared to spend time in an enclosed space with a woman who was slowly driving him insane.

During the ensuing car ride, Burke tried to follow Cady's conversational thread. Something about a retirement home, no more Bingo, strip poker, and a lonely man named Gerald. About the only thing he got out of it was that this was her way of explaining why she didn't show for their meeting at the library yesterday. Though honestly, she could have been reciting Latin hymns for all the sense it was making. Wishing for a pair of earplugs, he laid his head back against the seat and closed his eyes. The scent of her perfume grabbed him by the short hairs. He was going to cry, right here in this tiny tin can of a car. Forget the sexual tension. Every damned thing about Cady Eaton was gonna kill him.

Chapter 5

"Again, I am so sorry—"

"It's fine. Just don't ... no more apologies. Please?" Burke shook his head and accepted the glass of beer from the waitress.

Cady lifted her own heavy stein and took a few swallows of the pilsner. The hoppy flavor slid down her parched throat. It was enough to make her smile. Almost. Ending the day at Smitty's bar seemed a fitting choice after the day they'd had. And it had been her own stupid fault, of course. She drew a design in the condensation on her glass, too embarrassed to meet her new employer's gaze.

She'd insisted on taking her piece-of-crap car to show off her town. They'd made it to Shaky Bridge just fine. The wheezing started on the way to the cove, where she'd introduced Burke to some of the lobstermen that were coming back with the day's haul. Lucille had made it halfway up the narrow, winding road to the lighthouse when she coughed, sputtered, let out a sound like she'd eaten a whole pot of Saturday night beans, and died.

Of course, the tow truck driver was the same guy she'd turned down for the prom. She would swear there had been a satisfied gleam in his eye when he'd given her his exorbitant bill. Pat Murphy was now married and Cady had lost count of how many times he'd become a proud papa. With an impressive beer gut and more hair on his chin than his head, he just paid proof to the theory that there was someone for everyone.

She'd wheedled a ride back to Burke's cottage from Pat, feeling only slightly guilty that she made Burke sit in the middle. The cab of the tow truck was cramped and the look on Burke's face made it plain that she would regret the fact that he was forced to touch thighs with their burly driver.

Cady raised the glass to her lips, only to realize that it was already empty. She set it back down, a small moue pushing her mouth into a pout.

"Why do I get the feeling you could drink me under the table any day?" Burke watched her, amusement crinkling the corners of his eyes.

Cady opened her mouth to respond, decided it was better to let him believe this, and snapped it shut again. She flashed him a smile that she hoped looked mysterious.

The waitress approached then and Cady took the liberty of ordering the seafood platter for each of them. The food here was to die for.

When the server left, Burke's gaze was caught by something behind her and he frowned. He lowered his voice and leaned across the scarred table to be heard over the din of conversation and the crack of colliding balls at the pool table.

"So, at what point does a stranger stop being interesting enough to stare at?" He jerked his shoulder in a *see-what-I-mean* gesture. She whipped her head around to catch a group of locals staring at her ruffled tablemate.

"What? The attention doesn't flatter you?" Cady winked.

"Seriously. People greet you like you're their best friend, but they look at me like I've got three heads. I'm going to need them to let down their guard and trust me to tell their story for the magazine."

"This is good. They're curious. See the one with the bright red beard? That's Farmer Zach. In the summer he runs the biggest fruit and veggie stand. In the fall he sets up a really spooky corn maze. I say we put him on the list for tomorrow's research possibilities."

"It's just … the staring. Is it really necessary? I'm so used to people ignoring each other in the city." He hunkered down in his chair, turning his body slightly to the left.

"You're new, and you're interesting, but if you want the truth, you stand out."

"I'm just a regular guy. How do I stand out?"

"Take a look around the room. Is anyone else wearing slacks? Loafers? Button-down shirts—that are actually ironed—and aren't made of flannel?"

When she could see that he was starting to get defensive, she pressed on.

"You need to dress to fit in. Jeans, sneakers, a ratty old T-shirt." She leaned back in her chair to show off her own standard-issue Scallop Shores evening wear. She picked at the gaping hole exposing her entire left knee. Time to think about turning this old pair of jeans into a new pair of cut-offs.

"The only T-shirts I own are for running. I wouldn't wear them in public." He rubbed the back of his neck, clearly mortified to even think it. "And jeans. I've never ... Hell, I wouldn't even know where to buy jeans."

A fit of coughing wracked her as her second malt beverage went down the wrong pipe. She took a moment to catch her breath, wiped the moisture from her eyes, and gave him a frank look.

"You have never owned a pair of jeans? No denim? In your life? Nothing? And you can't see how you stand out in this town?"

"Until I came here, I would never have found it that unusual."

Settling into her creaky wooden chair, Cady lifted her chin. There was a story here.

"What kind of background do you have, exactly?"

"Hey, I'm just passing through here. You don't need to know my life story." Burke stuffed a hand into the bowl of pretzels on the table and came out with a pawful.

"I'm not trying to pry. It's okay if you're too scared to talk about yourself." She let the challenge hang.

He muttered under his breath, his eyebrows lowered so far she almost couldn't see the brilliant emerald of his eyes. They faced each other, neither speaking. She goaded him with her smile. The hard set of his jaw revealed that he had no intention of caving easily.

She reached out and patted his hand. Clearly he wasn't ready to trust her.

"Hey, don't worry about it. When you're ready to start interviewing people, they're going to be so proud to be in the spotlight that you'll have them eating out of your hand."

When their plates arrived, Cady groaned aloud at the scent of fried seafood. Burke eyed the greasy baskets warily. He picked up his fork and poked at a plump scallop like it was going to spring up and bite his nose. She plucked a fried clam from the pile, dug a trench in her tiny container of tartar sauce, and popped it in her mouth.

"The salt is right there, but I'd go with the tartar sauce. Total yum." She licked her greasy fingers.

"What is it covered with, besides 50,000 needless calories?" Distaste colored his words.

"Uh uh. You don't get to judge until you've tasted it. What do you like best? Shrimp, scallops, clams, or haddock?"

"I prefer to be able to see my shrimp, pink and veiny."

"Shrimp it is." Cady chose a piece from her own basket, stretched across the table and pushed it past Burke's lips before he could react.

His hand snapped up to grab her wrist. Only he just held it there. He worked the seafood around in his mouth, chewing slowly. His eyes held her gaze just as steadily as his hand held her wrist. Her breath lodged in her throat as she waited.

"It's different than I'm used to." He released her.

"But?"

"But it's good. Is that what you want to hear? No, wait, total yum. Wasn't that it?" The smile he graced her with was all the reward she needed.

Warmth spread through her veins and only part of that could be attributed to the alcohol in her glass. Burke was so unlike the men she'd grown up with in Scallop Shores. Sure, he was a bit of a food snob. And there was no doubt he came from money and was used to getting what he wanted. But he wasn't pompous or mean about it. He wanted to fit in with the locals but seemed lost as to how to go about it. He was out of his element and that vulnerability was doing distracting things to her libido.

"Fine, you win," he growled before abandoning his own fork and dipping a fried clam in tartar sauce. He licked his fingers and waggled them in her face but her concentration had been stuck on his tongue, sneaking out to bathe his greasy digits.

"Mmm-hmm."

"I'll tell you about me—on one condition. You go first." Burke continued to eat over his basket, clearly expecting a little entertainment with his dinner.

"What's to tell, really?" She nibbled on a French fry and tried to think of anything exciting that had ever happened to her.

"I've lived in Scallop Shores my whole life. I have an older brother who's a cop in town. He thinks it's a lot more thrilling than it is." She chuckled.

"It's good to have a job that you love. Not everyone can say that."

Cady found herself nodding. She had to admit she hadn't thought of it that way before.

"Anyway, my whole family grew up in this town, both sides. Would you believe that I'm the first one on either side to leave town, with the intent to permanently relocate, in at least four generations? Some have moved to the next town over, but no one has ever seriously traveled. Never been on a plane. Never seen the Pacific Ocean, and no desire to. See, I just don't get that."

"But they were happy to just spend time with each other, here?"

"What? Yeah. I mean, we're really close. We love hanging out. Holidays, birthdays, any excuse to cook, bake, and yak it up." The dopey grin slid off her face when she realized Burke wasn't smiling along with her.

He was in another place. And it wasn't a happy one.

"Tell me about your family," she whispered, silently praying that he wouldn't shut her out.

"I'm an only child, so that should be cool, right? My parents have tons of money so I was spoiled. My dad worked a lot. I didn't see him much. But my mom didn't work at all, and I didn't see her much either." His smile was sad.

"Dad would travel for work. He got to see some pretty amazing places. He'd bring me back a snow globe from each city he visited. I've got a huge collection. Mom did all her traveling for pleasure. Shopping. So she pretty much stuck to Paris and Milan. She didn't do kitschy things like snow globes."

Cady realized their hands had instinctually found their way to each other under the table. She ran a comforting thumb back and forth over the top of his hand.

"I'm going to go out on a limb and guess that you weren't invited on any of these trips?"

"Boy, for a townie, you sure are smart." He squeezed her hand.

"All right, poor little rich boy. Ever played darts?" She tossed back the rest of her beer and set the mug down with a clunk.

"It would seem this is a night of firsts." Burke rose, tugging her up so fast that for one brief moment, their bodies were flush against each other. Too soon he broke contact and allowed her to lead the way to the dartboard. She kicked his butt four games in a row before Burke surrendered, conveniently blaming it on his need for an early start the next day, and they left the bar.

Cady sang along with the radio the whole way home, but nerves took over by the time Burke pulled into the small parking lot behind Logan's Bakery. A single glaring light bulb attached to the loading dock dimly illuminated the inside of his rental car and the sculpted planes of Burke's face. An awkward silence fell and Cady racked her brain to fill it, another apology for the tow truck debacle, earlier that day, forming on her tongue.

But she didn't get to deliver it.

Burke suddenly leaned in, his sweet, warm mouth covering hers. The kiss was tentative, as if he expected her to push him away or slap him.

The hell with that.

Cady grabbed him by the shirtfront and nearly hauled him into the passenger seat with her. The taste of beer still on his lips, the woodsy scent of his heated skin, was driving her crazy. It was a damn good thing the good folks of Scallop Shores were snoozing in their beds at this hour. Because any onlookers would be getting quite a show.

She sucked on his bottom lip, and his hand started searching out bare skin beneath her shirt when a sudden caterwauling from the Dumpster a few feet away had them jumping apart. Damned cats!

Burke blinked at her, looking dazed, and she was selfishly glad he seemed as rocked by their kiss as she felt. For a second, she wished she were the type of girl to invite a man she barely knew back up to her apartment. But she wasn't. She'd have to settle for getting to know him much better—and *then* inviting him upstairs. Because after experiencing the way that man kissed, Cady could only imagine what he could do in a bed.

• • •

Eight hours later and Burke still could not get the taste of her off his tongue. Nor did he want to. Which is why he'd abandoned his fruitless attempt at sleep and had joined the birds and the scampering chipmunks at oh-my-God o'clock, lugging his laptop out to the back deck to settle in and watch the sunrise. Snatching up an insulated travel mug from the wide arm of his Adirondack chair, Burke took a big sip. His eyes watered when the scalding liquid blazed a path down his throat. Wow. There was more than one way for coffee to wake a body up. He rested his head against the back of his seat and took another tentative swallow. Much better.

He opened his laptop, slipping in the memory card from his camera, and uploading the photos he'd taken on their outing yesterday. Cady on the suspension bridge, the sunlight pulling out all different shades of blonde in her playful braids. A group shot of Cady with a bunch of gruff lobstermen. Her eyes had danced with merriment as she made bunny ears behind their heads. Cady holding up a wriggling, mottled lobster, stacks of lobster traps piled behind her.

The women he knew in New York would be horrified to get anywhere near a live lobster, much less actually hold one in their hands. Cady lifted hers like a prize trophy, her grin nearly as large as the crustacean she gripped proudly. Burke had nearly squealed like a girl when she tried to hand it off to him. Okay, so he was more like the women in the city than the men in Scallop Shores. He needed to work on that.

Balancing the laptop on his knees, Burke flipped open a steno and tried to come up with a comprehensive series. What would his readers like to learn about this hidden gem of a town? He chuckled to himself. Where had that come from, "hidden gem"? He was supposed to be here under duress. He wasn't supposed to be enjoying himself.

He'd actually found himself disappointed when Cady's car had crapped out on them, dumping them on a curvy, narrow lane, just minutes from the famed lighthouse. He'd seen tons of photos but the idea of seeing it in person suddenly held an odd appeal. Maybe he would take her back there today, in his much more reliable car.

But first on the agenda today, he'd let himself be talked into clothes shopping. God, there was another thing he couldn't believe he was looking forward to. When Cady had learned that he'd never owned a pair of jeans, she'd made it her mission to outfit him, the better to keep from standing out in town. He shouldn't care what people thought. Let them stare. Only he found himself wanting to blend in, to be accepted.

Besides, denim was soft and comfortable. Everyone looked good in it. Especially bubbly little blondes. Burke shifted in the Adirondack, trying to focus on the task at hand. Cady in the photos. Cady in his brain. If it wouldn't complicate things all to hell, he'd just take her to bed and be done with it. He couldn't remember the last time he'd had sex. That was all this was. A raging case of blue balls.

Maybe he could talk her into a quickie in the changing room, wherever they ended up shopping? A frown slowly pulled Burke's face into a dark scowl. Cady was a good girl. She had principles. She wasn't the type a guy took advantage of just because he was horny.

Great. He'd just spent a sleepless night replaying their kiss over and over. Now he was trying to figure out the best place for a clandestine rendezvous. She was a small-town girl, an innocent looking for fun and excitement in the city. He was a jaded jerk, who was used to getting whatever he wanted—and discarding it when he got bored. Money did that to a person. He was a shark. Cady would do well to steer clear of him.

The sharp trill of his cell phone sounded from his pants pocket. Who the hell would call at, what time was it? Six a.m. Who called people at six a.m.? Checking the screen, he snorted. His mother. He'd lay odds she was in Europe again and hadn't even bothered to take the time difference into account. Shoving the phone back into his pocket, he let it go to voicemail. No, thank you.

Burke closed the laptop and concentrated on the small amount of coffee he had left. It was profoundly quiet out here. Just a few days ago, this would have sent him into a panic attack. He needed chaos, cacophony—or at least, he thought he did. Now, staring off into a row of thick pines, he was stunned to find that the lack of hustle and bustle on his current assignment was actually relaxing. His eyes widened as he spied a small brown bunny nibbling at a clump of clover just feet from where he was sitting. Okay, so make that relaxed *and* charmed.

Gathering his things as slowly as possible so as not to disturb his new little woodland friend, Burke headed in to take a shower. An undisciplined writer was an out-of-work writer and he had a series of articles to shape. It was time to get focused.

The cottage's shower could barely manage tepid water at the best of times, so today's chilly dribble was not altogether unexpected. And it worked to chase the fuzziness from his brain and tamp down the hormones raging through his body.

Re-energized, he settled at his desk, glanced longingly at the ocean view from his window and flipped up the screen on his laptop to get to work. He checked his email first, to see if there was anything from Meredith, his editor. This assignment being her baby, she was a lot more involved in the day-to-day than he was used to.

Just an email from his mother. God, the woman didn't quit! Ah, crap. The subject line read "Your father." Had something happened and she called to let him know? And he'd just blown her off. Way to go, jerk! Burke tapped the mouse to open the missive.

> "I know very well you were awake, just now, when I called. Must we play these games, Burke? Honestly, sometimes you still act like a small child."

Really? Something was wrong with his father and she was taking the time to scold him? If he could flip off the computer screen with any hope of the gesture reaching his mother's shocked face, he would. Well, okay, he wouldn't, but he'd want to.

"As you are aware, we have been most indulgent of your little writing hobby. You have had yourself numerous adventures all over the world. Hurrah for you, darling. However, you are nearly thirty years old and it is time for you to become a responsible adult. Enough of this globetrotting nonsense. It is time for you to take your position as head of the company."

Burke felt his stomach fall, down, down, hurtling into a chasm with no bottom.

"Your father has announced to the board that he will retire, effective this September. We need you to come back immediately, so that he can sit down with you and explain your duties."

Aw, hell no!

"I am certain whatever assignment you are working on can be passed along to the next available writer. If there are any exceptionally ruffled feathers, let your father or I know and we can send a check. Money talks, dearest, especially when your little publication is far from being Condé Nast."

Burke pried his fingers from the mouse he couldn't do without, even with a laptop, before he accidentally crushed it. Little publication, indeed!

"Your father will be expecting you within the week. Unfortunately, I will not see you until the week after, or possibly later. Make us proud, son."

And it ended just like that. No "I love you," or "Miss you lots." Not from Evangeline Sanders, wife of Prescott Sanders, CEO and owner of one of the largest luxury hotel chains in the world. They thought he'd just drop what he was doing and go home like a good little boy? Burke's parents were about to become very disappointed.

Chapter 6

It was just a minor setback. If you want something badly enough, you have to be willing to accept that sometimes you have to take a few steps back when you're eager to move forward. Blah blah blah. Platitudes were not going to turn Cady's mood around. She'd had to say goodbye to Lucille this morning, boxing up her personal effects and leaving her precious car in a scrap yard.

Okay, so it wasn't like she was emotionally attached to her car. It got her from point A to point B, or at least it had until it bit the dust on the way up to the lighthouse. The car hadn't provided her with any truly memorable experiences. She had run over a skunk (already dead) on her inaugural drive. Every time it rained over the following year, Lucille had reeked with the smell of skunk. Cady had lost her muffler flying over potholes out on Bartlett Road. You couldn't really catch air on those potholes unless you were breaking the speed limit by at least twenty miles per hour. This memory finally put a grin on her face.

In need of transportation, her dad had taken her to pick out a used car from Sergeant Gerry, Chase's boss, who bought and sold vehicles impounded by the town. They'd both tried to talk her into something compact and girly. But Cady had spotted a gray beater pick-up and she knew it had to be hers. Her dad had groused that it wouldn't be fair if she got a truck before he did. Pulling him aside, she promised to take him to McCloskey's field after the next good rain and they could take turns doing doughnuts. He'd promptly told the Sergeant that Cady was buying the truck.

After dropping her dad off at home, Cady drove next door to Chase's and Amanda's house. Sitting in the truck for a minute, she looked to her right. Her parents' white raised ranch was just visible through a stand of birch trees. On the same plot of land,

Chase had designed a log home for Amanda, based on pictures she had kept in a scrapbook. It really was stunning. To Cady's left was an acre of forest just waiting for the day she and her future husband would break ground on their dream home. Or at least, that was the plan according to her parents, back when they had bought enough land to share with their children.

Cady felt a twinge of guilt, like she was breaking up a matched set. Oh, that was ridiculous! She shoved open the door of her new-to-her truck then slammed it for good measure.

"Hey, anyone home?"

A mouthwatering aroma led Cady straight into the kitchen, where she found Amanda stirring a giant stockpot on the stove. She took the offered spoon and sampled the beef stew. Closing her eyes, Cady savored the flavor of the thick broth, softened vegetables, and melt-in-your-mouth beef. The bitter tang of turnip tasted so much better in this mixture than it did when her mom mashed it up for Thanksgiving and Christmas.

"Doesn't that just hit the spot? It looked like it was going to rain this morning, so I thought it would be the perfect time to make one last batch of beef stew."

"Only you've made enough for an army, Amanda."

"What we don't eat today, and you're invited for dinner, by the way, I'll freeze in a few containers. Then when the baby comes we'll have something easy to heat up and eat."

"Yeah, I suppose even Chase couldn't screw that up." Cady winked.

She helped herself to a bowl from the cupboard beside the sink and spooned a serving of stew into it. With any luck, she'd be out with Burke at dinnertime, so she'd have to snag some right now. Amanda was right. It may be spring, but Mother Nature hadn't made New Englanders tough for nothing. It was downright chilly out today. Cady tucked into the warm meal.

"Can I help you with anything today?" she asked between bites.

"I thought you were supposed to be helping out Burke with his magazine articles."

"He's writing right now. We'll meet up later." Somehow the fact that they weren't meeting up to work on the travel articles, but to shop for jeans, felt too private to share. Even with her best friend.

She hadn't seen him since he'd dropped her off after that kiss. Cady's eyes drifted closed as she remembered the heat of it, and the most embarrassing groan rumbled out of her throat.

She coughed, scraping the last bite of stew from her bowl and swallowing quickly. She took the bowl to the sink, rinsing it out and placing it inside the dishwasher.

"I've got a couple of hours to kill. I could do some heavy lifting, or scrub some floors. What do you say?"

When Amanda didn't respond, Cady turned around. Her best friend stood in the middle of the kitchen. She wore an apron stretched taut across her growing belly and she pulled up a corner of the fabric, twisting it tightly. A single tear rolled slowly down her cheek. She looked scared to death.

"Sweetheart, what's the matter? Are you in pain? Should I call Chase? Come sit down."

Cady wrapped the young woman in her arms, guiding her through the kitchen and into the living room. She helped her friend to the couch and positioned the ottoman to support her feet. By the time she had her comfortable, the poor pregnant woman was sobbing.

"Damned hormones," Amanda sniveled.

Looking around desperately, Cady snatched a box of tissues from a side table and shoved it in Amanda's lap. She waited for the tears to subside, still unsure whether she should be worried or not. She debated calling Chase to let him know his wife was having a meltdown. She wasn't used to being around pregnant women and didn't know when to raise the alarm. Eventually Amanda's sobbing dwindled to nose-blowing and quiet sniffling.

"Has the crisis passed?" Her voice was gentle, her expression concerned.

"I'm so sorry. I hate acting so foolishly in front of you, Cady. This is so embarrassing."

"Hey, it's me, remember? I'm here for you, honey."

"But that's just it. You're leaving. I'm going through one of the biggest moments of my life. I am completely freaking out about what to expect ... and you're going to leave me." Amanda shook her head like she was disgusted with herself.

"Sweetie, you are going to have that baby long before I leave. You know I'll be right by your side the minute you go into labor, Chase and I both." Her words didn't seem to have the calming effect she'd intended.

"What about after? What happens when the baby is sick and I get worried? What about when I start talking baby babble and no sane adult can understand me anymore? Who's going to remind me to put on my makeup and comb my hair? How are we going to have our girls' nights?"

Amanda gripped both of Cady's hands tightly in hers.

"I'm scared. You are my anchor, my link to everything that came before motherhood. When you leave, I worry that I'm going to drown. I need you here, Cady. As horribly immature and selfish as that sounds, I need you here."

Once again, Amanda dissolved into tears, turning to bury her face against the couch cushion. Cady rubbed her friend's back, trying to keep from crying herself. They had talked about this since they were kids. Amanda knew she wanted to leave.

This was emotional blackmail! The whole town represented a support network that would be more than happy to help the new mom. Cady was only one person. Surely her presence wasn't *that* important. She bit her tongue, telling herself that pregnancy did strange things to a woman's emotions.

Chase had complained to her just last month, that his wife had totally flipped out when he brought home the wrong flavor of ice cream. He wouldn't have minded the tirade, except that it had been the *right* flavor, and his reason for running to the store just a short twenty minutes before. At the time, Cady had found the story amusing. She'd reminded her brother that it took two people to make a baby and that his part was infinitely easier.

Realizing that this was one of those moments when she would have to set her own feelings aside, Cady rose to make them both some tea. By the time she brought the mugs into the living room, Amanda's hysterics were through. She waited quietly on the couch, massaging the bump in her belly, as Cady added sugar and cream to one mug and then handed it to her friend. They sat in silence for a few moments.

"It just never seemed as real before as it does now—you moving to the city, that is."

"What makes now different than any other time?" Cady settled cross-legged in a corner of the couch and sipped her tea.

"I'm not sure. It's something in your eyes, in your face. It's like this powerful determination, like nothing is going to get in your way."

Except having to shell out 5k of my hard-earned Get Out Of Dodge savings on a new-ish pickup truck, Cady thought.

Cady wished that her best friend, her confidante since kindergarten, could understand the excitement she felt when contemplating a new life in the city. The thrill of a fresh start. The new experiences that would start the very second she drove over the town line.

Burke would understand. He'd been there. She needed to see him. Their kiss, that delicious kiss, had been interrupted by a couple of stray cats fighting for dominance over the Dumpster.

It had made a lovely evening a tad awkward. He'd had enough writing time. He'd earned a break. Maybe she'd drop by.

Heat spread up her neck and across her cheeks as she thought of the brief time she'd spent in Burke's rented cottage, the big cozy bed taking up most of the bedroom. Yeah, it was probably best that she stick to a phone call. It was becoming difficult to remember theirs was a working relationship.

• • •

That evening, after insisting Burke slip into one of the new pairs of Levis they'd picked up at the outlet mall the next town over, Cady introduced him to one of the town's lesser-known attractions. Brownie's was a tiny ice cream stand, only open from Memorial Day weekend through Labor Day. They didn't even have indoor seating. Everyone placed their orders at the screened-in window and took their frozen desserts to a scattering of picnic tables and benches scattered on the grass. The shop was at the top of a winding road and the picnic tables were placed in full view of the lighthouse and the powerful surf that slammed against the rocks below.

The sun was beginning to set and Cady lifted her face, the last lingering rays stroking her cheeks like warm fingers. Her grin crooked, she realized the sky was painted the color of rainbow sherbet. She closed her eyes briefly, savoring the moment, then turned her full attention back to her companion.

"Mm ... ice cream therapy. Just what I needed." Cady swirled her tongue through her triple-chocolate double scoop, closing her eyes as the sweet flavor danced across her tongue. Yeah, it didn't get much better than this.

"Rough day?" She looked over to find Burke watching her, his eyebrow cocked in interest.

"You could say that." She smirked. She hadn't intended to dump on him. She'd just needed a break from her loved ones.

Then he scooted closer. The late evening sun brought out golden flecks in his eyes. He was inviting her to open up. She'd be crazy not to take advantage of a unique opportunity like this. Cady blinked, curious as to his motives. Darting her tongue out to lick the perimeter of her sugar cone, she saw the moment his expression changed from interested, sympathetic even, to hooded and—hungry.

Burke grasped her wrist, holding it steady while he leaned down and pressed his open mouth to her ice cream. His eyes never left hers. *Oh my heavenly Lord!* It didn't take a very great leap to imagine his mouth in other places. Warmer places that he could melt just as easily. The only physical contact between them was his hand on her wrist—but she couldn't help shivering.

"Hey, you've got your own!" She laughed, her voice shaky, breathless.

"But yours is so good," he growled.

Working relationship. Theirs was a working relationship. Cady pursed her lips and blew out slowly. Oh, the things she wanted to do to this man!

"Tell me what prompted this 'ice cream therapy' field trip." He let go of her wrist and focused on his own dessert.

"Ugh. Family. It's nothing. I'll be fine after a healthy dose of chocolate." She rolled her eyes and waved her free hand in the air.

He caught her hand in his own, squeezed it before drawing it onto his thigh and holding it there.

"I wouldn't have asked if I didn't genuinely want to know." Burke took a couple of largish bites from his ice cream. Cady waited for him to wince when the brain freeze hit, but apparently it never did.

"Sometimes you have to look elsewhere for support. Family can be more of a hindrance when you're trying to chase down your dreams."

"Exactly!" She sat up straighter. "I mean, it's not like this is a surprise to any of them. But suddenly it's all about them. Chase is upset that I don't want to live in town. Amanda has made it all about her—I'm leaving her, she says. I'm leaving her to raise her baby all on her own. Really?

"What about 'We're so proud of you, Cady'? Or, 'You must be nervous, taking this monumental next step in your life. How can we help?'"

"They love you. They don't want to lose you." His voice was gentle.

"But they aren't losing me! They're trying to hold me back. Staying here would be like living in a cage—a roomy cage the size of a town—but a cage, nonetheless."

"They want you to live the life they'd like for you, not the life you need in order to be happiest." His voice drifted off, thoughtful.

"They don't care about my happiness." Chocolate was no longer working. Disgusted, Cady pitched her ice cream cone in the trash bin beside their wooden bench.

"No, that's not it. Believe me. Your family loves you. They want you to be happy. They want to be with you. They want to be part of the exciting memories you make. They want to belong in your life." He let his words hang, while frowning into the dying rays of sun.

Cady shook off the pity, trading it for a healthy dose of shame. Her family loved her. Of course she knew that. From what Burke had told her of his parents, she had no right to complain.

"Are you living your dream? Traveling, I mean? Telling the world about the places you visit? Is that what you want to be doing?"

She studied his profile. His jawline was hard, as though he were gritting his teeth. His nose long and angular. He had eyelashes any woman would envy. And he looked so profoundly sad.

Cady shifted until they were touching, shoulder to thigh. Noticing that he'd seemed to have forgotten about his own melting ice cream, she reached out and tugged it loose, tossing it into the garbage without even looking. Burke turned to face her, his expression mildly confused. Had he forgotten what they were talking about?

"Are you living your dream?" she prompted.

His smile was bitter.

"Funny you should ask."

She let him set the pace, sitting quietly as she listened to the shriek of the gulls and the chatter of the families at the surrounding picnic tables enjoying the early summer evening. As the night crept in, so did a chill that had nothing to do with the drop in temperature. She leaned into his body, trading her own warmth and comfort for a little of his.

"I thought I was. Yeah, I wanted to write. But I've got these stories in my head. They need to come out. And lately they've been nattering at me, louder and more insistent."

"You want to write novels? That's so exciting!"

"I don't know. I mean, Stephen King seems to have cornered the horror market in this state, wouldn't you say?"

"Stephen King has made a name for himself. But that doesn't mean you can't too."

"I've been sitting at my makeshift desk every morning. That view of the ocean. It's awe inspiring."

"You want to write books, exclusively. Are you saying you want to stay in Scallop Shores?"

"What I want and what I get to have are two very different things." His frown deepened, his chiseled countenance grew even stonier.

A tiny seed of selfishness was trying to take root in her heart. It wanted Burke to move back to the city with her, once summer was over. Sure, finish the article series and then focus on a book—but not in Scallop Shores. Yeah, moving to the city was supposed to be Cady's time to make new memories and discover herself. But plans change. She could still make new memories and be her own person with Burke in her life.

"What aren't you telling me?" Her voice was barely a whisper, yet she knew he heard her from the slump of his shoulders.

Burke sighed, sliding a few inches to the right. Cady had to catch herself or she would have tumbled right into him. He was looking for distance right now. She needed to give it to him. He turned, finally, and faced her. His smile was for her benefit, she knew. Oh, how she longed to reach out for him. But he didn't want that. Her fingers flexed uselessly in her lap, so she sat on them.

"I told you a little about my parents and my whole 'poor little rich kid' story. My dad owns a chain of hotels. I've lost track of how many different countries he's invaded. I don't care. It was his thing. His business. His legacy. I wanted no part of it.

"I needed to make my own way in the world, do something for myself that had nothing to do with my dad's name or money."

He gave her a look that said he knew she'd understand that better than most. He was right.

"So good ol' dad is retiring. And as his only son and heir, it has been brought to my attention that I have a responsibility to the family business. I am to abandon my job, shrug off my dreams, and report for duty as the new CEO of Sanders Resorts."

"Sanders ... Resorts? Oh my God, are you kidding me? I didn't even make the connection. They're ... huge!"

"Ah, then I was doing my job well. Look at me. Okay, I might be a city guy. I know more about how to tip the valet than where to catch the best lobster. But I'm no titan of industry. Do you even realize how many people would report to me?"

Burke ran a hand through his hair. His eyes snapped angrily. This was good. This was better than the defeated look that had made Cady long to comfort him. This Burke was ready to fight. And she would fight alongside him.

But if he were CEO of a company based in Manhattan? She'd have it all. The little seed of selfishness was trying hard to take root.

Not gonna happen. Cady would much rather hang on to Burke as a friend, in Scallop Shores, where he would be happy and living his life to the fullest, than to dream of a relationship with him in New York, where he would be but a mere shadow of the man he once was. She'd do anything to help him get out of this familial duty.

"What will they do if you tell them no?" She could tell by the determined glint in his eye that he had a ready answer.

"There are probably a dozen men more qualified to take over the position. My father would have no problem naming a successor. But they'd cut me off. I'd lose my monthly stipend, any inheritance I stood to gain. I'd be penniless."

"Excuse me? You have a job. Or am I missing something? Your magazine is paying for you to stay in that cottage by the shore. They're paying your expenses. They're paying for a freaking assistant." Her eyes widened.

Burke pressed his lips together tightly, suddenly finding the lighthouse so fascinating he couldn't tear his eyes from it. Darkness had descended and the automated light winked on and off.

"Oh, Burke," she whispered.

"It was worth it." He still wouldn't look at her. His voice came out gruff.

"But it has to stop. The paying part. Not the work."

Now he gave her his attention. His face in shadow, she could still read the intensity in his gaze.

"Why would you offer to help me like this? Unpaid? You barely know me. You have your own goals. You have somewhere you're meant to be."

"And I'll get there. But you first. Screw Sanders Resorts! Let's finish your magazine series and find you a job in Scallop Shores that gives you plenty of time for writing."

He reached out a finger and lifted her chin, leaning in close enough for her to feel his warm breath on her face.

"You still haven't told me why."

Her heart ricocheted in her chest. She could have come to love this man. Perhaps she already did, to some degree. But he was right. Theirs were different goals, leading them on very different paths. Maybe someday she'd find someone who made her feel as alive as Burke did.

"Because you're my friend. And I would do anything for my friends."

"Your friend?" She hardened her heart against the tone in his voice, the look in his eyes by the light of the nearby lamppost.

It was better this way.

Chapter 7

The large LCD display on the bedside clock read two eleven A.M. Burke rolled over, punching his pillow, though it was more from frustration than an effort to make the cotton more pliable. Friends. Is that what they were? Had his kisses had so little effect? He was more out of practice than he thought.

They had something. He wasn't imagining it. There was a hum, an intensity that drew them together like magnets. Yet Cady was so fixated on getting out of Scallop Shores that she refused to do anything about it.

So now he lay sleepless, in the dead of night. His body ached for a woman who seemed intent on testing the very limits of his endurance. He'd come to this town for a story, for a job that, until recently, had seemed satisfying and quenched his thirst for writing. And now, because of Cady, he was ready to throw away a cushy inheritance and a career that would set him up for life. All for a woman who intended to leave him at the end of the summer. He was insane.

From the far side of the house came a muffled crash. Burke sat up straight, scrambling to the edge of the mattress and feeling for the steel baseball bat he kept under the bed. Damn it! This wasn't his apartment in Manhattan. He was in a rented cottage with no accessible weapon. Another crash came, this one a little closer to the back porch. He searched wildly for something to fend off the intruder. Coming up empty in the bedroom, he padded stealthily toward the kitchen in his boxer briefs.

The bright light from a nearly full moon shone a path to the counter and his cell phone, sitting on the charger. Burke snatched it up and dialed 911.

"911, what is your emergency?"

"I need to report an intruder." He rattled off the address of the rental cottage.

"Someone is inside your house?"

"Well, no. He's breaking in."

"Could you be more specific? Have they broken a window? Are they attempting to get in through the door?"

"Seriously, lady? Are you going to wait until the guy gets inside and kills me before you send someone out here? Maybe I could explain this better to your supervisor."

"That won't be necessary. A patrol car was dispatched to your address as soon as you said intruder. The officer should be there shortly. Please stay inside and do not attempt to engage them."

"Officer? As in one?" Burke's eyes widened as he swore his would-be assailant stood up straight on the porch, casting a shadow on the living room wall. The guy was nearly seven feet tall! Oh, they were never going to be able to tackle this behemoth on their own.

"I assure you he will assess the situation and call for backup if needed."

"Fine. But make sure he's got his weapon drawn when he gets here. This guy is big. He's like some freakin' Sasquatch or something."

There was a pause on the other end of the line and the 911 operator cleared her throat loudly.

"Try to be patient and the police officer will be there within a few minutes."

Now he could hear the scuffling that issued from the back porch. The intruder was going to try to get in through the sliding glass door! Unbelievable. He wondered why the jerk wasn't more careful about being quiet. It was clear the cottage was no longer vacant. The rental car was parked in the driveway. He couldn't believe the balls on this guy!

Spotting the knife block sitting beside the cutting board, Burke felt a little queasy. The thought of slicing through living flesh was enough to make him hurl. But he grabbed the largest one anyway. Hanging over the stove was an array of pots and pans. He reached up and pulled down a frying pan. Maybe he could catch the guy unaware, and knock him out cold as he entered through the back.

Headlights speared the night, nearly blinding him as they lit up the kitchen. The cavalry had arrived. No flashing lights or sirens, but they hadn't made any attempt to sneak onto the property and catch the intruder in the act. So now he was probably running through the woods, long gone. Wasted trip. Burke shook his head in disgust and went to let the patrolman in.

"Officer, he was trying the back door. You might still be able to catch him if you're quick." Burke gestured for the man in uniform to hurry, leading him through the house with his kitchen weapons held out in front of him.

"Mr. Sanders, are you certain someone was trying to break in? You heard them try the door?"

The officer trailed behind, not bothering to keep up with Burke or even take the lead. "Listen, I heard him on the back porch. The idiot wasn't even trying to stay quiet. Come on, we've got to catch him. I don't care if it's just a couple of stupid teen pranksters. They need to learn a lesson. I intend to press charges."

Burke reached the sliding glass door that opened out onto the back porch. The police officer followed, his service revolver firmly encased in its holster. Unfortunately, there was no way to hide their approach. So Burke hurried to the door and flipped the switch on the side of the wall, bathing the deck in light. He dashed to the side of the door, in case the would-be robber opened fire. Before he could take a look to see if their quarry was still in sight, the patrolman let out a bellow of laughter.

Seated on the deck, in front of the gas grill and looking quite comfortable, was a bandit all right. A fuzzy, fat raccoon. He had managed to climb up to the surface of the grill and pull down the leftover hamburger and hot dog that Burke had forgotten to remove after dinner. At the moment, he was washing down his late-night snack with a bottle of Corona.

Burke glared. Could this night get any worse? The cop was wiping tears from his eyes, nearly doubled over as he was still convulsing with laughter. Awesome. This would be all over town by morning. Burke peered at the man's name tag. Officer Eaton would enjoy relating this late night rendezvous. Aw, crap! Eaton. It couldn't be. In this small town? Double crap!

"Tell me you aren't related to Cady. I know Scallop Shores is small, but please tell me you're another Eaton."

The man grinned wide, showing a set of beautiful white teeth. He slapped Burke on the shoulder and laughed some more.

"Cady would be my baby sister, Mr. Sanders. The name is Chase. I'm sure we would have met in town, eventually, but I have to say—this is much more interesting."

"Well, seeing as I'm standing here in my underwear and you have just witnessed the single most embarrassing experience of my entire life, I guess you should call me Burke."

Turning off the porch light, they left the raccoon to his dinner. Burke walked Chase back to the kitchen door and held it open. He rubbed a palm over his face while he shook his head.

"Is there any chance we can keep this between us? Say the guy got away?"

"Not a chance! This will keep the guys at the station entertained all summer—hell, probably into the first snowfall." Chase flashed him a huge grin and chuckled as he trotted down the steps. "Welcome to Scallop Shores, Burke." He opened the door to the cruiser and was about to get in when he turned. "Hey, what's going on between you and my sister?"

"Sadly, not a thing, man. Not a thing."

"Yeah, well, I've got my eye on you. Don't make me sic that raccoon on you!"

Burke slammed the door on one of Scallop Shores's finest and went back to bed.

• • •

"Mornin', sis! Your boyfriend stop by yet?"

Cady rolled her eyes at Chase, her fingers plucking a dozen assorted cake doughnuts from the display case to pack in a box. She folded the lid down and taped the box shut. Her customer, Hazel Davenport, raised an eyebrow. Clearly she was just as interested in the answer.

Cady shook her head and smiled patiently, trying to indicate that Chase was just being a pest. Hazel waited a few moments longer, but when no new information was forthcoming, she sighed and took her doughnuts to go.

"Would you cut it out? Burke is not my boyfriend." She slapped at the counter with a wet rag. "You want some coffee, or what?"

"You want to work in a coffee shop in the city? You need to work on your customer service skills, baby sis." Chase slid onto a stool, taking off his cap and setting it on the counter beside him.

Knowing this exchange could go on indefinitely, Cady turned her back on her brother. She poured a mug of coffee and set it in front of him. Before he could reach for it, she sent the sugar dispenser sliding to the far end of the counter. Chase would have to get off his duff to go get it. Score two points for her!

"So we had a little excitement last night. A 911 call down at the rental cottages off Sandy Point." The dramatic pause would have been comical, had she not known exactly who he was referring to.

"Oh my God! Is Burke okay? Is he hurt? What happened?" She was too concerned with what might have happened to let the triumphant look on Chase's face set her off.

"See! I knew there was something going on between you two." He waggled a finger in the air.

"Damn it, Chase, did something really happen or not?"

She'd been warming a blueberry muffin for her brother and turned to see that the handful of customers in the bakery were eagerly hanging onto Chase's words. She hurried around the counter, and practically shoved the plate in his lap. Standing over her brother, lips pursed, hands wringing, she waited. He blinked, seeming surprised at her reaction. Okay, maybe he hadn't really meant to scare her.

"He called in an intruder, about two o'clock in the morning."

Cady's eyes widened. Who on earth would break into one of the summer rentals in the middle of the night? Petty crime wasn't unheard of in Scallop Shores, but robbing a cottage that was occupied? It would have to be a very stupid crook, or—

Oh, poor Burke.

"Let me guess. The intruder wasn't human?" She cringed, hoping like crazy that she was wrong. The jubilant look on her brother's face told her otherwise.

"It was Mr. Masked Bandit himself. He helped himself to some food Burke had left on the grill. Hell, he was even washing it down with a brewski. Classic! I almost peed myself. There was Burke, a frying pan in one hand and a carving knife in the other. Ready to take down the perp in just his skivvies."

"Oh, no," Cady groaned. "He must have been so embarrassed."

"Nope, the little guy looked quite content. He was polishing off a beer, eating a little late-night snack."

"Shut up, Chase!" She cuffed her brother upside his head. "I imagine you had a ball, letting him know you were going to spread this all over town."

"He did ask me not to say anything." Chase nodded. "But he didn't try too hard. Maybe if he'd offered money—"

"God, you can be such a jerk sometimes!"

Cady closed her eyes, feeling awful for Burke. It was a common occurrence, the further from town you got, to receive late-night visits by wild animals. She should have warned him not to leave any food outside. Of course, that wouldn't stop raccoons from examining the contents of a trash can. The little guy had probably started with that, and then his keen sense of smell led him to the leftover barbeque on the back porch. Wait until Burke woke up to deer grazing on the flowering shrubs in his front yard. He was probably a little too close to shore for that, but Cady wouldn't rule it out entirely.

"I wouldn't worry about Romeo, sis. It's not like he's gonna live here permanently. We'll tease him for the summer and then he'll be on his way. By the time he gets back to the safety of the city, he'll have concocted a clever story about the rabid raccoon that attacked him in his sleep." Chase smiled and nodded toward his audience as the bakery erupted in laughter.

"Go easy on him, Chase. He didn't know."

"You should have heard the 911 call. The guy seriously thought someone was on their way into his house to kill him. He met me at the door with his badass kitchen weapons like he thought he was going to help me 'take him down.' I couldn't have had an easier target."

Okay, so the image of Burke trying to fend off a harmless raccoon with a butcher knife was pretty funny. Cady tried to hide her grin by scratching an imaginary itch on her nose. Chase caught her eye and winked. She lost it. Laughter bubbled up from her belly and the undignified snort she produced made her laugh even harder. Tears sprang to her eyes and she sat down hard on the stool beside her brother. Everyone in the place was laughing so hard, no one heard the bell over the door ring.

"Hey, is there any way a dumb city guy could get a latte this morning? I didn't sleep very well last night."

Burke's grumpy question was met with a fresh gale of guffaws. His green eyes narrowed to dark slits and he did not look amused. Cady coughed and dabbed at her eyes. She focused her attention on the floor as she rounded the counter. Another fit of giggles was just too close to the surface and she couldn't look him in the eye until the moment had safely passed.

Quickly, she fixed him a double shot soy latte and handed it across the counter. He took the cup, slipped a few dollar bills into her palm, and headed for the door. He was leaving? Good grief, he wasn't *that* thin-skinned, was he? Cady searched frantically for something to say.

"There's a big lobster bake at my parents' house tomorrow. Everyone will be there. You're welcome to come." Burke paused, his hand still on the doorknob. "I'd like you to be there."

He turned around slowly, eyeing the crowd of regulars before giving his full attention to her.

"I don't know. I'm awfully busy."

Her disappointment must have been obvious, because it didn't take long for the petulant frown on his face to morph into a hesitant grin.

"Aw, why not! I'd love to hang out with your family. I would love to interview them, see how their view of Scallop Shores differs from yours. I can even bring some Coronas. I think I may have one or two my uninvited raccoon guest didn't drink." He winked. Then he turned a devilish smile on Chase. "See you tomorrow, Officer." Burke gave a mock salute and left the coffee shop.

"I do not like that guy. He thinks he's some smooth city slicker who can come into town and sweep my sister off her feet. You're smarter than to fall for the likes of him, right, Cady? Cady?"

She had been staring out the window, watching as Burke backed his car out of the space and pulled out onto the street. Blinking owlishly at the empty space in front of the store, Cady turned a guilty face to her brother. Seeing him roll his eyes was enough to set her off.

"Look, big bro, I'm a grown woman who is allowed to make grown-woman decisions. If I want to let that smooth city slicker sweep me off my feet, that's my choice to make. How do you know it's not the other way around? Maybe I'm going to sweep him off *his* feet!" She folded her arms across her chest and glared at Chase.

Her blush was deep and immediate as the bakery filled with hoots from the customers she'd conveniently forgotten about. That was the problem with small towns. No one respected private conversations. She sighed, picturing a coffee shop in the city, where folks were kind enough to at least pretend not to overhear something unless they were explicitly invited into a conversation.

"Don't you gentlemen have someplace you need to be this morning?" She glanced pointedly at the peanut gallery lining her bakery counter.

"Can't help it if you make things too dang entertainin' here!" Earl Duffy chortled.

"Well, by all means, stay and enjoy the entertainment." She swept a grand bow. "But I'm charging five bucks a head."

Cady laughed out loud when Old Man Feeney took out a five-dollar bill and slapped it on the counter. Okay, they were nosy cusses, but she loved these guys.

Chapter 8

Part of him felt like he was giving in too easily, giving up a part of himself just to belong. He walked out of the cottage and strode to his car, the new jeans Cady had picked out feeling like an extension of his body. He slipped into the car, sliding a hand across his soft denim-clad thigh before chuckling to himself and putting the Lexus in gear. Maybe he was just being introduced to a better way of living.

If his parents could only see him now. His grin wide, he backed out onto the road and headed toward town. For years he'd just blocked out any thought of family responsibilities. It was something he'd deal with when the time came. And to be honest, *dealing with it* meant that he'd been resigned to his fate, putting it off as long as possible, making memories he could carry with him into the boardroom.

Cady made him want more. Or less, depending on how you looked at it. She knew he wanted to write—not magazine articles, but novels. She knew it and she didn't laugh it off. She encouraged him to pursue his dream. It meant he'd be broke—a situation he'd never had to deal with and one that, frankly, scared the crap out of him.

As scared as he was, Burke had never felt more alive in his life. While the little blond spitfire was showing him around town, she was also teaching him to let go of his insecurities, face his challenges, and go after what he wanted. And today she was inviting him to a family gathering. Did she know how much he wanted a family? He was only just starting to realize it himself. He couldn't wait to meet the people who shaped the woman he'd come to—what? Care for? Respect? Lust after? How to describe what he felt for Cady? It was a tangled bundle of Christmas lights, that's what it was.

Surprisingly, there was an empty spot right in front of Logan's Bakery. Burke parked, sat for a moment, and then wondered if he should go in and let Cady know he was there to pick her up. They still had to stop by the nursing home. They were bringing her elderly aunt to the festivities. Would Cady have locked the door? Couldn't hurt to try.

The closed sign was up but the door to the bakery was unlocked. Burke let himself in, hoping the jangling bell over the door would alert Cady to his presence. He could hear voices in the back. As they weren't getting any closer, he figured they must not have heard him come in. He shuffled closer.

"... waste of damned money. Nobody wants your stupid fancy drinks with that fancy espresso machine. It's taking up my counter space."

"I spent my own money on that espresso machine, in the hopes of drawing in a bigger crowd for you. I bought the syrups and all the supplies. I don't ask anyone else to take it apart and clean it. It's on me."

"Well, it needs to leave. We're a simple town. We don't need cappuccinos, lattes, and soy-anything. We cater to fishermen and teachers, moms, and postal workers. No one is asking for the fancy crap."

"Respectfully, Mr. Logan, the tourists ask for it all the time. And I have talked a few of those teachers, moms, and postal workers into trying something new."

"If you have to talk someone into trying something, it ain't worth it. This is my bakery and I won't have my customers feeling like they're being browbeaten into ordering something they don't really want."

"I'm not browbeating anyone! This is the twenty-first century. You're treating this bakery like it's a '50s diner. I feel like I should throw on a pair of roller skates and chew bubblegum while I serve up my drip coffee."

"Mind who you're talking to, Missy! I've let you have the run of this place while I've been busy, but you take too many liberties. There are going to be changes around here. My changes. Not yours."

A door slammed in the back, presumably to the outside. A moment of silence and then Cady's frustrated yell carried into the front of the store. Burke backed up until he was nearly at the door. Did he have time to sneak out? She stalked through the doorway from the back area, swiping angrily at her eyes. Nope.

"Stupid ignorant, old-fashioned ..." She looked up sharply when she realized Burke was in the bakery. "Awesome. You heard that, then?" Blowing out a long sigh, she whipped off her apron and threw it on the counter. "Come on, let's go. I'm ready to have some fun."

Cady eyed the display case, and pulled out a tray of brownies and a strawberry pie. She handed the pie to Burke and fixed a quick box of macaroons to go. At his raised brow she shrugged.

"My sister-in-law is pregnant. Can't have enough sweets. And heaven help us if we don't have the right choices on hand."

Burke nodded, shifting the pie to one hand and picking up the tray of brownies with the other.

Cady held the door open and locked it shut behind them.

"Don't you need to set an alarm? Fiddle with some fancy keypad?"

"Pull down the big iron portcullis?" She giggled. "It's Scallop Shores, silly. Who's going to break in? A raccoon?"

He could tell how hard she was trying to keep from laughing. Her lips were folded in over her teeth and she wasn't breathing. He cocked a brow and waited. Sure enough, a belly laugh erupted from deep in Cady's gut. She slapped at her leg with her free hand and stopped to draw in a few lungfuls of breath.

"Whew. Couldn't resist. I'm sorry."

"No, you aren't. But you needed to smile so I'm taking one for the team." He set the pan of brownies and then the pie in the backseat of his rental car.

"Oh, you mean that little kerfuffle with Mr. Logan? We have that same argument every time he waltzes back into town. He just wants to make sure I don't get too comfortable in my managerial position."

"Does he know you plan to leave town soon?"

They were on the road and headed to the nursing home, Kittredge Manor, where Cady's aunt lived.

"I don't flaunt it. He knows, but he's in denial. I run that bakery better than anyone he's likely to find as a replacement. The thought of having to train a new manager is probably giving him hives.

"If giving me a hard time about my 'fancy coffee' gives him his jollies, more power to him. If he can dish it, I can take it. And it will give me that much more satisfaction when I do finally give my notice."

The stubborn jut to her chin told Burke she protested just a tad too much. She loved her espresso machine and the fancy drinks she got to make. Of course it was going to upset her when her boss attacked something that meant so much to her.

"He pulls that machine out, he's going to hear from this disgruntled former customer," he grumbled.

They parked at the nursing home and headed inside. Cady certainly was popular here. She stopped to say hi to an elderly gentleman shuffling slowly toward them. Burke hung back, waiting for Cady to take him to her aunt's room. He yelped in surprise when a shaky hand grabbed a handful of his ass.

"Doris! You need to behave yourself. And anyway, hands off—this one's mine." Cady shook her finger at the elderly woman. Her eyes danced with merriment.

They continued to the end of the hall, Burke checking over his shoulder every few feet.

"What the heck was that all about? They've got some randy old women here."

"It's those sexy new jeans. Even the geriatric set can't help but cop a feel." Cady chuckled.

"So ... I'm yours, huh?"

"Of course not! I was just saving your butt—quite literally—and you're welcome, by the way." She blustered, refusing to make eye contact.

"Her ears turn beet red when she's lying, you know."

"Auntie!"

They were standing in the doorway of the last patient room on the left. An old woman waited for them in a recliner by the window. A giant purse sat in her lap.

"You must be him, then. The city man who has our Cady, and half the town of Scallop Shores, all aflutter."

"Burke Sanders. Nice to meet you."

"Cadence Eaton, the first. But you can call me Auntie."

If the rest of Cady's family were anything like Auntie, this was going to be an interesting evening. Burke offered the woman his hand and helped her to her feet. Together they started back down the long hallway, and if he used the ladies Eaton to shield him from Doris Grabby Hands, so what? The old biddy scared him.

• • •

When they arrived at Cady's parents' house, Burke was met with an unusual sight: the women sitting out on the big deck while the men crowded the kitchen and stood over huge pots of boiling water.

"We were wondering when you'd finally get here. Foster just put the lobsters in. Won't be long now."

"Sorry, Mom. Burke was busy flirting with all the old ladies at Kittridge."

He shook his head, the urge to slap her on the ass for that remark only curbed by the fact that he would have proved her point. This teasing, the back and forth, it's what Cady did with Chase too. Was this her way of welcoming him into the family? He didn't know whether to be honored or embarrassed. He wanted to preen, but then he wondered if this was her way of saying she thought of him as a brother.

"Let me guess. It was either Doris or Abigail?" Cady's mother tapped a finger to her chin.

"I believe Cady referred to her as Doris," Burke confirmed.

"Well, feel lucky she only grabbed your butt. Abigail stuck her hand in Chase's front pocket one time." The very pregnant woman seated before him must be Chase's wife.

All four women on the deck must have found his expression highly amusing, because they could barely breathe for all their laughing. Burke shook his head. The women he knew in the city were not this blunt.

"I'm sorry, Burke. This is my mother, May, and my sister-in-law, Amanda."

May stood, and before Burke could hold out a hand in greeting, she wrapped him in a hug. Amanda was slower, struggling out of her plastic deck chair. She, too, introduced herself with a hug. Her big belly got in the way and Burke was stunned to feel a slight tap to his middle.

"Oh, excuse me! I guess Baby Eaton is saying hi, as well." Amanda giggled.

Cady led the way into the kitchen, setting the pie down on a section of counter that wasn't filled with paper plates, bowls, or bags of potato chips. She took the other desserts and found homes for them as well, turning to give Burke a bright smile before sidling over to the stove and laying a loud kiss on her father's cheek.

"Daddy, this is Burke Sanders. Burke, this is my dad, Wallace. You've met Chase." There was a snort of laughter that made it very clear that everyone in the room was well aware of Burke's famous 911 call.

"And that gorgeous man fixing us dinner is Foster Duncan. He's Amanda's brother. Their parents own The Lobster Pot, a restaurant in the harbor. Best seafood on the East Coast."

Burke nodded his head toward the man who was probably as close to thirty as he was. Gorgeous, huh? He supposed, if you liked dark hair, darker eyes, and a dimple in one—no, make that two—cheeks. Instinct had Burke wanting to dislike the guy on principle. He kept looking from Cady to Foster, searching for some sign that would reveal they were more than friends. Not having experienced jealousy before, Burke found his first taste bitter.

"We're almost done in here. Cady, love, why don't you start taking things out to the patio table? Probably should light up the citrine candles now, too. Mosquitos will be wanting to eat us alive." Wallace handed her a stack of plates and a long-handled lighter.

Before he could offer to carry something out, May pushed a large covered salad bowl into his hands. She tossed a big bag of potato chips on top and patted his arm. Burke tried to navigate past a huge gray cat that looked as though it was doing its best to trip him up.

"Daisy! Scat!" Cady stuck a toe out and convinced the cat to leave him alone.

"Thanks. I think it was trying to break my neck." He chuckled.

"Probably." Cady wasn't laughing.

The long plastic table had already been covered with a red checked tablecloth. May and Auntie were following close behind, each carrying more food. Burke tried to lift covers and peek under glass lids, but he kept getting his hands slapped. It all smelled so good. His own parents would have cheerfully dropped dead before dining al fresco.

He hovered as the ladies set plates out, filled lemonade glasses, and uncovered bowls of potato salad and homemade cole slaw. Cady had gone back inside to help carry out the lobsters, clams, and drawn butter. Burke hurried over to help Auntie and Amanda into their seats.

"Woo hoo! Check out those city manners." Chase chortled as Burke pushed in Amanda's deck chair.

"You could learn a thing or two from this gentleman, Chase Eaton." Auntie narrowed her gaze at her nephew.

This time the laughter was directed at Chase, and Burke was happy to join in.

Everyone found a seat at the table. No stranger to lobster, given his extravagant lifestyle, Burke was happy not to have to be instructed in the ways of extracting the succulent meat. He didn't need another reason for a good ribbing from Chase.

"So, what do you think of our humble little town?" Wallace asked, sinking his teeth into a juicy ear of corn.

"High crime rate," scoffed Chase.

"Enough with the raccoon jokes. It's getting old." Amanda rolled her eyes.

Burke pushed his fork through his pile of homemade potato salad and tried not to smirk at the man who made needling him almost a full-time job.

"I really like it here. I can definitely see the attraction." He left it at that, knowing that the protective older brother in Chase would pick up on the double entendre, while hoping it was subtle enough that he didn't piss off Cady's dad in the process.

"Yeah, he's even thinking of staying. Isn't that exciting?" Cady squeezed his knee.

"So, wait … you'd choose our quiet little town over the Big Apple? Maybe you'd have better luck than any of us have had, convincing my stubborn little sister that she doesn't need to move all the way to the city to be happy. There is plenty of excitement right here in Scallop Shores."

"Burke will need the quiet," Cady interrupted, no doubt to deflect yet another raccoon joke. "He's writing a book."

"A travel book?" May asked him.

"Fiction, actually. Horror."

His head was beginning to spin at how fast the conversation was being pulled in different directions. It was clear Cady was using him to avoid a fight with Chase. Yet the pride in her voice seemed genuine. He had to admit, he liked it.

"Ooh, our own Stephen King!" Auntie's quavering voice trilled.

Burke's chest felt tight as he struggled with emotions that were so foreign to him. He'd only just met most of these people, and not only did they accept him for who he was, they were interested in his dreams of becoming an author. How could Cady want to leave this? Familial support, it felt like being pulled into a warm embrace. Good Lord—men were not supposed to get the warm fuzzies like this.

"Well, my editor would have my hide if she found out about my little moonlighting job." Burke waggled his brows as he looked around the table. "I sure could use some local perspective from someone who isn't desperate to flee the area. Maybe from someone who actually spent time in the city and chose to come back to her hometown?"

He'd been going for lighthearted, funny even, but the silence that descended over the table told Burke he'd crossed a line. Cursing inwardly, he was about to apologize to the elder Cadence when she smiled warmly.

"Young man, you are more than welcome to come visit me any time. I'm sure I have a story or two to share."

He let out the breath he'd been holding.

"So if you're gonna hang around, you should join our poker nights." Foster—God love the guy for stepping in and changing the subject—punctuated his point with a lobster claw.

Out of the corner of his eye, Burke caught Chase making a throat-slicing gesture with his hand. Yes! Poker, beer, gambling, and trash talk. Now, that was manly. The fact that Chase didn't want him there? Icing on the cake.

"I'd love to." He shot Chase a toothy grin. "Let me know if you want to carpool, buddy."

"Oh, I like you." Amanda looked from her husband to Burke and back again, amusement crinkling her eyes.

Cady, too, seemed to be watching the exchange like it was a tennis match. She plucked at a fluffy buttermilk biscuit, sitting back in her chair and looking relaxed. Burke understood with sudden clarity that Cady had everything he wanted: a supportive, loving family, a close-knit community, a job she loved (at least as far as he'd seen). And she was willing—no, eager—to leave that behind and start a life on her own in the city. It didn't make sense.

She was happy here. He'd have to be blind not to notice that. Surely it wouldn't take much convincing to get her to stay. The wheels started to turn and Burke tried to come up with ideas on how to incorporate the parts of city life that Cady seemed to feel she needed in order to make her life complete.

Step one: Appease Mr. Logan by convincing more Scallop Shores residents to order Cady's espresso drinks, so she could keep her machine at the bakery.

As if on cue, Cady traded out Burke's empty plate for a slice of pie. He forked up a piece of flaky, buttery crust and placed it on his tongue. Heaven. The town could not afford to lose such a talented baker.

He looked up to find that she was waiting for his assessment. His heart stuttered as he watched her expression go from nervous to hopeful and back again. She cared that much what he thought? Why him? Burke gave her a thumbs-up and a satisfied groan. Her face lit up. Joy, pure joy. It was contagious. He couldn't afford to lose her, either.

Chapter 9

Three orders for cappuccinos, five for lattes, one for an Americano, and another for a macchiato—all from people who lived and worked in Scallop Shores. Cady was starting to wonder if she was on some *Punk'd* type reality show. Seriously bizarre.

"Hey, Cady, what's up? I've got thirty glorious minutes to myself and I plan to indulge. Can I get a mocha with whip?" Talia, owner of Tumble Tots and mother to the cutest twin boys, had sidled up to the bakery counter.

Cady blinked. Talia always ordered a large French Roast, extra cream, and a brownie bite on the side. Without exception. Something was definitely going on.

"I'll make you a mocha, on one condition." She raised a brow, folding her arms across her chest. "You tell me who put you up to this."

The bright smile fell from Talia's face. *Gotcha!* She glanced toward the big plate-glass window as though she were afraid she'd be caught. Cady nodded in satisfaction.

"He's just trying to help you out. Honest."

"Who is? What are you talking about?"

"Burke." Talia lowered her voice and leaned in closer. "He's around the corner, convincing people to try something from your espresso machine, instead of the usual drip coffee."

"Why on earth would he do that?"

"He said Mr. Logan was going to make you pack it away if you didn't sell more. He asked if we'd support you in this. And of course we would. Our community rallies together. You should have asked us sooner, Cady."

"Oh, Lord ..." Cady slapped a hand to her head and rolled her eyes.

This had to stop. She prepared the mocha—because no one touched her espresso machine but her—then gestured for her part-time employee, Sophie, to man the counter. She'd have a little chat with the overstepping new man in her life.

Because he'd annoyed her, and because she was feeling a little evil, Cady slipped out the back door and made her way around the building. Sure enough, Burke was at the end of the block, head down, talking to a couple of older women. *Ha! Good luck with that.* Those two never frequented the bakery. Known for their penny-pinching, the Allen sisters refused to eat out and only bought food they could prepare at minimal cost. To her stunned disbelief, Cady watched them each pat Burke on the arm, nod, and walk into the bakery. Forget *Punk'd*; maybe she was on an episode of *The Twilight Zone*.

"How are you doing it? Cash incentives? Offering up dates? Kisses? What?" Cady took some small satisfaction from the startled jolt that nearly had Burke tumbling over his own feet.

"What does it matter? You need the customers and I'm bringing them in. Most people would use this moment to say thank you."

"It matters because I didn't ask for this. And I do not need the customers. These people—well, most of them—were customers to begin with. This situation with Mr. Logan is my problem, not yours."

"You should probably get back in there. The lovely Allen sisters seemed quite excited to try out a hazelnut latte. Just one. They said they were going to share it."

"Fine. But you're coming with me. I need to keep my eye on you. You're stirring up trouble!"

"That's just your way of saying you like me and you can't keep your eyes off me. It's okay, you can admit it." Burke winked.

"Oh, you're insufferable!" Cady grabbed the man by the hand and dragged him toward the entrance to the bakery.

"You're the one we're supposed to be focusing on. We need to figure out how to keep your parents off your back, get you a job so you can afford to live here, and then finally get you started on your dream career."

As the bell jangled over their heads, Cady caught Sophie madly waving her arms to get her attention. The Allen sisters were waiting for their drink.

"We, huh? Why are you so hell-bent on helping me?" Burke stopped her with a firm hand on her shoulder.

"Because I like you and I can't keep my eyes off you." Cady tossed him a saucy grin and hurried to slip behind the counter.

"Hey, City Guy! You're always good for a laugh. Come sit with us." Old Man Feeney slapped the empty stool between him and one of his cronies.

Behind the espresso machine, Cady watched Burke bristle. His back went ramrod straight and he shot Feeney a look that made the old man squirm. *Way to stand up to him, Burke!* She wanted to cheer out loud but settled for a huge smile. He just stood there, waiting.

"Fine. Burke. Okay? Would you like to sit with us, Burke?" Old Man Feeney capitulated.

"I'd love to. Thanks." He slid onto the proffered stool and slapped his new friend on the back.

The Allen sisters took their drink to a table by the window to wait for their warmed up croissant. Cady watched them, bemused. This was, indeed, an odd day. The Allen sisters' purchase plus Feeney making nice with—anyone, really, was headline-worthy.

Handing the pastry to Sophie to bring to the women, Cady made her way to the end of the counter, where Burke sat with his new buddies.

"What's your pleasure? The usual?" She stuck her tongue out at the lascivious wink he favored her with.

"You know what? I'm celebrating today. The BBQ with your family helped me make up my mind. I've decided to stay in Scallop Shores. So I'd like to buy my new friend here a drink." He turned and fixed the old man with a challenging stare.

"How about it, Feeney? You got the nerve to try one of Cady's fancy citified drinks?" Burke arched a brow.

"You callin' me out, boy? You think I'm chicken? Just because you're moving here now doesn't mean the rest of us have to get all fancy."

"I don't think you're chicken. I think you're cheap. This one's on me, pal. Celebrate with me. I'll buy you whatever espresso drink you want."

"Kid's got balls! Fine. Gimme the plainest dang fancy coffee you can make with that contraption." He answered gruffly. "But I ain't tippin'."

"You've got it!" Cady leaned across the scarred Formica counter, stole the ball cap off the old man's head, and kissed him right on his bald pate.

"Aw, geez. You see what you made her do? She's gonna think I'm some kind of freakin' teddy bear now."

"Don't worry, Mr. Feeney. I'll always think of you as a grizzly bear."

"See that you do." He harrumphed.

Cady quickly made two more drinks, silently debating whether or not she ought to train Sophie to use her precious espresso maker. It was probably just a one-time aberration. The locals would be back to their plain old coffee tomorrow. She looked at the empty tip jar perched near the register and couldn't help but chuckle. Her sleepy little town was anything but predictable today. And now Burke was making his stay in Scallop Shores a permanent one. He looked so excited to share his news with anyone who'd listen. She couldn't be happier for him. Really. However, her own dream of a new life in the city didn't look quite so bright and shiny.

"So tell us about the Big Apple. Cady's got it stuck in her head that it's the best place in the world to be. The streets lined with gold, or something?" Old Man Feeney eyed the drink she put in front of him with suspicion.

"Nah, nothing like that. The streets are wall-to-wall cars, the sidewalks so crowded with people you can't walk without knocking into someone. The horns honking, jackhammers from road construction, I'm talking major noise pollution."

"It can't be that bad. It's just a busy city. People have to work. They have to get from place to place." She set Burke's latte in front of him with a frown.

"But they could be friendly about it. People here are so friendly." Burke winked at Feeney while purposely avoiding her glare. "Folks in the city can't be bothered with so much as a 'good morning.' Everyone is staring at their phones or hooked up to their iPads. They avoid each other."

"What's the real estate like out there? Would Cady be able to find an apartment right away?" Cady looked over to see that Talia was still in the bakery and had wandered over to join the conversation.

"The affordable places aren't in the safest neighborhoods. No doormen, no locks on the front of the building. Anyone can walk in, which means she'd be sharing the building with vagrants." Burke frowned sadly at Talia, his expression surely meant to convey concern.

"Don't worry, most of them are friendly."

"Oh, for the love of Pete!" The man was a storyteller—that was for darned sure!

"And I don't even want to tell you about the biggest problem with New York City apartments," Burke told his ever-increasing audience.

"What problem is that?" Sophie asked him, pretending to wipe down the counter near his elbow.

"The cockroaches. They're everywhere." He shuddered.

The women in the group squealed, just as Cady knew Burke had hoped. This was no longer amusing.

"So the first thing I'll buy is an industrial-sized can of Raid. Big deal. I doubt I'll be spending much time in my apartment, anyway, what with all the exciting things I'll be doing."

"It's just that these are your friends, and they want to know that you're safe and happy out there. I feel honor bound to make sure you're aware of the panhandlers and shysters. Oh, and of course, the pickpockets."

"I suppose the big, bad city has gangs of homeless children running around like the Artful Dodger?" Cady rolled her eyes. "I guess I'll just have to keep rolls of cash in my bra, then."

"Those pickpockets are so skilled, you'll be lucky if they don't steal your bra too."

The entire room erupted in laughter. Cady turned her scowl from Burke to see that he held every single patron in his thrall. Well, she didn't have to stand here and listen to this. She waited for the noise to subside.

"Thank you, folks. He'll be here all week." She clapped her hands and gestured toward Burke, like she was suggesting he take a bow.

"I, however, am leaving. If you need anything else, Sophie's in charge. Thank you for all the orders of espresso drinks, but it's really not necessary. No one touches my machine." She shot a warning glare at the young woman.

"Cady ..." Burke started to slide off his stool but she held out a hand to stop him.

"No. You've already said quite enough."

Mustering as much dignity as she could, with an entire store full of patrons watching her retreat, Cady flounced through the swinging door to the storage room. A set of stairs led to her apartment above the bakery.

She waited until she'd slammed her apartment door before giving in to tears. How dare he? Burke had made light of her plans, her dreams of a better life. He'd used her to get in good with the locals. Well, she hoped it had been worth it because she was done with him. If he wanted help finding a new job or support against his overbearing parents, he could ask one of his new friends. Cady curled up on the couch, clutched a pillow tight to her chest, and sobbed.

• • •

"I messed up. I messed up bad." Burke lowered his head into his hands. His body was squished into one of the tiny chairs in the children's section of the public library.

"You weren't trying to belittle her dreams. You were trying to convince her to stay."

He peered out of bleary eyes at the librarian whose observation skills were far keener than he'd realized.

"Your motives were pure—selfish—but not malicious. She can forgive you. But I think it's going to take more than just an apology." Bree rested a hand on his shoulder before settling into one of the pint-sized chairs across the equally short table from Burke.

"Yes! Grand gestures. I can do that." Burke drummed his fingers on his knee as his mind raced to conjure the perfect apology scenario.

"I'll buy her another espresso machine! She loves the one she has. Why wouldn't she love to have a second one?" Eagerly, he awaited Bree's opinion.

"Because she only has one set of hands? Because she had a hard enough time convincing Mr. Logan to let her bring in the first one? Because her espresso machine is her baby and if you give her a second one, that's making the first one less significant, less special. Because—"

"Okay, I get it. No fancy coffee maker." He blew out a sigh, his lips flapping with the motion.

They sat quietly for a moment. Burke was happy with whom he'd chosen to approach for help apologizing to Cady. Amanda, being Cady's best friend—and a hormonal mess due to pregnancy—was likely to rip him another one. Chase would happily blacken his eye on a normal day, just for kicks, but given how Burke had hurt his sister, well, he was steering clear of that particular officer of the Scallop Shores police department. Bree was a calming influence. He could see how she'd be a good children's librarian. He could also see how she'd be a good friend.

They'd had the children's section to themselves for a while but now a little dark-haired girl with bouncing curls dashed in. She made a beeline for Bree, wrapping her arms around the woman's neck and giving her a loud, smacking kiss on the cheek. A blond woman wasn't too far behind, holding a chubby-cheeked baby on each hip.

"No picture books this time, Lily. Your teacher said you're ready to try easy chapter books." The woman knelt and set the babies on the floor. The little boy crawled off toward the floor pillows. The little girl plopped down on her bottom, content to stay with her mama.

"Hey, Lily, I think it's time to introduce you to the Rainbow Magic series. You still get to read about fairies, but these are chapter books." Bree stood up from the table, then paused.

"Oh, I'm sorry. Burke, this is Quinn. Quinn, Burke. Quinn lived in New York for a while, so maybe she could help you with your dilemma." And with that, she was off to help Lily choose a new book to read.

"You're the one doing the series of articles on our town." Quinn's brow drew together in confusion. "But what's the dilemma? You need some help coming up with ideas? I thought Cady was helping with that."

"She was." He frowned, hating the pathetically defeated tone of his voice.

"Uh oh."

"My dilemma doesn't have to do with my work. I upset Cady—in a big way. Now I need to come up with an equally big way to tell her how sorry I am." He chewed at his bottom lip, concentrating. "She's fascinated with New York City. If I could recreate some of that here."

"The crowds? The noise? Really?"

"Well, no. I was thinking of the culture, the food."

"Is that what she likes about it? Are you sure?" Quinn asked, gently.

Burke paused. He couldn't answer that. If he were honest, he'd admit that he was projecting his own ideas about what he missed in the city. He really had no clue what Cady was hoping to discover there.

Bree rejoined them at the little table, holding a wriggling little boy in her lap and bouncing him on her knees.

"Little Mason decided to climb Mount Magazine Rack. You and Jonah sure have your hands full. Is Cora a little explorer too?"

"Thankfully, no. She's a shy one." Quinn smiled down at the baby who sat quietly beside her knee, playing with Quinn's car keys.

"So how are we going to get Burke back into Cady's good graces?" Bree looked from one adult to the other.

"He needs to get her alone and give her the time she needs to explain to him just what makes her dream about moving to New York so special."

"Without judgment or preconceived notions about the city. And no using family or anything about the town to make her feel guilty about not staying." *Or the fact that he wouldn't be returning to the city in September as he'd planned.*

"So no special dinner at the lighthouse?" His words were hopeful.

"She's most comfortable in her bakery, among her things," Quinn added.

"But Old Man Feeney and all the rest of them—"

"Won't be there at night, when the bakery is closed." Bree slowed her words down so Burke couldn't miss her meaning.

"I get in and, what, ask her to make me a latte because I know she loves using her espresso maker?"

The two women looked at each other, their expressions flashing between exasperation and amusement. Burke pressed his lips together and hunched his shoulders. He couldn't help it if he was going into this blind. He was used to dealing with shallow women. When he had to apologize to one of the women he usually dated, all he had to do was buy her jewelry and a fancy dinner. Then they'd go back to his place and have make-up sex.

Only this was Cady. And he wasn't dating her. And she wasn't shallow. And though make-up sex sounded like a terrific idea to him, that wasn't how he wanted their first time together to be. He wasn't even sure why he felt this desperate need to make things right again. Embarrassed, he realized he'd been just as shallow as all those women he'd dated. He had only apologized for accused slights with the goal of make-up sex afterwards. Again, he put his face in his hands and groaned. He didn't deserve to be forgiven.

"You really care about her." Bree's voice was a soothing balm on his battered emotions.

"Yeah, I care so much about her that I want her to sit down and tell me all the reasons why she wants to leave when I've only just come to realize that this is where I want to build my future." And if that wasn't crazy messed up, he didn't know what was.

"You could buy her flowers and jewelry, a big fancy dinner ..." Quinn let the suggestion trail off.

"But that would insult her," he finished.

"I believe he knows Cady better than he realized." Bree's lips twitched at the corners.

"I believe he's in love." Quinn shot him a calculating look.

"Love sucks." Burke grumbled.

"And sometimes it all works out in the end." Quinn took Mason in one arm and slipped Cora onto her knee with the other. She dropped a kiss on top of one head and then the other, giving both babies a quick squeeze.

"Mommy, I have bunches of books to read. Can we go home now?" Lily dropped a huge stack on the table at Quinn's elbow.

"And that's my cue, folks. Burke, good luck. Bree, work your magic." She nodded at them both, adjusted the two babies higher on her hips, and stood with practiced ease.

Once Quinn and her children were gone, Bree got to work explaining exactly how Burke was going to win over Cady. He had to admit, her plan was better than anything his shallow brain could come up with. Even if didn't involve make-up sex.

Chapter 10

Cady sat at her kitchen table, inputting the deposit slips from the checks Burke had written her into her budgeting spreadsheet. The plan for the evening being how she'd deal with expenses once she moved to New York. Okay, part of that plan involved a pint of Ben & Jerry's and a spoon. There may have been a glass or two of wine involved in that scenario, as well.

But Shannon Patterson, mom to triplets and wife to one of Scallop Shore's newest residents, Dean Patterson, called. She'd been waiting on the results of a major exam and had stress-baked again. Now she had a mountain of whoopie pies she didn't know what to do with. Could she drop them by the bakery tonight? It wasn't like Cady could say no. Whenever she stocked Shannon's baked goods, they always sold out faster than hers. She agreed to meet her friend downstairs at six o'clock.

While she killed time, Cady made the rounds to each room, turning on fans. The humidity was at an all-time high and her energy at an all-time low. The limp curtains lay still; not a single breath of air stirred through the multitude of open windows.

Dressing for the weather didn't seem to help. Wearing her skimpiest pink tank top and a ratty old pair of cutoffs, she still felt overdressed. She'd piled her hair up on top of her head just to provide a little relief.

A few minutes before six, Cady left her sweltering apartment and headed down the back stairwell to the bakery. Maybe she'd slip into the walk-in cooler and bask in the glorious refrigeration until Shannon arrived. A noise alerted her to activity in the bakery and she hurried to see what was going on.

"Shh, she'll hear you."

"Um, too late. She already has."

Bree and Foster looked up guiltily from the table they had been setting. Cady's eyes swept from one to the other, puzzled. Movement in the corner of the room revealed Burke, a vase of tall roses in his hand. His smile was sheepish and she couldn't help but be charmed.

"Thanks for all the help, you two, but I think I can take it from here." He set the roses down on the counter, offered Foster a handshake and Bree a quick hug.

They both waved to Cady, neither saying so much as a word as they let themselves out of the bakery.

"I'm going to go out on a limb here and assume that Shannon is not meeting me at six o'clock." Cady put her hands on her hips and waited for an explanation.

"Oh, she was already here. See? She left a plate of whoopie pies for dessert." Burke pointed to the counter beside the cash register.

"And ... Foster made us dinner?"

"He brought the wine too. Excellent vintage."

"Burke, what are you doing?" She stepped into the bakery-proper and took a moment to study the set up. The table in the far corner had been set with a gorgeous lace tablecloth. She assumed that was Bree's doing. Crystal wine goblets had already been filled with some kind of Chardonnay or other white wine. Dinner was waiting in a chafing dish on an empty table. He would have needed a lot of help to pull this off.

"I am trying to apologize. I embarrassed you in front of your friends and customers. I made light of your plans to move to the city."

He came up beside her, taking her hands in his, and waited until she looked up before continuing. "I was being selfish. I thought if I could make city life sound less than ideal, you'd want to stay. But you deserve more. You deserve to follow your dreams. I have no right to take that away from you." Bringing her hand to his lips, he brushed a kiss across her knuckles. She shivered.

"You mean that?" Cady eyed him dubiously.

"I mean that." He gestured to the table. "Sit down. I'll serve dinner."

Her lack of clothing suddenly making her self-conscious, she slipped into the chair Burke held out and tried to cover her over-exposed thighs with the cloth napkin he placed in her lap. An embarrassing rumble issued from her empty stomach, causing them both to chuckle. Whatever Foster had made for dinner, it smelled incredible.

"There was a salad somewhere. Oh, and a loaf of bread. I can check behind the counter."

"Don't worry about it. I'm starved. What is in that chafing dish? Just set it in the middle of the table. I might share." Cady frowned at the amusement in Burke's eyes.

"Okay, okay, let's get you fed already."

Rather than doing as she suggested, and putting the warming pan right on the table, Burke spooned the entrees onto two plates and slid one in front of Cady. He sat down with the second one, pausing to gauge her reaction to the menu choice before placing his own napkin over his legs.

He needn't have worried. Scallops were her favorite shellfish. She should have been sick of them, as often as her father had brought them home. Earning a living from the sea, the Eatons had learned to love all forms of seafood. And Foster had his own recipe for broiled scallops—one he refused to share with anyone. It said a lot about Burke that her friend was willing to make this dish for him.

"Mm ... This is so good." Cady moaned, licking a drop of buttery sauce from her lip.

She peeked under her lashes to find Burke watching her, intently. Her scalp prickled and heat that had nothing to do with the summer humidity had her breathing faster than normal.

"You aren't eating. Don't you like it?" She gazed pointedly at the fork that hung midway to his mouth.

He blinked a few times, taking a deep breath and then letting it out slowly. "I guess I'm a little distracted this evening."

Awareness hummed through the air between them like a live wire, raising the hair on her arms. Burke's irises grew darker, his attention leaving her face to slowly travel downward. Cady had half a mind to swipe the dishes from the table and use the lace tablecloth as a bed sheet. With trembling fingers she reached for her wine and took a healthy gulp.

"Tell me about New York."

"What are you going to do when you get to New York?"

They spoke simultaneously. Cady giggled, the wine rushing to her head and making a slightly embarrassing situation more than a little amusing. She took a bite of rice pilaf, chewing slowly as she waited for Burke to pick up his thread of the conversation. He shook his head, smiling.

"Tonight is about you. We've talked about my dreams, but we've never really talked about yours."

"Why do you care?" She wrinkled her nose and leaned across the table a bit. "Seriously. No one else has ever bothered to ask. No one in my family. None of my friends. They let me talk about moving to New York, but no one has ever asked me why."

"I don't know." Burke broke eye contact, lowering a troubled gaze to his plate. "This is uncharted territory for me. I'm used to women whose greatest ambition in life involves snagging a rich husband and figuring out the most exorbitant ways to spend his money."

Cady snorted. "You won't find *any* women like that in Scallop Shores."

"I think the city could use more women like you. Independent women, determined to make their own way in life. Brave."

"Some would say I was too ignorant to know when I should be frightened."

"I disagree. You stand up to what scares you. I wouldn't be surprised if the biggest reason you wanted to move to New York is because the idea of leaving your family behind terrifies you."

Wow. Cady cocked her head to the side as she let the chilled alcohol slide down her throat. She'd never thought of it that way, but it actually made a lot of sense. She was terrified of leaving her family, leaving everyone and everything that brought her comfort. Yet threaded into the fear was a thrill that she couldn't deny. A spark of adventure that spurred her on.

Burke's phone chirped in his pants pocket. He looked down briefly, and continued to eat.

"Oh, for goodness's sake! See who it was. It may be important."

"I have a feeling I know who it was, and I don't really want to deal with it."

His parents. Crap. She'd forgotten about Burke's troubles.

"Let me check it for you. Give me your phone. You keep eating." She stuck her hand over his plate so he couldn't take another bite until he did as she'd asked.

He rolled his eyes, rummaged around for his cell phone and slapped it in her palm. Cady woke up the screen, tapped on the message button, and read.

Where are you? I expected you here for a meeting with the shareholders this afternoon. This is not acceptable! You have responsibilities, B. Call me.

Cady frowned. Burke was watching her intently. He wasn't going to eat until she told him what the text had said. Just then, her own phone started ringing.

"Grand Central Station," she answered.

"Cady?" It was Fran at Kittredge Manor.

"Fran? Is something wrong? Auntie?"

"No, sweetheart, nothing is wrong with your aunt. I didn't mean to give you a scare. It's just that you are our go-to person when things get crazy here. Are you busy tonight?"

She looked across the table at Burke, his expression one of concern. Was this supposed to be a date? Or was it just an "I'm sorry, be my friend again" dinner?

"Are you still there? Cady?"

"I'm here, Fran. What do you need?"

"Most of our kitchen staff called in sick. You ask me, there is a big party out at Folley Pond tonight. We have a mountain of dishes that need washing and Carl is about to quit if I don't call in reinforcements. Is there any way you can help us out?"

Well, if this was truly supposed to be about her tonight—

"I can do you one better, Fran. I'm coming—and I'm bringing an extra set of hands. We'll be there in a few minutes."

"Bless you, sweetheart. We'll see you when you get here."

She ended the call and looked up guiltily.

"You volunteered us for some kind of grunt work?"

"Right on the first guess! My goodness, you're a smart one." Cady realized she still clutched a cell phone in each hand, her gaze going from the roses to the wine to the delicious food.

"I can call her back and cancel. I should." She shouldn't have been so quick to ruin their evening. She handed Burke his phone back and shoved hers in her front pocket.

"Don't you dare! It sounded important and we're not going to let this person down. If they called you to come and help out on a Saturday evening, then they were desperate." Burke swept his napkin from his lap, swiped at his lips, and tossed it on the table before standing up. "So, where are we going and what are we doing?"

"Kittredge Manor Nursing Home. We're washing dishes." She may as well have said they were scrubbing toilets, by the look that came over his face. It took supreme effort on her part not to laugh.

"Awesome. Love that place. Let's go."

"Hey, I really appreciate this. But don't think it gets you out of answering your dad. The guy is pissed."

The poor guy looked miserable, though whether it had to do with washing dishes on a Saturday night or having to face his father, she couldn't be sure. But for the moment, he was giving up his time for her. If she weren't careful she could easily fall in love with Burke Sanders. Who was she kidding? Part of her already had.

...

"So I told you once how Auntie spent a summer in New York? She was a nanny for this rich family that lived on Central Park West."

Burke was more than familiar with that area of Manhattan. It was where he'd grown up. But he'd finally gotten Cady to open up to him, and he wouldn't interrupt that for the world. He nodded.

"She still talks about those few short months as if they were the best of her life." Cady's voice was soft, full of wonder and emotion.

"I can see it in her eyes whenever she goes back there, in her memories. She loved it all. The kids she took care of, the days spent playing in the park. It was like a dream. She fell in love there too."

This gave him pause, and Burke looked up from the inside of the giant pot he'd been scrubbing. The tip of his nose itched and he was forced to scratch it with a huge yellow glove-encased hand. Unbeknownst to him, he'd inadvertently filled the glove with dishwater, and when he raised it to his nose, he got a shocking surprise. The front of his borrowed white apron was soaked.

"So why didn't she stay?"

"Class differences. She was the nanny. He was the younger brother of her well-to-do boss."

"Did he love her back?"

"Yes. Apparently they were quite mad about each other." Cady sighed, the copper lid she'd been drying stilled in her hands.

Ever the romantic, thought Burke.

"But if they loved each other—"

"It was different back then, Burke. He had a responsibility to marry within his station. Auntie says his family already had someone in mind."

"So she just left?"

"Once school started again, they didn't need her. They sent her home. Her love married a girl whose family was even richer than his and they had three children."

"She kept tabs? That must have been painful."

"I totally agree. But it's like she just had to know." Cady tugged the freshly scrubbed pot from Burke's hands and began to wipe it dry.

"He died recently. I remember when she learned about it in the paper. Auntie was just devastated. She has never stopped loving him. He was her soul mate. She never married. I guess if she couldn't have him, she didn't want anyone at all."

"So ... you're looking to head to Manhattan to find your true love, and when you do, you'll hang on to him no matter what the obstacles?" Burke plunged his rubber-gloved hands into the thinning bubbles of the lukewarm dishwater.

"No, silly! I'm going to the city to carve out my own experiences. I don't want to get to be Auntie's age and have any regrets. I don't want to be sitting here at Kittredge Manor on Bingo night, chatting about the good ol' days that weren't really all that good to begin with. I want to know that I worked my hardest to get everything I wanted—that *I* made it happen."

"You don't have a plan on what you'll do once you get there?"

"Do *you* have a plan on what you'll do to earn money in Scallop Shores?"

"Fair enough." He paused, unsure of how she'd take what he needed to say next. "It's just that Manhattan is one of the most expensive places in the country to live. I just want to be sure you know what you're getting yourself into." He cringed, waiting for her to take offense.

"I'll figure something out. Thanks for looking out for me." She giggled as she'd clearly seen him bracing for a proper set-down.

"We're rebels, you and I. I'm breaking the mold that my ancestors made years and years ago. I'm going to go out and see the world. I may have to occupy an apartment with a colony of cockroaches and share my Ramen noodles and brown tap water with them, but that's going to be my choice."

"Sounds appetizing. Here, pack this wet noodle to take with you when you go." Burke held up a bedraggled piece of wet spaghetti. He flung it at Cady, who squealed.

A loud snap was the only warning Burke had before she cracked the dishtowel against his ass. Oh, it was on! He scooped up a dollop of soap bubbles hanging out near the sink drain, waiting until Cady turned to face him. He blew them into her face, where they scattered and settled in her hair. She reached around him and grabbed the long hose that served as a faucet. Aw, crap! Before he even had time to hold up his hands in surrender, she'd doused him good.

Burke backed away, making the sign for timeout. They were both nearly breathless from laughing. Water dripped all over the floor, but the dishes were finished, stacked neatly on the counter. Grabbing a second dishtowel, he dropped it to the tiled floor and used his foot to mop up the excess water. Cady did the same with hers and, for a minute, it looked like they were doing a funny dance.

"I think we're done. Thanks for doing this with me, Burke. I know it's not how you'd planned to spend your Saturday evening, but I really appreciate it."

"You want to thank me? I know a good way." He wiggled his eyebrows suggestively.

"Burke!" Her eyes went wide as saucers, her cheeks suddenly stained a bright pink.

"Whoopie pies. We brought the container with us, remember?" He winked. "What were you thinking?"

"Ooh! I can do you one better." Cady scrambled around the industrial-sized kitchen sink and rummaged inside a cupboard at the back of the room. Spinning around, she held up a half-empty bottle of Jack Daniels.

Now, this was his kind of woman!

They slid to the floor, backs against the cabinets. Burke held a Tupperware container of whoopie pies in his lap and Cady opened the whiskey, took a swig, and passed the bottle to him. He cracked open the lid on the sweets and handed one to her nicely.

Cady stuck out her tongue and licked her way around the circumference of the chocolate pie. Burke banged the back of his head against the cabinet, refusing to let out the moan that burbled just on the other side of his lips. She sucked the chocolate from the tip of one finger, grinning evilly as she caught his eye.

"Witch!"

"You love it."

"Doesn't mean I'll put up with it for long," he warned.

"What if someone were to walk in?" A saucy smile curled her lips.

"Should have thought of that before."

Tossing aside the plastic container, Burke leaned over and grasped Cady's face in both hands, claiming that saucy smile and the sweetness that lay behind it. He groaned into her mouth as her greedy fingers plowed through his hair, tugging just enough to hurt but not so much that he wanted her to stop. She tasted of sweet sugar and the burnt wood of Tennessee whiskey. It was far more intoxicating than the one swallow of JD that still burned his throat.

As the kiss intensified, Burke pulled her roughly into his lap. His hands moved down to that ass he'd been dying to touch ever since Cady had sashayed out into the bakery in barely there cut-off jeans. So warm. So firm. His lips moved to the column of her neck, on his way to even greater treasures.

"God, I didn't realize how wet I'd gotten you." Cady struggled in his grip.

Panting, Burke raised his head, his sex-addled brain unable to make sense of her words.

She was pushing against him, simultaneously plucking at her damp tank top that had soaked up excess water from his shirt.

"Yeah. I should just take it off." He reached for the top button, frowning when Cady covered his hands with one of hers.

"Slow down, cowboy. This isn't the time or place." The look in her eyes suggested there would, eventually, be a perfect time and place.

Sliding out of his lap, Cady slumped down beside him once more. They sat side by side, chests rising and falling rapidly. Burke didn't dare move. Even his teeth ached from how badly he wanted this woman.

"What are we going to do?" Her voice was still breathy.

"F—" She placed a finger over his mouth before he could finish the word.

"About the text you got from your dad, Burke. What are we going to do about that?"

She was going to kill him. Only Cady could dash cold water on him, both literally and figuratively. Burke closed his eyes, resigning himself to the fact that they were no longer talking about them.

"I've ignored him this long. He's a smart guy. Eventually he'll get the message."

"You know you owe him an explanation. And he deserves to hear it from you face to face."

Just because she was right did not make her words any easier to hear. Burke thumped his head against the cabinet again for good measure.

"I could take a puddle jumper out of Port Kitt. Be back in town before dinner."

"Or you could take me with you, show me a real night out on the town."

"Hey, I was trying for special. That dinner, the roses—" Again, a finger across his lips was all she needed to shut him up.

"Were all beautiful and incredibly special and I love the thought behind them, even if it meant you were groveling." Cady wrinkled her nose, an irrepressible grin making her eyes dance. "Okay, I may have liked that part the most."

"Perhaps I was mistaken. Could be you aren't so different from the women I knew in the city." Burke chuckled, jerking back as she punched him in the arm.

"Have to grovel often?"

"I plead the Fifth."

This time he was faster, and caught her tiny fist in one of his hands. He pried the fingers open, one by one, until her fleshy palm was revealed. Raising Cady's hand to his mouth, Burke maintained eye contact. He kissed the center of her palm, his lips lingering, and tongue darting out to taste the skin. He wanted to roar, beat his chest in manly conquest at her gasp.

A trip to the city was looking downright appealing. Especially if it included an overnight stay. Burke kissed his way up Cady's wrist, enjoying the tinkling sound of her giggles. He'd never invited a woman to spend the night at his place before. He refused to dwell on just how big this was. Or how scared he was that this visit would only cement her resolve to leave Scallop Shores.

Chapter 11

"What do you think?" Cady held up two silky nighties for consideration. The pale pink gown was a simple sheath, beautiful without being too in-your-face. The black one was much more revealing with plunging lacy bra cups. The length barely covered her butt

"Innocent flower or sultry vixen?"

Amanda rubbed at her lower back, arching to stretch out the muscles as she lowered herself to Cady's bed. She shot her friend a contemplative look, chewing on her bottom lip as she carefully chose her words.

"You guys have an understanding, right? This is just for fun? No one gets hurt?"

"Yeah, of course. I mean, we haven't exactly had a conversation about it. *'Hey, just FYI, we aren't in a relationship. Don't go getting attached or anything.'*"

"It's just that, the more time you spend with Burke, the more you talk about him. And the fact that he was able to hurt you so badly in front of everyone at the bakery, well, that kind of tells me that you're already in over your head."

"Nothing is happening between Burke and me. Nothing can happen. We want different things." Cady dropped the silky nightgowns on the foot of the bed and turned to the open drawer.

"The funny thing is, Burke is the one wanting the white picket fence, the house, all of that. I'm the one wanting freedom and fun times, excitement."

"You don't think you could talk him into staying in the city? He could find a job at a different magazine, one that wouldn't have him traveling all the time."

Though there had been no need, Burke had asked Cady not to mention his parents to anyone. He was just starting to become involved in the community and he didn't want everyone to look at him differently because he was the heir to a multi-billion-dollar hotel dynasty. Fitting in here, in town, was important to him. He was discovering a sense of belonging in this small town that he'd never had in the city. No, she wouldn't be able to talk him into staying in New York. And she didn't want to.

"This is his dream, Amanda. If anyone knows what it's like to chase after dreams, it's me. I just want him to be happy."

Cady scuffed across the worn carpet to the tiny opening that served as a closet. Reaching into the corner, she pulled out an old L.L. Bean tote bag and carried it to the bed. The straps were bright red, her initials embroidered in matching thread across the front.

Amanda laughed in delight. "You still have that old thing? I remember when you used to stuff it with Barbies and Beanie Babies when you came over for sleepovers."

"To be replaced in later years with nail polish and teeny bopper magazines." Cady chuckled.

"I used to try to get you to talk about what it would be like when we were married, raising our babies together. Our girls were going to have matching outfits, remember?"

"I remember that you knew you were going to marry Chase as far back as second grade. We were what, eight years old? You wanted me to marry Foster. One big happy family."

"It could have been," Amanda muttered.

"You know I love Dimples, right?" Cady referred to the nickname she'd given Amanda's brother years ago.

"But he lives in Scallop Shores and is therefore out of the running." Her friend sighed. They'd had this conversation many times.

"Look at you, though. You got Chase. You're having his baby. All your plans are coming true." Cady wiggled her brows and grinned wide. "You had your wicked night. Now it's time for mine." Sticking her tongue out at her friend, she unzipped the tote bag and peered inside.

"Ah yes, and what a night it was." Amanda's deep chuckle told her more than she wanted to know.

Cady stuck her fingers in her ears. "La, la, la. No details. I don't want to think about my brother doing nasty things to my best friend."

"Your poor brother is getting nothing but the brush-off lately, so it's good for both of us to be able to remember what put this little one in my belly."

"Aw, poor little Chase. He never was very good at being told no."

"He's inviting Burke to the poker game next week. He loves to torture the guy, but I think Chase really likes him."

Cady paused, midway between the dresser and the bed, a stack of shirts in her hands. Her brother was making nice with Burke. Damned if that didn't make her all teary. She couldn't look at Amanda, knowing that the other woman would feed off her emotions and it wouldn't be long before they were both blubbering idiots. And for no other reason than Chase was making an effort to include Burke in the community.

"That's awesome. They'll have a great time." She stuck her head in the closet again and pretended to study her choices, taking a moment to get herself under control.

"Will it be weird to come home for visits? Or will you maybe want to come home more often, now that Burke will be here?" The hopeful lilt to Amanda's voice left no question which answer she wished for.

"I hadn't even thought about that yet. I should probably leave town before I think about coming home for visits." She turned slightly and threw a wink over her shoulder.

Right now she didn't want to think about her impending move. She didn't want to think about life without her friends, her family, or Burke. She wanted to live in the moment. She wanted to think about her trip with Burke, pretending that it was more about getting to see the city she wanted so much to move to and not about spending time with a man who was starting to become a necessary part of her life.

Cady needed this trip. It would be good to regain her focus, build up her excitement. Just her and Burke on a whirlwind tour of his stomping grounds. She'd get to see him in his element. The preppy, *GQ* guy who'd first walked into her bakery and snagged her interest. Except Burke had changed a lot since their first meeting. He was really fitting in and finding his place as a local. And for the first time in her life, Cady found herself falling for a resident of Scallop Shores.

• • •

There was no backing out now. Burke had made an appointment to meet with his father at ten o'clock the following morning. The fact that he'd had to make an appointment to be seen made his decision that much easier. He'd booked a couple of tickets for a puddle jumper leaving out of an old Air Force base-turned-commercial airfield in Port Kitt. This time tomorrow, he and Cady would be up above the clouds.

But for now, he sat at his makeshift desk and worked on his latest article. Meredith was loving the off-the-beaten-path angle, and Burke felt more than a little guilty at taking full credit, since he'd never gotten around to officially asking to hire Cady on as his assistant. This week he was writing about a small mom-and-pop business that rented out boats, canoes, and kayaks by the hour to folks looking to spend a little time on Scallop Shores River.

He was sure his readers would delight in the humor aspect, as he described his icy plunge into the river. It turned out canoes were easier to get into than out of. He recalled the spectacularly embarrassing moment when his arms were pinwheeling wildly as the foot planted firmly on shore and the foot still in the canoe drifted further and further apart, turning him into a human wishbone. Not his finest moment. Burke rolled his shoulders and thought about the email awaiting an answer.

Meredith was pushing for an answer. Where was he going from here? What fabulous locale had he chosen for his next assignment? She'd given him carte blanche (within reason) as she'd been so pleased with his articles on Scallop Shores, the seaside town she'd been so certain he'd fall in love with. She'd offered up some suggestions: Monte Carlo, Santorini, and Jamaica, to name a few.

That was another overdue visit he'd have to make while he was in the city. It was one thing to cut ties with a family that he'd never felt he belonged to. But the magazine, his editor, they'd always been decent to him. He had no complaints. Up until a few short weeks ago, he'd hounded Meredith for the plum assignments. Now he was telling her 'thanks, but no, thanks'. The idea set his stomach churning like a pit full of snakes.

What the hell was he going to do for a living? He knew if he asked to do freelance from Scallop Shores, the answer would be no. It was a travel magazine, after all. No. If he wanted to stay in this town, he had to quit his job at the magazine. He'd have to find a nine-to-five, probably working weekends and most definitely pulling in a minimum wage. How the hell much *was* minimum wage? Could anyone even live on that?

Burke had never wanted for anything in his life. While other college-bound kids straight out of high school were eating boxed macaroni and cheese or Ramen noodles, and buying secondhand furniture at Goodwill, Burke's parents had bought him an apartment—a penthouse apartment—complete with an interior designer named Maurice, who had spent more time checking out Burke's butt than fabric swatches.

Living in this tiny one-bedroom cottage was the closest Burke had ever come to slumming it. And once he gave his notice at the magazine, he was one step closer to sleeping on the street. Did Scallop Shores even have a homeless community? He could be the first. The thought of squatting in front of Logan's Bakery almost made him smile.

Okay, he had to snap out of it! He was following his dream, right? He was going to write the Great American Horror Novel. It didn't matter if he never earned a dime. He would be doing what he loved, in a town that he was learning to love. It was a new beginning, and damn it, he could do this!

Elbows on the table, Burke rested his chin in his hands and stared moodily out the window. The sun shone bright, everything outside awash in color. The sliver of ocean that he could see was placid. It should have been calming, that tranquil blue. But it made him feel weak. And being weak pissed him off. He needed a plan.

He needed to know just how bad things were going to be financially, once his parents cut him off. The penthouse was in their name. That issue had never bothered him before. It had allowed Burke his independence, while also ensuring that his parents could feel they were doing their part to support him, and still remain emotionally distant.

Hadn't a trust fund matured a couple of years ago? Did he have access to that? Was it already in an account somewhere? Maybe things weren't as dire as his panicked brain had made them out to be. Then again, perhaps there were strings attached and part of getting his hands on that money meant accepting a role in the family business.

Resigned to the fact that these questions were going to have to remain unanswered until he saw his father, Burke pushed his chair away from his workspace and stood up. His brain was too cluttered to do any kind of writing today. The beautiful summer weather was calling to him. Besides, living this close to the seashore and not spending more time at the water's edge was a crime. He'd enjoy a run down to the beach and cool off with an icy dip in the Atlantic.

Cady was working or he'd ask her to join him. It disgusted Burke how she'd had to beg for the time off. Two frickin' days! From what she'd told him, she never took vacations. That Mr. Logan really took advantage of her. He couldn't wait for the day she gave her notice.

As he changed into running shorts and laced up his sneakers, he grinned. Mr. Logan had made Cady train Sophie on making espresso drinks. It was his one condition in order for her to take the time off. Burke knew it was killing her to let someone else touch her precious machine. But it meant that the bakery owner was admitting that customers would order the higher-priced drinks. That had to be worth something, right?

The humidity wasn't quite as thick as it had been, but the sense of walking out his door and into a wet blanket was still something Burke had a hard time adjusting to. As he jogged out his driveway and down the short, unpaved road that held a couple of other rental properties, he tried to picture the area in winter. Cady told him the beach areas were pretty much deserted after Labor Day.

Burke ran past a roadside stand that sold local produce. He'd have to come back when he had some cash on him. He'd gotten addicted to fresh blueberries on his granola in the morning. They weren't big and plump, like you could buy in the grocery store. These were much smaller, growing wild in the woods around town. And they were so much sweeter. His mouth watered and he picked up his speed to put some distance between himself and the tempting fruit.

Taking a right, he passed a campground that catered to RVs and smaller campers. It would kill his father to know this, but

Burke liked that Scallop Shores didn't just cater to the well-to-do, like some of the ritzier towns up the coast. This town made it possible for people on any budget to vacation here. There were a couple of hotels that his father wouldn't absolutely cringe at. The B&Bs were quite popular, too. But there were motels and campgrounds of all kinds.

He watched a group of teens playing a game of volleyball on the cushiony grass at the campground. Mothers managed to hold a conversation from their webbed lawn chairs while keeping an eye on a group of toddlers splashing around in a kiddie pool. Oh, to have had summer experiences like this when he was growing up! Well, there was no sense lamenting the past when he had it within his power to change his future.

Burke arrived at the beach and knew that his plan to run the whole length before rewarding himself with a swim was not going to be possible. Had he really not been down here at this time of day before? Not a parking space to be had. Families were jaywalking between cars that were stuck in traffic as far as the eye could see. The sand was nearly nonexistent, covered in multicolored blankets and towels. A rental station had been set up near the lifeguard stand, though there weren't many floats left to be rented. He stood on the sidewalk, looking down over the chaos that was Scallop Shores overrun by tourists. It was glorious!

Chapter 12

Horns blaring and traffic rushing past. Voices raised in conversation over the myriad noises surrounding them. A jackhammer digging up concrete a street over. All of it wrapped Cady up in a cacophony of discordant pandemonium. It was glorious.

Spinning in a slow circle, she took it all in, a wide grin stretching across her cheeks. She'd promised to wait in the little coffee shop across the street while Burke met with his father. But he had her cell number and she was too excited to sit around twiddling her thumbs. The minute he disappeared behind the glass door of the high-rise, Cady had scrambled from her chair and out into the bustle of the city.

Before he had left, Burke had slapped a twenty-dollar bill on the table. It wasn't like she didn't have any money of her own, so she tried to push it back toward him. The tightness of his jaw and a quick shake of his head caused her to relent. He was worked up over this meeting with his father. If this was what it took to convince him she would be fine on her own for an hour or so, then she wouldn't argue.

Cady meandered down the street, stopping to admire a killer pair of heels on a well-dressed storefront mannequin. She wouldn't have any use for them in Scallop Shores. But here? In the city? She was starting to develop some dangerously expensive tastes. Lustily eyeing the shoes one more time, she sighed and moved on.

What an amazing day! Her first plane ride. Okay, so that hadn't been quite as thrilling as it had been nerve-wracking. Who knew she had a fear of flying? Burke had been so sweet, holding her hand and dropping soft kisses against her temple when her squeezes were probably close to breaking his poor hand.

Her first cab ride. Never mind that she thought the guy was going to kill them before they ever arrived at their destination. There might not have been multiple lanes in Scallop Shores, but there were stoplights. And rules. She was pretty sure that red meant stop—not zing through before anyone else had a chance to step on the gas pedal. Cady bit her lip. She'd have to get used to that now, wouldn't she? Oh, boy.

Bright sun found its way down to the sidewalk, bouncing off all the glass and chrome. Blessedly, the humidity in New York was not as cloying as it was on the coast. It was a gorgeous summer day. Fighting the urge to skip down the sidewalk, Cady giggled to herself. She was finally in the city.

A tall man in a business suit rushed past, knocking her shoulder and causing her to shuffle several inches to her left in order to keep her balance. If she hadn't been looking down already, she would have tripped over the legs stretched out in front of her. An old man, his scruffy beard filthy and his long trench coat entirely too warm for the weather, scowled up at her from the pavement.

Oh, the poor dear! On this day of firsts, Cady encountered her first homeless person. She gave him her kindest smile, wavering only slightly when it was returned with a toothless leer. Remembering the twenty-dollar bill that Burke had given her, she stepped closer, reaching in her pocket and leaning down to press it into the old man's hand. She refrained from wiping her hand on her shorts, but only just barely, after she'd had to yank it out of the old guy's grasp. Okay, that was only slightly creepy.

Patting herself on the back for having done her good deed for the day, Cady turned the corner to continue her exploration of the city. She'd probably just helped a homeless man feed himself for the whole week. Her jaded brother would have thrown a fit. Chase would claim it was just going toward booze or cigarettes. But Cady had to believe that someone as down and out as that poor man would see the money for the boon that it was and figure out a way to stretch every last penny.

Smiling at anyone who'd make eye contact with her, Cady practically danced along the sidewalk. It felt good to do for those less fortunate. This felt more rewarding than volunteering at the nursing home. Maybe she'd find a soup kitchen, where she could volunteer her time.

On the next corner she encountered another homeless person. This one was a young mother, with a toddler, and a scruffy little dog. No one else was stopping. How could no one care? The woman looked younger than her by at least five years. Her little girl, stringy hair and face streaked with dirt, was no more than three. Living on the streets? It was horrifying.

Scrambling in the tiny purse she had slung across her body, Cady drew out all the bills she could find. Thirty-six dollars. It was all she had on her. The young woman refused to make eye contact. She was probably too ashamed. Circumstances had forced her to beg on the street in order to feed her child. What that must feel like!

"Please. Take it. I wish I could give you more."

When the woman hesitated, Cady turned to the child, offering her the money. Eyes bright, she snatched at it like it was a shiny, wrapped Christmas present. Cady gave the dog a brief pat on the head and scratch behind the ears. She sent a watery smile to the mother and child and turned before she really started crying. She'd taken a few steps back in the direction she'd come before she heard the woman's raspy voice.

"Thank you."

Cady nodded and kept going, her footsteps heavier and her mood lower. Living in the city was going to be a lot harder than she realized. There were so many people who needed help. And as soon as she gave her money to one, she discovered another who needed it even more. How did she decide who was more deserving? As much as it killed her, she knew she'd have to harden her heart to the atrocities she knew she'd see on a daily basis.

On the way back to the coffee shop, Cady passed several other eateries. Pausing at one that had the cutest little bistro tables outside, she shrugged her shoulders and went in for an application. Couldn't hurt to get a jump-start on things.

By the time she'd arrived back at their original meeting place, she had five job applications and an offer for drinks to discuss "an ideal working arrangement." She'd tossed that application in the first trash bin she'd come to. Ick! She was ready to celebrate a productive and emotionally draining morning. Unfortunately, this coffee shop didn't serve Diet Coke, so she ordered a cup of hot chocolate and settled in to wait for Burke.

• • •

Pacing the downstairs lobby long enough to make himself dizzy, Burke checked the time on his phone. Five minutes after ten. Satisfied that he was officially late for their appointment, he stabbed the elevator button for the top floor. Catching a glimpse of himself in the mirrored door, he relaxed his features until the smug smile stretching across his face had disappeared. It wouldn't do to look so happy when one was about to get chastised.

Burke stepped off the elevator and into a plush lobby. It spoke volumes that he'd never actually seen his father's place of business. Though, looking around, it was really no surprise. The pale cream chairs, larger-than-life paintings, and sculptures all screamed "Don't sit there! Don't touch that!" He felt as though he were a small child again, uncomfortable even in his own home.

An older woman looked up at him from behind a curved half-wall, her hair pulled back so severely Burke wouldn't have been surprised if she couldn't close her eyelids. She nodded her head, a polite smile ghosting her lips.

"You must be Burke. Go ahead in. He's expecting you." She remained seated, extending a skinny arm to direct him toward a set of double doors to his right.

His footsteps made no sound as he waded across the thick carpeting toward his father's home away from home. A fresh pot of coffee brewed somewhere close by. His nose twitched, his mouth watered, and he suddenly longed to have Cady by his side as he entered his father's domain. She probably would not be pleased to know that he associated her with the smell of roasted coffee beans. Even if it was the really good stuff.

Two doors. Tempted to open them both with a flourish, making as grand an entrance as possible, he refrained. But only just. Unsure if he was supposed to knock first or just let himself in, Burke rapped lightly on the door at the same time as he turned the knob. It hadn't mattered either way, as his father was on the phone. The older man lifted a long finger, either to indicate that he'd only be another minute, or to remind Burke to hold his tongue.

Okay, then. So much for gaining the upper hand by arriving late. Burke ground his back teeth together and wandered further into the spacious corner office. Sun streamed in the floor-to-ceiling windows, bathing the room in natural light. The view was amazing, although wasted on Prescott Sanders, whose gleaming mahogany desk faced the doors and not the Manhattan skyline.

His father continued to bark into the phone, so he continued to explore his surroundings. A seating area in the corner looked only slightly more comfortable than the one he'd seen briefly in reception. Two wingback chairs in that same cream color, a thick glass coffee table, and a long, white leather couch that Burke suspected was used more for afternoon naps than meetings with clients.

On the opposite wall was a bank of bookcases, matching the desk, serving as a catch-all for knickknacks. Realizing he had a unique opportunity to gain some insight into the man whom he knew so little about, Burke began to peruse the shelves. There were plaques and trophies, several from other countries, for various hospitality industry awards. Ah, and a photo of Prescott with President Obama. Burke rolled his eyes.

The bookcase closest to the desk was the hardest to get to. He had barely enough room to slip between the furniture to examine the contents. If he didn't know better, Burke would have thought that this was because these were the items his father was fondest of, that he wanted to keep close enough to view on a daily basis, to take down off the shelf and hold. He nearly forgot that his father was still in the room, he had such an irresistible urge to snoop.

Not a speck of dust marred the polished wood. A few snow globes took center stage—swiped, no doubt, from Burke's own collection when he was a kid. He picked up the one from Anaheim. Yep, this had been his. A bitter reminder of the only time he had fought to accompany his father on a business trip. The man was opening a hotel mere steps from Disneyland, for crying out loud! But his father had insisted his school work come first.

Shoving the snow globe back in place, Burke knocked over a picture frame that sat in the middle of the shelf, hidden in the shadows. It was a photograph of a woman with long, platinum-blond hair. She sat in a meadow of daisies, cradling an infant in her lap. Burke didn't recognize her and was tempted to assume the photo was the original that came with the frame. Until his eyes lit on the next one, also hidden behind the row of snow globes. It was the same woman, her hair trimmed to just brush her shoulders. The infant was now an adorable little boy with his mother's pale hair but eyes that looked familiar. They looked like—his. Burke scrunched his nose in confusion. The child looked like him, but not.

Moving on to the next item tucked toward the back of the shelf, Burke felt a burning in his gut that intensified with each labored breath he took. A Little League trophy. He'd never been allowed to play baseball. His mother had insisted sports were too dangerous. His father was too busy to argue on his son's behalf. Or he just hadn't cared. Either way, it didn't matter. This was not his trophy.

"If you're quite through poking around in my belongings, I have a meeting with finance in twenty minutes."

"Who's the kid?"

"Excuse me?" His father waved off the question with an impatient hand. "Your cousin. On your mother's side."

"What's his name?" Burke's voice was careful, measured.

"Scott."

"Clever." He set the trophy back in place before he could be tempted to use it as a weapon.

"I have no idea what you're talking about."

"How old is he?"

"Who? The kid? I don't know. I guess he'd be about five years old in that picture."

"How old is he now, Dad? Your other son? How old is the kid you actually wanted?"

His father sighed, pinching the bridge of his nose as he turned to stare out at the billion-dollar view laid out in front of him. He didn't look guilty, or ashamed, even. Just tired.

"This isn't what I called you here to discuss."

"No, of course not. You called me here to discuss taking over the family business. But for how long, I wonder. Just until your namesake comes of age? Then I'd get kicked to the curb?"

God, he didn't even want the job, so why did this hurt so much? He'd come in here with his own agenda. Burke couldn't take his eyes off the fucking trophy.

"What do you want? More shares? I'm giving you the reins, Burke. It's yours now. It will always be yours." Whatever the man had been about to add, he bit off at the end.

"Ah, that's it, then. I'm the rightful heir. The son born on the correct side of the sheets." His short laugh was cruel.

"Just name it. Name it and be done. I shouldn't have insisted you come down here. I should have come to you. Where is your latest dalliance? Cape Cod?"

"I've already told you what I want. I want nothing to do with ... this." Burke spun in a circle, his arms flung wide. "I want to write. I want to live a quiet life in the beautiful little town I've discovered. And now, more than anything, I want to pretend I was born into another family—any other family."

"And just who am I supposed to get to run this company so I can retire?"

Everything suddenly became crystal clear to Burke. The reason he was being pushed to take over a position he had absolutely no formal training in, no background whatsoever. His father had another family, one that he actually wanted to spend time with. And his mother? He had a feeling that if the woman had any idea at all, she'd thrown up blinders so she wouldn't have to acknowledge the truth. If she didn't acknowledge it, it didn't exist.

"Mother deserves a divorce. Your kid deserves your name—your *last* name."

"I didn't ask your opinion. Things are fine exactly the way they are. No sense dragging the media in and creating a circus. Your mother doesn't deserve that."

"Yeah, it wasn't like she did anything wrong."

"You don't know anything about my life. Don't presume to judge me!"

They faced off, father and son, Burke's expression carrying more disgust than real anger. His father was right. He didn't know him at all. And he had no desire to.

"Bottom line? I want out. You want to do something to assuage your guilt, sell off a couple of hotels and set up a cozy little trust fund. You wouldn't even miss them. I want someone else—anyone, really—to step up as CEO. I want to start my life over in my new town, with my new friends."

He spared one last look at the Little League trophy and headed for the double doors. "I don't want to be contacted in any way, for any reason—not even a Christmas card. And you can be the one to explain to Mother why I have cut you out of my life."

"She won't understand." The older man's voice sounded higher than normal. Burke had no sympathy for the rising panic he detected.

"She will if you tell her the truth."

Turning at the doors, Burke speared his father with one last hard look and added, "Oh, and I want the deed to my penthouse changed. It now belongs to a Ms. Cadence Eaton. I'll leave an address with your receptionist on where you may send the proper paperwork for her to sign."

"Burke, wait." His father rounded the desk and started to approach. "I'm sorry."

"That's funny, because I'm not. You made this a lot easier than I thought it was going to be."

The door barely made a sound as it closed behind him.

Chapter 13

"Was he at least happy to see you?" Cady had been trying all day to get Burke to open up about the meeting with his father. He'd been trying just as hard to avoid the conversation.

He steered her away from a man selling designer purses on the sidewalk in Times Square. Okay, perhaps designer was too strong a word. She shrugged. Prickly as he was today, she appreciated him looking out for her.

"I wouldn't say so, no. He was in a hurry to get to his next meeting."

"Well, the guy needs to slow down and appreciate what he has." She slipped her hand into his, giving it a quick squeeze.

"That's exactly what he's trying to do."

"Oh, that's wonderful!" She looked up at Burke, the smile fading from her face when she saw that his own expression had gone from grumpy to downright pissed off.

What the hell was she missing? She didn't even dare ask how his meeting with his editor had gone. This was not how she'd envisioned their adventure in the city.

"I need to get my mind off things." His voice was clipped. "What do you say we go all-out touristy and visit the Statue of Liberty?"

He closed his eyes, composing himself, and when he opened them he was able to smile. Just a bit. She'd take it.

"Sounds fun—if you aren't completely sick of seeing it."

"I've never been, actually. My parents avoided the tourist spots around the city. Said they were all tacky and they wouldn't be caught dead there."

"But surely your school took a field trip? She's an icon—Lady Liberty!"

Burke shook his head. "I didn't go to public school. I didn't even go to private school in the city. My parents shipped me off to boarding school in Connecticut."

A shudder went through Cady at the thought of being raised in such a cold, impersonal environment. She didn't know what to say. He didn't want her pity and she didn't want to piss him off any more than he already was. Chewing her bottom lip, she concentrated on the sidewalk.

This time it was Burke who squeezed her hand, then slipped his arm around her shoulder and kissed the top of her head. Uncertain, Cady peered up and was happy to see the twinkle back in his eyes. Well, if seeing the Statue of Liberty was all it took to snap him out of his funk, then she was all for it.

"I'm sorry. I was being a grouch. I owe you an explanation." He paused, pressing his lips together as he stared intently into her eyes.

"Of course you don't. I shouldn't have pushed."

"I want to tell you. Really. Another time." Swinging her around, Burke waved an arm and hailed a cab. He helped her in and slid beside her, letting the driver know where they were headed.

"We'll talk about it. I promise. Right now I want to be happy. I want to see the Statue of Liberty. I want to take cheesy pictures and buy stupid souvenirs and make sappy memories with you. Is that all right?"

Relief washed through her now that he was making an effort to be happy again. And something else, too, a deeper feeling that made her slightly breathless. He didn't owe her anything, yet he'd promised to tell her what had happened that morning. He was trusting her with his feelings, with his heart. Cady knew this for the huge deal that it was.

Heart tripping in her chest, she raised her head in time to be met with a kiss that stole her breath. Burke threaded his fingers through the hair at her nape and pulled her up against his chest.

Instinctually she opened her mouth, moaning as his tongue swept in and took possession. Oh, the man could kiss! Her blood heated and her muscles loosened. She looped her arms around his neck, becoming frustrated with their awkward positioning in the cramped back seat of the cab. The back seat of the cab!

With a low squeal, Cady pushed at the wall of Burke's chest. He broke off the kiss, his deep chuckle doing delicious things to her insides. His eyes were still hooded, darkened with passion. His tongue sneaked out to lick his lips and she followed the movement until it disappeared back into his mouth. She braced her head against the back of the seat and closed her eyes.

"We could always skip the sightseeing."

When his voice got like that, rough and growling, it was all Cady could do to keep her clothes on and remember they were in a public place. She peeked out of one eye and, sure enough, the driver leered at them from the rearview mirror. She was ashamed to admit that she was so aroused, she was torn between telling the man to mind his own business and giving him the show of a lifetime.

"Tonight. When we don't have an audience."

Again with that low laugh that she could feel all the way to her toes. How did he do that? Cady turned her head and concentrated on the city life zooming by outside the window. Sure, a big part of joining Burke on this trip into the city had been about the "sleepover." But she was in New York City and she should be soaking it up!

It turned out that the Statue of Liberty wasn't the only "first" for Burke that day. They'd ordered falafels off a food vendor truck, spent a fortune on tacky Big Apple souvenirs, and photo bombed a group of Japanese tourists on the Staten Island ferry. He'd taken Cady into his arms and showed off some pretty impressive ballroom dance moves when they'd stopped to listen to a street performer playing the violin. The guy had been so grateful at the crowd that had gathered, he'd offered a portion of his tips to Cady and Burke. They just shook their heads and waved goodbye.

The sun was setting in Central Park as they strolled down a path that would eventually lead them to Burke's street and his fabulous apartment on the top floor of his building. They shared a gelato in a large waffle cone, taking turns leaning in to swirl some up onto their tongue. It was—perfect.

"I had meant to take you out for a fancy dinner, you know."

"How many times do I have to remind you that I am not like any of the other women you've dated?" Cady frowned, biting her tongue and wishing she could take back that last word. Crap!

"Are we?" Burke kept walking, holding the cone up to her mouth for a lick.

"Are we what?" Feigning ignorance, she took a bite of the gelato and smiled at him innocently.

"Dating." His voice was quiet and she knew a lot rode on her answer. Had she just ruined their perfect vacation?

"We are ... enjoying spending time together. We are getting to know one another. We are about to go upstairs and trust that the other person is not going to laugh when they see them naked."

Make light of it. Refocus his mind on the sex and he'll forget the "D" word. Cady wasn't even sure if he'd asked because he was hoping they were or because he was hoping they weren't dating. Too bad life didn't come with a rewind button. This was definitely one of those moments she'd rather undo. Uncomfortably, she waited for his response.

"I plan to be paying close attention when you get naked. But I won't be laughing."

Whew, close call! The awkward moment was diverted. And by the look on his face, she was suddenly very happy she had decided to go with the sexier black teddy instead of the safer pink nightgown.

A tiny part of her brain tried to fixate on the amazing day they'd spent together. No other man had ever made her laugh so hard. He had a fun, goofy side that was wildly entertaining. She felt carefree and giddy around him. Perhaps that was enough. If she stayed in Scallop Shores, and if they became a couple, would Burke be enough to keep long-held regrets at bay?

Cady sighed. It wasn't his job to keep her happy. That job was hers and hers alone.

"Here we are. Right across the street."

For tonight, anyway, being happy meant being with Burke. She'd worry about any long-term damage to her heart another day.

• • •

A girl could get used to a place like this.

Cady slipped her shoes off at the door, practically tiptoeing across the gleaming hardwood floor because she didn't want to sully the polish. Drawn to the view, she almost couldn't decide which direction to turn. For it was all windows, all skyline and all beautiful.

"Do you like it?"

"I love it," she breathed.

"Good."

She wrinkled her nose at his satisfied nod. He was giving up this apartment for a permanent home in Scallop Shores. It shouldn't matter what she thought. She shrugged it off and continued her self-guided tour.

The living area was huge, with two buttery soft, black leather couches and a couple of matching chairs in a modern, whimsical shape. Even the huge square that served as a coffee table/footrest was the same black leather. It screamed style and money but didn't strike Cady as something that Burke would have chosen for himself. Turning in a slow circle, she saw it more as a designer's touch.

To her left, behind a beveled glass partition, was the kitchen. The first thing she noticed was the shine. She'd never seen such a well-lit kitchen. Light reflected off the industrial stainless steel appliances, glass cabinet fronts, and gleaming granite countertops. There was even a small refrigerator-type thing just for wine. And it appeared well stocked. Wow. The kitchen island, alone, was almost as big as her entire apartment back home. Oh, to be let loose in this room! Cady turned around before she could start to drool.

"I want to show you the rooftop." Burke took her hand and led her up the winding marble staircase to the second floor.

The upstairs of the apartment was carpeted with a deep, cushiony white pile. She barely had time to peek in any of the bedrooms they passed as he dragged her to the end of the hall, to what must be the master bedroom. Swallowing hard, she prayed that Burke wouldn't notice the slickness of her palm. He gave her a reassuring smile, as though he'd read her thoughts. Being here, surrounded by the best that money could buy—it was a tad overwhelming.

He'd pulled her into the master bedroom but didn't even pause at the king-sized four-poster bed; instead he flipped on the light switch as he crossed straight through the room and toward a thick glass slider. Cady was intrigued by a blue light that glowed on the other side of the door. What did he have out there?

"Oh my freaking wow!"

She saw the pool before Burke even had a chance to open the sliding glass door, and danced in place as she tried to keep herself from shoving him aside so she could get to it faster.

"You … How did … This is all yours? Do you use it?" She was breathless, her words jumbling together in her hurry to get them out.

"Yes, this is mine. I love to swim. It's the one sport my mother deemed safe enough to allow me to participate in. My school had an excellent swim team."

Burke slipped his polo shirt over his head and tossed it onto a nearby chair.

"When my parents were looking for a place for me, I insisted it have a lap pool. I would have been happy sharing a common pool with the rest of the tenants, but my parents ..." He trailed off, rolling his eyes.

"Wow, and here I was, happy to have a door lock that my brother couldn't pick, when I got my place above the bakery."

"He broke into your apartment?"

"No. He would sneak into my bedroom when we lived at home. He always seemed to know where I kept my diary. He used to pick the most embarrassing moments to quote the juiciest stuff."

Cady's eyes widened as Burke reached for the button on his khaki shorts. She glanced around, though it really was impossible for anyone to see him at this height. Unless they were straight above them—in a helicopter. She craned her neck and peered up, just to make sure.

"What kind of things did you write about in your diary? Who you made out with? How far you let them go?" His voice was a sexy purr.

"I'll have you know, I was a good girl." She pulled her bottom lip between her teeth and tried to keep from moaning when he shucked off his shorts and underwear in one fluid motion.

"Have you ever been skinny dipping?" Burke stepped back, giving her an eyeful before taking a running leap out toward the center of the pool.

Cady squealed as droplets of cool water splashed her exposed skin. Burke treaded water in the middle of the pool, the smirk on his face challenging her to let her guard down. She had very little doubt that, should she chicken out, he'd haul himself straight out of the water and throw her in fully clothed. Jutting out her chin and giving him a little nod to show she accepted his challenge, Cady slipped out of her tiny black denim shorts.

An appreciative whistle had her turning around and doing a little wiggle in the sexy black lace thong she'd bought just for this occasion. Burke sounded as though he was choking and Cady whipped around to make sure he was all right. He watched her with an intensity that turned her blood to fire in her veins and took away all desire to tease. Swallowing hard, she scrambled out of the rest of her clothes, kicking them under a chair before diving neatly into the water.

"Impressive," he complimented her as she surfaced inside the circle of his arms.

"Can't live in Scallop Shores, surrounded by ocean, lakes, rivers, and ponds, and not pick up a thing or two."

"Mm, less talking."

Burke took her mouth in a rough kiss, infusing her with his impatience until they were a slippery, writhing knot of limbs. She could taste the chocolate gelato still on his tongue and sucked greedily. His large hands grasped her buttocks and lifted her against him. Unbidden, Cady wrapped her legs around his waist. So close. If she just moved a little to the left.

Walking forward a few feet, he pressed her back up against the edge of the pool. This gave her more room to maneuver and, feeling bold, she tried to take him inside her. Burke swiveled his hips, resting his forehead on hers as he caught his breath.

"My little wildcat. We've got all night."

He lifted her slightly, propping her buoyant body with a strong thigh between her legs. Nerve endings already frustratingly sensitized, it took all her willpower not to hump his leg. Cady gasped when Burke lowered his head and lapped at one turgid nipple. She arched her back, letting him know she wanted more attention. She could feel his throaty laugh deep inside her as he gave her what she craved.

"More." *Had she said that?*

Nails raking down his back hard enough to leave marks, Cady tried to draw his mouth toward the other peak. She mentally cheered when he complied. Head thrown back, she shivered as his mouth traced a hot path up her cool, wet skin. She reached down between them, sheathing his steely hardness in her small hand and squeezing hard.

"Baby, yes!"

She used long, slow strokes, guiding him ever closer to her entrance. Burke bit softly on her earlobe, eliciting a cry that didn't carry far over the noise of the traffic below.

"I need ... We have to ..." Burke lifted Cady until she sat on the edge of the pool, then hauled himself over the side, wet feet slapping the concrete as he hurried over to the shorts he'd abandoned earlier.

Her head spinning as she tried to keep up with his movements, Cady swung her legs out of the pool and tried to pretend she looked more like a sexy siren than a drowned rat, as she sashayed toward him. He was scrambling in his pockets, tugging out his wallet to search inside. She bit her lip, fearing the moment would be lost if he found he did not have a way to protect them. Her sigh of relief echoed his when he pulled out a single foil wrapper. He turned and gave her a sheepish smile.

"I really didn't plan for our first time to be out here, in the open."

Cady looked around, feeling more wicked than exposed now, and gave him a reassuring grin. She adjusted the back of the lounge until it was completely supine, then lay down, patting the space beside her.

"That's okay. I thought I'd be showing off some sexy lingerie about now. But I'm all for spontaneity."

"Promise me you'll model it later." His chest rose and fell rapidly.

"My big wildcat. We've got all night."

With a wicked gleam in his eyes, Burke tore off the wrapper and sheathed himself before hopping on the cushioned lounge chair. Cady squealed as the metal chair slid a bit across the cement, screeching as it went. She laughed out loud. Being with Burke was like being on the most thrilling roller coaster in the world.

No sooner had she had that thought, Burke shifted on the cushion and yanked her over him. So he was handing over the reins, huh? Cady didn't mind one bit. Wiggling down until their bodies were aligned perfectly, she reached for his hard length to guide him inside. She'd been looking down and was momentarily surprised when Burke hooked a finger under her chin and directed her focus back up to his face. Yes, he was right. This was better.

Staring into his soulful eyes, she took him in, inch by agonizing inch. Fully seated, neither moved for a moment. Burke reached for her hands, pulling them up above his head and causing her breasts to brush against his chest. The contact was electrifying. The angle put delicious pressure on all the right places and Cady set a rhythm that she hoped was mutually satisfying.

A tortured moan escaped his lips and she knew she had nothing to worry about. Her hips picked up speed, her breasts slapping a rhythm against his chest. Neck muscles straining, Burke lifted his head off the cushion and kissed her like his life depended on it. He let go of her hands, only to grip her thighs, shoving up with his hips at the same time as he pulled her against him as hard as he could.

Senses on overload, Cady reached for that peak, the pinnacle that would take her straight into bliss. So close. A crescendo building inside. Up, up, and—there! Every muscle in her body trembled as she took and took. Like a wild man, Burke moved fast beneath her. His entire body went stiff and his exultant shout made her lady parts want to weep in satisfaction.

He tried to lower her onto his chest, but as he remained inside, the friction was too much, her sensitive nerve endings almost raw. With no small amount of disappointment, Cady lifted herself off his body and slid to the edge of the cushion to lie beside him. They lay there, panting and laughing. Always laughing. Burke swept her hair away from her face with a big hand, leaving a gentle kiss on her temple. A girl could really get used to this.

Chapter 14

"Game's five card stud, deuces wild. Ante up, gentlemen."

Chase sat with his back to the garage door. He shuffled the deck like a pro, dealing the cards out to the group seated around the small folding table. His friend, Foster, sat on his left, Wallace on his right. Burke was across from Chase, his chair butting up against the work table along the back wall. If he didn't know better, he'd think the seating arrangement was deliberate.

The other two men in the game tonight introduced themselves as Curtis and Jonah. Burke had seen them at the bakery but had never been formally introduced. Their casual rapport with each other led him to believe they were father and son, though they looked nothing alike.

This was going to be an expensive night. Burke slid a chip toward the center of the table. When Chase had invited him to join them for poker night, he'd been quick to accept, eager to be accepted into the fold. Never mind the fact that he'd never played a game of poker in his life. One could only learn so much about the game through the Internet. The rest he'd have to pick up on the fly.

"Burke? Another beer?" Wallace had tipped his chair back to reach the small fridge in the corner of the garage behind him.

"Yeah, thanks." He accepted the can, cracked it open, and took a deep guzzle, careful to avoid eye contact with the man.

Okay, so maybe he shouldn't have accepted the invite so readily. Walking into the garage tonight had felt a little like entering the lion's den. Of course, that was his own guilt talking. Not two nights ago, he'd been spending some quality naked time with a woman probably anyone in this room would kill to protect.

Damned if he wasn't already trying to figure out when he could get her alone again.

The first few rounds of bets went by with little talking. These guys took their poker seriously. Chase set a bowl of pretzels on the table and everyone dove in. Cady had insisted he take along a batch of her peanut butter brownies. Was it too soon to mention sweets?

"So how was your little vacation to the city?" Chase sent Burke a cryptic look over his cards.

"Well, it was ... I had business. I had meetings." Burke slid a finger beneath the collar of his shirt and tugged a little. Was it getting hot in here?

"Our little Cady was quite impressed. Hasn't stopped talking about it since she got home." Wallace watched him closely as he popped a pretzel into his mouth and chewed hard.

Was that why he'd been invited here tonight? Was this a set-up? They were going to beat the crap out of him. A thin bead of sweat trickled down the side of his face, alerting everyone at the table to his discomfort. Burke pretended to study his cards while he struggled to come up with a way to diffuse the situation.

It wasn't like she was a kid. Cady was a grown woman and could sleep with whomever she wanted. They had a right to live their lives without public scrutiny. What had she said to her father, her brother? Whatever it was—he was a dead man!

Unaware of the tension zinging back and forth across the table, Curtis doubled the bet. Jonah folded. Well, the sooner he lost his money, the sooner he could leave. Burke pushed a stack of chips in. Chase grinned, lifting his ball cap from his head only to plunk it down low over his eyes.

"Looks like things are getting interesting, boys." He waited for Foster to fold, then matched Burke's bet.

"Too steep for my blood." Wallace tossed his cards on the table, face down.

Back to Curtis, who looked a tad uncertain about his chances to win now that the pot had grown this large. *"Don't throw it now. I'll never get out of here,"* Burke screamed inside his head. The older man looked back down at his cards, frowned, and called, adding more chips to the stack. *Thank God!* One by one they revealed their hands. Chase swore under his breath when his two pair turned up nothing. Curtis proudly showed off his three aces and everyone at the table waited for Burke to flip his cards over. He had three of a kind and a pair.

"Son of a bitch—full house," Curtis moaned.

Damn it! He'd won a sizeable pot, the opposite of what he'd set out to do. So much for going through his money quickly.

"Heh. Beginner's luck." Burke jumped when Jonah slapped him on the back.

"Dude, who brought the brownies? Are these peanut butter? Sweet!" Foster had stepped away from the table and was prowling the goodies set on the woodwork surface. He carried the plastic container to the table and the group of grown men descended on it like vultures on carrion.

"See, I knew inviting my sister's boyfriend would be a good thing." Chase held a brownie victoriously in the air.

"Even though he's taking all your money?" Jonah laughed.

"Yeah, well, there is that. It's all good. The night is young and I intend to make him cry." Chase's laugh held nothing sinister. It was almost as though he were genuinely joking around.

"We aren't officially dating," Burke felt the need to point out. Though if it were up to him, they would be.

"And I'll bet money it's my daughter holding you at arm's length, isn't it?" Wallace folded his muscled arms across his chest as he leaned back in his chair.

"I wouldn't exactly say that. Amanda said Cady had big plans for that fancy weekend getaway." Chase wiggled his eyebrows suggestively.

"I thought we were here to play cards." *That's it. Remind them of the business at hand.*

"What's the matter, Burke? Why can't you tell us about your cozy little trip?" Chase flipped a poker chip back and forth between his knuckles, like a Vegas pro.

"Dude, he probably thinks you're gonna take him out back and shoot him for messing with Cady." Foster shoved Chase in the shoulder, knocking the poker chip to the table. He may have been trying to help Burke out, but the guy still wore a shit-eating grin.

"Son, we know you're sleeping with my daughter. Why do you think we asked you here tonight?"

Aw, hell. It was an ambush. A poker table and five grown men stood between him and the nearest door. Burke couldn't take all of them on. Maybe he could outrun them? He reached into his khakis for his keys. How to get a running start?

"You idiots are never going to get Burke to go along with what you want if you make the poor kid piss his pants." Curtis rolled his eyes toward the ceiling.

Wait, what?

"I can't help it if the guy has a guilty conscience." Chase shrugged.

"Okay, yeah, I slept with her, all right? She's a big girl." Burke wiped a big hand across his face, blinking.

"That girl of mine knows what she wants and she goes after it." Wallace harrumphed. "She wants to move to the city. But she wants you, too. And that's a good thing."

"Excuse me?" This conversation was starting to give him a migraine.

"You seem to be carving out your own space here in town. You intend to stay, I take it?"

Burke nodded.

"You make my little girl happy." It was a statement, not an order, no matter how gruffly it was uttered.

"Cady doesn't date. She can't be bothered with locals. I didn't think she even cared about sex until you came along." Chase put his palms on the table, leaning forward over his elbows.

"She prefers to play matchmaker," Jonah added, the others nodding and murmuring their agreement.

"Then you came along and she finally starts acting like a woman ... with needs." Chase screwed up his features, shuddering his disgust.

Jesus. Beam me up, Scotty. Anywhere but here.

"Bottom line, guys? 'Cause you all are seriously making me uncomfortable."

Burke stared Chase down, waiting for him to get to the real reason they'd invited him to poker night.

"You like her, right? You want to date her, but she's got her own agenda and she's pushing you away?"

"Yeah, that's about it."

"Convince her to stay. Convince her she has everything she needs right here in Scallop Shores." Wallace had scraped his chair back and moved to stand over Burke.

"This was why you invited me to play poker with you guys? To help you emotionally blackmail Cady into giving up her dreams so you don't have to give up your daughter, your sister?"

"Aw, don't get upset. You're an okay guy. We were gonna invite you anyway. Just thought we'd kill two birds with one stone." Chase puckered his lips, making kissing noises to the amusement of the others seated at the table.

"That and we knew Cady would send some of her goodies with you." Wallace reached across the table for another brownie, nodding at Burke as he stuffed nearly the whole thing in his mouth.

So this is what it felt like to be a part of something? Burke downed the rest of his beer and settled in as Foster dealt another round. What the hell had he signed on for? On the one hand, he had to admit that it felt good to be needed. On the other, he knew he didn't have it in him to manipulate Cady that way. Even if it was to his own benefit.

Hell, he even planned to make her transition as easy as possible, by offering her the penthouse so she wouldn't have to worry about a place to stay. As much as it killed him to think it, he was going to have to get used to the idea of saying goodbye. Like it or not, so would they.

• • •

"How about this one?" Cady held up a tiny navy blue sweater with a sailboat embroidered in the center.

"Too boyish. What if it's a girl?" Her mother tsked.

Sighing, Cady slipped the hanger back onto the rack. She shouldn't even be here. She'd already spent far too much of her precious savings on Baby Eaton. But the little squirt needed something better than a matching onesie and bib that read "I heart the Big Apple" from his or her favorite aunt.

She wouldn't be spending much time with them once she moved to the city. So the gifts she chose would say a lot about who she was, right? Did she want to be the funny aunt, who sent silly, meaningless gifts? Or did she want to be the beloved aunt, whose gift choices were thoughtful and from the heart?

A frail hand dropped onto her shoulder and Cady turned her head to smile at her own aunt. Amanda's baby shower was later this afternoon, so they'd sprung Auntie from Kittredge Manor for the day. Auntie didn't need to be in this baby boutique either. She'd worked so hard on a handmade gift for the shower.

Cady covered the old woman's hand with her own and squeezed gently. Auntie's talent with a crochet hook never ceased to amaze her. Stiff as her fingers now were, her aunt had turned a simple skein or two of yarn into a beautiful layette for the newest member of the Eaton family.

"Your mother needs to spoil her first grandchild. We'll let her have her fun now, won't we?"

"I was so excited to buy the baby his or her first New York souvenirs. I thought it might be a way for them to remember me. But now I just feel foolish. You made that gorgeous blanket, with the matching sweater and hat and booties. Mom is buying everything under the sun."

Auntie pointed a gnarled finger to a display in the corner of the store. Cady followed with her eyes. Keepsakes, tins, albums, oh! Picture frames. They shuffled together as one, their hands still clasped, until they stood in front of the frames. She let go of her aunt's hand to pick up a sterling silver frame, flowering vines decorated the edges. In beautiful script at the bottom it read: *Only an aunt can give hugs like a mother, keep secrets like a sister, and share love like a friend.* This. This would be her gift. The photo would be their first moments together, when she finally got to hold her precious niece or nephew.

The price tag on the back made her wince. It was sterling silver, not eighteen-carat gold, for crying out loud! Cady shook her head and started to put the frame back on the shelf. Sure, it was perfect, but sometimes perfect just wasn't practical.

"Buy the frame, Cadence. You know it's exactly what you want to give." Auntie nudged her shoulder.

"I can't justify it. It's too expensive. I'm going to need every penny I have to float me until I get a job in the city."

"Trust me, young lady. Buy the frame. Do you honestly think I would let my favorite niece make the biggest decision of her life without helping her out?"

A mischievous smile transformed her wrinkled face and put a twinkle in eyes that had been more rheumy than clear for many years now. Cady paused, still holding the photo frame, wondering what her aunt was up to. She appeared tickled to be the bearer of a delicious secret that she wasn't quite ready to divulge.

"Fine. I'm buying the frame. But don't think I'm going to let you off the hook that easy. How are you helping me out, hmm? Are you going to carry furniture into my new apartment? Do you have contacts in the city that are going to give me a job?"

"I have an inheritance to leave that I am willing to part with now, so that I may see it enjoyed while I am still on this Earth. But if my lippy grand-niece is going to get fresh with me—"

"*You* have an inheritance?" Cady clapped a hand over her mouth the minute she'd uttered such a tactless question. She cringed as the older woman cocked her head to the side and gave her a look that showed her just how inappropriate that question was.

"I'm so sorry, Auntie. It's just that ..." She was about to put her foot in it again, she realized. "No, you're absolutely right. Why wouldn't you have some sort of nest egg? You've been an intelligent, independent woman your whole life."

Auntie had only taught elementary school, giving piano lessons on the side to make ends meet. Maybe she was a shrewd investor? Cady bit the inside of her lip as she pondered this surprise revelation.

"And now you're sucking up. Close your mouth, child, and go buy the damned picture frame. Your mother beat you to the register." Auntie nodded toward the counter at the front, where Cady's mother was leaning over the top, probably getting ready to deplete the shopkeeper's supply of gift boxes.

Cady pressed her lips together, fighting to keep from laughing out loud. She spun on her heel and hurried to the register to rescue the poor cashier from her pushy mother. Bumping a hip against her mother, she looked pointedly from the stack of sweater boxes on the counter to her mother and back again.

"What? It just looks trashy if I wrap all her gifts without using proper boxes."

"And if you wrap each one individually, we'll all be watching Amanda unwrap presents until it's time for the baby to graduate high school." She patted her mother's shoulder. "You can fit three outfits in one box, easy. Don't take her entire supply."

The storeowner smiled gratefully at Cady. She returned the smile with a covert wink, carefully separating a stack of gift boxes and sliding them back across the counter. Her mother's defeated sigh was comically melodramatic. Cady chuckled.

"Here, let me get that for you. You need to save your money." Her mom tried to take the picture frame from her hand.

"It's all right. I've got it. Auntie told me not to worry about the money." Cady shrugged.

"Oh, your aunt ... Oh!" May nodded her head and turned to share a look across the store with the elderly woman.

What was she missing here? It wasn't like Auntie was a wealthy woman. Where she got this secret stash of money that she was willing to share with her grand-niece, Cady had no idea.

The three women stepped out into the bright August morning that was already shaping up to be a scorcher. Cady glanced at her aunt, gauging whether the woman was up to the walk back to the car, or if she should leave them here and run back for it. Gripping her cane firmly, the elder Cadence took the lead, heading around the block to where they had parked May's older sedan.

They passed the florist shop, a small real-estate office, a one-man law firm, and the coin laundry that had been in business since before Cady had been born. Across the street more shops greeted them with their bright awnings and beautifully hand carved signs. They passed the hardware store, waving to Mr. Pettridge as they walked by.

Wynter Grayson stood inside the display window of The Book Nook. She was already designing a back-to-school theme. Cady's heart beat a little faster as she realized just how quickly her time in

Scallop Shores was winding down. Another month, perhaps? She said she'd give herself until Labor Day weekend.

"Oh, Cady, look at this!" Her mother stopped short in front of a shop with a big "for lease" sign in the window.

She'd been disappointed to see the little family-run restaurant close a few months back. The husband and wife were getting on in years and their children had long since left the area, with no interest in taking over the establishment. Unable to continue on their own, the elderly couple had let the lease run out and, last Cady had heard, moved to a retirement community in Boca Raton.

"I know, it's sad. Just sitting here empty."

"No, it's exciting, silly! It's just sitting here empty. Waiting for you to start a business here in Scallop Shores. So you don't have to move to the city."

"What kind of business would I start?" She eyed her mother quizzically.

"A coffee shop, of course. Though you could have an expanded menu, given that this is already set up as a restaurant. You could hire a cook and a waitress. Feature your espresso drinks and all the baked goods you are so good at making."

"And steal business away from Logan's? Mom, that's a terrible idea. He might not be the nicest guy, but he's pretty much given me free rein to run the bakery as I see fit."

Cady cupped her hands over the glass and peered inside. She'd never considered owning a business. But to stay in Scallop Shores? Maybe this was a sign that her dream wasn't big enough? Maybe she was meant to run her own coffee shop in the city? Her eyes grew wide as she considered the possibilities.

"I think this would be perfect for you." Her mother was still talking about this building, in particular.

No, she had zero interest in starting up a coffee shop in her hometown. And, quite frankly, the idea of running her own business in the city was too overwhelming to consider at the moment. She'd settle in and think about it—in her own time. Cady caught Auntie watching her closely. She sensed the woman was living vicariously through her, and she wanted to make her proud. She only hoped her baby steps were enough for now.

Linking arms with her mother and Auntie, Cady guided them toward the car. She had a lot to think about.

"And you and Burke can stay a couple."

Wait, what?

"Mom, how many times do I have to tell you that Burke and I are not dating?"

"Of course, darling. Friends with benefits."

Good Lord, where had her mother learned that term? Friends. Cady sighed. She'd be lying if she said she didn't want more than that. She did. She desperately did. But their lives were going in opposite directions and they wanted such vastly different things.

Sparing a last glance at the "for lease" sign, Cady stiffened her spine and pasted on a fake smile. Yes, she had a lot to think about.

Chapter 15

Being in charge of Logan's Bakery had its perks. Cady stood off to the side, taking in the balloons and streamers, the crowds of people milling around with glasses of punch as they nibbled on the platters set out on the long counter. Amanda held court at the table closest to the window, her cheeks wet with a fresh batch of happy tears. Chase and a group of his buddies sat at the end of the counter, where they had sneaked in a keg. *At a baby shower? Really, big brother?* Cady sent a look heavenward.

One person in Chase's little posse caught her watching them and smiled devilishly. It had been a few days since she and Burke had come back from their trip to New York. A few busy days. Now that the post-coital glow had dimmed and they were back to their normal routines, Cady wasn't quite so take-charge and confident. Her cheeks grew warm as he studied her from across the room until she had to turn away, suddenly uncomfortable with the intense feelings that just being near him produced.

"Sweetheart, I heard a couple of people mention we're running low on coffee." Her mother whispered in her ear.

"On it." Happy to have busy work to do, Cady patted her mother's shoulder and rounded the corner.

She emptied the last package of grounds into a filter and set the coffee to brew. Heading into the supply room for another box, she flipped on the light and let out a tiny squeal as Burke pushed his way past her and closed the door behind them. His focus was on her mouth.

"If I were a paranoid guy, I'd almost think you were avoiding me."

"Almost?"

"Well, yeah. See, I look back at all the times, at the penthouse, that I made you scream my name and I think, 'Who would want to avoid that?' And I realize that's just crazy." He slowly backed her against the wall.

"You're pretty sure of yourself." The fact that her chest was already heaving and her skin itched to make contact with his implied that he had every right to be.

"Yup." Slapping his palms against the wall, on either side of her head, Burke lowered his head and took her mouth.

Without any coaxing on his part, Cady opened for him, drawing him in and joining their tongues in a sensual dance that started slow but quickly fanned out of control. Her fingers clutched at the back of his shirt, running up and down the slippery fabric until she'd had enough and tugged it loose from his pants so she could reach his bare skin. He slid one hand down to pull up her thigh, yanking it against him as he ground their bodies together.

"Think—" Burke didn't have time to finish the thought as the knob rattled and the storage room door swung inward.

"Jesus, get a room!" Chase pretended to cover his eyes, leaving a wide gap between his fingers, as he cleared the door frame.

"We did. But some people don't bother to knock." Burke pushed himself away from the wall.

"What do you need, Chase?" Cady needed to move this party elsewhere, before the testosterone level got any higher.

"Ice." He paused, grinning. "Come to think of it, you could use some of that yourself. Burke? Cool things down a bit?"

Cady blew out a sigh on her way to the ice machine. One would have hoped that becoming a father would have instilled a sense of maturity in her big brother. But so far all she saw was a 12-year-old trapped in a man's body. She filled a bucket with ice and passed it off to her brother, who looked like he intended to wait for them to leave with him.

"Oh, for crying out loud, Chase! We're right behind you." She slammed the door shut on the ice machine and swiveled, hands on her hips.

Chase gave them one last lecherous grin, waggled his brows, and left the room. Burke was watching her closely. She lifted her chin and met his look head-on. She hadn't been avoiding him. Much.

Turning to the back wall, Cady lifted down a box of French Roast, one of Hazelnut and one of Breakfast Blend. Burke had sneaked up behind her. She could feel his hot breath on her neck as she contemplated which other flavor to bring out front. A heavy hand branded her hip and his lips found that sensitive spot just behind her ear. Her knees nearly gave way.

"We good?" He whispered.

Oh, they were more than good together! But that wasn't what he was asking. He wanted to know where they stood. He wanted to know that they were a couple now. That they were together. And she had to tell him they weren't.

They *were* good together. And she enjoyed every second she spent with him. But Burke was putting down roots in town and she was leaving. What they had was temporary. It was addicting and it was amazing and she would be smart to break it off now, while she could still walk away with her heart intact.

She twisted around, pushing the stack of boxes into Burke's arms. *Don't make eye contact! Stay strong!* Before she could return to the shelf for another box of coffee grounds, she caught his worried frown. He didn't say another word; just watched her sadly. He understood how things were and he wasn't pushing her to stay. God, why did he have to be so damned perfect?

"We're good, Burke. Of course we're good." She focused on a point just over his shoulder. "We should get back out there before Chase brings reinforcements."

Grabbing a box of decaf, Cady lifted it to her shoulder and led the way out of the storage room. She poured the freshly brewed carafe of coffee into the near-empty urn and started another going.

Burke had dropped off the boxes he'd carried out and retreated to the group of men in the corner.

Would it be so bad, if she were to stay? She could think of much worse places to live. Her family was here. Her life, her history, everything she knew and everyone she loved. Again, her eyes lingered on the newest full-time resident of Scallop Shores. It must have been the occasion, because all of a sudden she was thinking happily-ever-after, raising a family with Burke and living out her life in the same town she swore she had to leave in order to grow. She was nuts.

"Amanda, I am dying to see what's under all this adorable wrapping paper. I say it's time to open presents. Mine first!" She couldn't wait to see what her friend thought of the picture frame. They could choose just the right photo together.

Cady swiped an order pad and pen off the counter, lifted the topmost gift from the pile on the table and set it in her friend's lap. Her mother quickly cleared the leftover food from the table and everyone started to gather around to watch the festivities.

The next half hour was full of oohs and aahs, as the women cooed over tiny baby outfits and cuddly stuffed animals. Chase whined over all the items that would have to be assembled and Cady laughed to see him wrap his mind around the breast pump as he gingerly picked up the parts. Her parents looked so proud. Amanda's family hovered around her, refilling her lemonade, kissing her brow, and showering her with attention.

This could be her someday. Cady wrote down the last gift, a plastic bathtub filled with baby soap, bath toys, hooded towels, and washcloths from Sergeant Gerry and his wife. Standing up, she went in search of trash bags to help carry out all the smaller gifts. A slight smile tugging at the corners of her mouth, she caught Burke's eye. To be fair, the guy had every right to feel out of his element here. She wouldn't have blamed him for bailing early. He winked at her. He was actually enjoying himself. Hope weaved its way through her chest, cinching it tighter.

Chase had recruited a few guys to help move the bigger presents, like the car seat, stroller, and electric swing out to his truck. Cady's and Amanda's mothers were packing up refreshments for people to take home with them. Amanda had disappeared into the restroom. Auntie sat at the little table by the window, alone. In her hands she held a small scrap of cloth, a yellow sleeper.

The old woman didn't know she was being watched and Cady was stunned by the sorrow etched into her elderly aunt's wizened visage. Her wrinkled hands stroked the soft fabric, back and forth. Regret. It was so tangible, Cady felt like she'd been bludgeoned in the stomach. It hurt to breathe.

Cadence Eaton had come back home to Scallop Shores. She'd left the man she loved behind. And she'd regretted her decision. Looking at the woman now, all Cady wanted to do was wrap her arms around her and comfort her. Was this what she had to look forward to if she stayed? Would she look at Burke one day and resent him for convincing her to choose him over her dreams of life in the big city?

The shattering of glass brought Cady back to the here and now fast. Ice skittered down her spine and she stared in horror at the remains of her New York Dream tip jar now in hundreds of pieces on the cracked linoleum. The sole contents of the jar, the money Burke had deposited on his first day in town, lay amid tiny shards of broken glass. Was this a metaphor for her life? Tears burned behind her eyelids, but Cady refused to let them fall.

"I'm so sorry, sweetheart! I was just moving the deli platter. I had no idea your tip jar was so close to the edge." Her mother dropped to her knees and began to pick up the larger pieces of glass.

"Hey, no, it's no big deal. Please let me do this. I don't want you to cut yourself."

Cady pulled her mother up off the floor and gently pushed her away from the tip jar carnage.

"Mom, why don't you take Auntie back to Kittredge Manor? I think she's had a long day."

Still haunted by the look on her aunt's face as she sat caressing the baby outfit, Cady shuddered.

"I'll help you clean up." Burke was suddenly at her elbow.

"No. I've got this. Really. You go on home. I'll call you later." Knowing the wounded puppy dog look that was sure to be on his face, she kept her gaze focused on the broken glass.

If she looked at him now, she'd cave. She would let him help her clean up the mess. She'd invite him back up to her apartment and they would spend the rest of the night making love. And tomorrow she would be wondering if she'd just lost a little piece of herself.

So, no. She had some thinking to do. And she needed to do it alone. Putting her blinders on, Cady went in search of the broom and dustpan. She returned to the front of the bakery to find that everyone had cleared out. He'd actually left. He had listened and was respectful of her needs. So why had she immediately turned into a blubbering idiot? Sniffling, she swept up the broken tip jar, wiping her tears away with the back of her hand.

•••

She should be here with him. Well, no, that was a poor choice of words. He would have liked her to be here with him, to share this moment, to give her input. Burke followed the Realtor through the raised ranch, knowing the woman was chattering on about the features of the house, but too absorbed in his own thoughts to be able to hear anything but a garbled buzz.

He knew the baby shower was rough on Cady yesterday. He could see that she was starting to waver. Family meant so much to her. It would have been so easy to take advantage of that, to be selfish and take what he wanted for himself. Chase had pulled him aside at the party and said the same thing. Cady's big brother claimed to have her best interests at heart, but Burke knew better.

They were upstairs now. Burke left the large master suite and stepped into the smaller room beside it. *The nursery.* He blinked. It was a bare room, white walls and no furnishings, so why his mind automatically went there he wasn't sure. But the harder he stared, the clearer the picture came to mind. The walls were a smoky blue-grey; no pastels for his son. Sports memorabilia decorated the room. A rocking chair would sit by the window, overlooking the thick woods at the back of the house. He could almost hear Cady crooning a lullaby as she nursed their infant.

"There are three bedrooms upstairs and the guest room downstairs. Do you and your wife have any kids?"

The Realtor's words finally penetrated and Burke whipped his head around. Wife? Kids? He'd caught her covert looks at his left hand as they were walking up the driveway so he knew she was fishing. Just a few months ago he would have been flattered, probably would have played along. Today he had zero interest and was mildly irritated that a professional Realtor could be so transparent.

"Not yet. But we're trying. That's the fun part." *Take a hint, lady!*

She pursed her lips into a semblance of a smile and turned away. Burke took one last look around the room before joining the woman in the hallway. Sure, it was impulsive, but something about this big house called to him. It was close to town but still had the illusion of isolation. It didn't have the incredible ocean view that his rental cottage did, but it had an even better one of the river.

Cady would tell him he was making a rash decision. She'd say this was merely a reaction to the discovery of his father's "other" family. She'd tell him to hold off, wait until he'd calmed down and could think rationally. She would cringe at the thought of him throwing so much money into something as permanent as a mortgage.

That is, if she knew about what went down during that meeting with his father in New York. He'd meant to tell her by now. It just hadn't come up. And the longer he sat on it, the worse he felt. He'd talk to her today. Right after he signed those loan papers.

The meeting with his editor had gone much smoother than the one with his father. Meredith must have heard Burke's story a lot, someone writing for a magazine but dreaming of making it on their own. She was nice about it, offered him her best wishes and thanked him for his years of hard work. He'd stayed up all night last night, finishing up the last few articles for submission, and after a last cup of coffee, sent them off first thing this morning. It was done. He was staying in Scallop Shores.

There was nothing left for him in New York. Burke had turned his back on his family, his past. He belonged to a new town now. He had new friends. Granted, he didn't feel close enough to anyone but Cady to reveal his connections to Sanders Resorts— yet. Sure, he'd get razzed for it, especially by Cady's older brother. But these were good people and he knew that he could trust them.

After he left the Realtor and the house that was now his, Burke headed toward town. Cady would be closing up the bakery about now and if he sneaked in, she'd have to talk to him. He wanted to celebrate. He wanted to share his good news with her. He was officially unemployed and was about to purchase his first home. Yeah, she'd think him insane. He'd need to come up with a different way to break this to her.

Taking a left at the Civil War monument, he drove toward the cottage instead. He was going to miss the tiny place with a peek at the ocean. Hell, he'd even miss his little bandit-friend. Though, now that he'd be living in such a densely forested part of town,

Burke imagined he'd discover lots of new woodland creatures traipsing through his yard. He wasn't sure if he should be thrilled or terrified.

Dusty dirt crunched under the tires as he pulled into the rental's short driveway. He parked under a tall pine, peering up at the small porch that led to his front door. For the last few days Burke had spotted a small dog running around his property and the surrounding rental cottages. He'd assumed that it belonged to a family vacationing nearby. Today the furry guy lay on his porch, head on his paws, looking like he'd lost his best friend.

Not wanting to startle the poor pooch, Burke slipped out of the car and edged up toward the stairs, holding his hand out in front of him. The little dog had longish black fur that stuck up in all directions. His snout was short and piggish. He didn't know anything about dogs, never having so much as a goldfish when he was growing up, so he couldn't tell what breed it was. Judging by the look of him, he was a mixture of several. Purebred mutt.

"Come for a visit, have you, buddy?" Burke sat down on the top step and was welcomed with the steady thumping of a shaggy tail.

He reached out and stroked the silky head. The little dog stood up, stretched, and rubbed up against Burke's side. Cute little guy.

"What's your name, huh, fella?" He was surprised to find that the dog wasn't even wearing a collar.

Who did he belong to? Would the vet have a way of finding the owners? Impulsively, Burke picked up the dog and pulled him close. He laughed as the dog bathed his cheek in doggy kisses.

This poor little guy needed a champion and suddenly Burke couldn't think of anything more important to do with the rest of his afternoon than help his new friend. Carrying the furry mutt to his car, Burke drove to the vet clinic that he'd seen in town. He hoped they wouldn't mind taking a walk-in.

A couple of hours later they were back home. The vet had searched for a microchip that would help them locate the dog's owners. Unable to find one, and based on the fact that the dog also had no collar, the vet had come to the conclusion that the dog had been left behind. He said this sad occurrence happened several times over the course of the summer, families abandoning their pets like garbage left behind at camp sites.

Horrified that anyone could be so cruel to someone so helpless, Burke had decided then and there that he would give the dog a home. The scrappy thing was so small that no one had given him a hard time when he'd brought him inside the grocery store, setting him in the top of the cart usually reserved for babies and small toddlers. Burke had bought enough food and toys for several dogs. He'd bought a collar and a leash at the vet.

When he got into the house he took a pillow off the bed and the threadbare green blanket off the couch to fashion a dog bed on the floor. The dog walked cautiously through the cottage, as though he were unsure what to make of all this kindness. Burke didn't blame the little guy for finding trust a little hard to come by.

"We've got a lot in common, you and me." He sat down on the couch and patted his lap, encouraging the dog to hop up. After a moment's hesitation, he did.

The vet had told Burke that the dog appeared to be about a year old. He guessed that the family had gotten him as a puppy, and now that the cute stage was over, the idea of dog ownership had begun to bore them.

"Well, I have no idea what you were called before, but I figure you're young enough that I can give you a new name and you can adapt." Burke ruffled the dog's fluffy ears as he pondered.

Chuckling, he thought of his little midnight visitor and the first time he met Chase Eaton. As embarrassing as that night was, it was also the moment he began to feel as though he were a part of the community. Burke grinned down at the hairy little beast who was fast worming its way into his heart.

"I think I'm going to call you Bandit. What do you think? Bandit?"

Placing his paws on Burke's chest, Bandit stretched up to lick his new master's chin.

"Bandit it is, then."

They sat together on the couch for a long time, Burke scratching the dog between the ears. He'd said goodbye to his old life and his job. He'd bought a house and been adopted by a dog. Life was good and he really had no right to be asking for more. But what the hell? He'd come this far. The only thing missing was Cady.

"Wait until you meet her, Bandit. You're going to love her." *Just like I do.* Burke sighed. It probably shouldn't have come as such a surprise that he would fall for the one woman in town determined to leave it.

Chapter 16

Old Man Feeney was the last customer out of the bakery that afternoon and it was all Cady could do to keep from slamming the door behind him. She flipped the sign to *Closed* with more force than necessary and watched to see if it would fly off its hook. When it stopped swinging, she had half a mind to tear it off the door and throw it across the room.

Taking a deep breath and blowing it out as slowly as possible, Cady tried to shake off her funk. She rubbed at the back of her neck as she slipped behind the counter, grabbed a Diet Coke out of the cooler, and carried it to the table in the corner. Swinging the chair around, she straddled it, cracked open her can of soda, and took a deep swallow.

Oh, how she loved the smell of her precious espresso beans, but there was just something about Diet Coke that calmed her soul. Another swig and she settled down to the mundane task of reordering napkins, to-go cups, and plastic cutlery. She flipped through the pages of the catalog, familiar enough with the contents that she knew exactly where to find everything she needed.

It meant less browsing and more efficient work time. She could send off her order, finish the day's paperwork, and enjoy the rest of her day guilt-free. What she would do with that day, she hadn't the foggiest. Everyone was busy with their own lives. She may as well have left Scallop Shores already. Cady winced at the sound of paper tearing as she turned the page a little too aggressively. Guess that funk hadn't quite gone away.

Smoothing down the glossy page, she did what she told herself she wasn't going to do—she browsed. Whenever she ordered for the bakery, she did it on Mr. Logan's dime. She sought out the best deals, found items on clearance, and bought the most generic, boring supplies that were offered. But there were some really cool things in here. She scrambled up from her chair, sent a covert glance toward the plate glass window before racing behind the counter for the bakery supply catalog. A sneaking thrill raced down her spine as she began to peruse the pages, not for Logan's Bakery supplies, but for items—for her own place.

Firstly, it wouldn't be a bakery, but a coffee shop. After all, it was the coffee that brought her regular customers in at seven a.m. every day, and free refills that kept them in their seats for the better part of the morning. Cady looked around the bakery, mentally rearranging the glass display cases and adding furniture like cozy armchairs and a scattering of bistro-style tables. Oh, and a fireplace! Old Man Feeney could warm himself by the fire instead of sitting on a hard stool at the counter, with no support for his back.

Cady blinked. Only this fictitious coffee shop wouldn't be in Scallop Shores. It would be in New York City. Right now it was just a fantastic, exciting dream. Feeling a little like a deflated balloon, she pushed the order forms aside and rested her elbows on the table. She was going to miss this place. She'd been a part of Logan's Bakery since she turned sixteen and needed spending money for books, music, and new clothes.

Had it really been more than ten years since she'd started as a part-time cashier? Cady had waited far too long to start saving for her eventual move to Manhattan. In the Eaton household, if you wanted something badly enough, you saved up for it. That was how she earned her first phone, and the TV in her bedroom. She'd saved up and paid her own way through college courses at the local community college in Port Kitt.

This glaring reminder of the passage of time did nothing to make her feel nostalgic. Instead, it fueled her determination. She had been talking the talk long enough. Ripping the top page off the notebook she'd brought to the table, Cady began to pen her resignation letter. She was giving Mr. Logan one month to find her replacement. It meant he'd have to stick around long enough to actually make a decision or two regarding his own business. She wasn't sure he was up to the task. But he didn't have a choice. She was leaving.

It wasn't like anyone was asking her to stay. Amanda and Chase were so excited getting ready for the baby that they'd ceased giving her the guilt treatment. Her parents equally so. Their worlds revolved around the newest Eaton-to-be. And Cady didn't begrudge them this special time at all. Okay, not much. But Burke.

She didn't have to look at her blurry reflection in the napkin dispenser to know she was pouting like a spoiled child. She'd expected him to fight for her to stay, especially after their incredible night at his apartment. Had she read too much into that evening? Hell, that whole weekend! Was it too much to hope that he'd want to continue their relationship? Enjoy more—nights? She blew out a sigh that lifted her long bangs off her forehead and away from her eyes.

A light tap on the door elicited a grouchy groan. She was closed. Hello? She was also in a snit and if they valued their lives, they would turn and walk away. Another rap with a knuckle, this one on the window, caused Cady to look up with a sneer. Perfect. Speak of the devil. Burke peered through the window, waving once he knew he'd been spotted.

Cady took her time getting out of her chair, taking another leisurely sip of Diet Coke and meandering toward the door to let him in. She knocked into the closed sign, setting it swinging and hoping it would catch Burke's eye.

"Hey, I've missed you." He leaned into the doorway and kissed her softly on the lips, but made no attempt to cross the threshold.

"I've been right here." She held the door open and gave him a pointed look.

"Would it be okay if ...?"

Burke looked down and Cady gasped when she realized he wasn't alone. Attached to a leash was the craziest-looking mutt she'd ever seen. The dog had a wicked overbite. And his fur couldn't seem to decide which direction it wanted to grow in. But if dogs could smile, this one had the biggest, happiest grin in the world. The damned thing was so ugly he was cute.

"Oh my goodness!" She squealed, snatching the leash from Burke's hand and dragging them both into the bakery.

"Are you sure he can be in here?"

"Just don't report me to the health inspector."

Settling on the floor, Cady chuckled to see the dog needed no encouragement. He jumped into her lap, snuffling, sneezing, and lapping her silly. She stroked his ears and kissed his little pug nose.

"What is your name, sweetness?"

"Bandit."

"Ah, like your little midnight visitor." Cady laughed to see that Burke seemed pleased she understood the source of his new pet's name.

"You got it. And besides, this guy's kind of a thief in his own right. He stole my heart and he looks like he's well on his way to getting yours too."

"I haven't had a dog since I was a kid." Cady sighed, ruffling Bandit's perky ears and losing herself in his adoring brown eyes.

"Well, this is a first for me." Burke's voice was quiet, contemplative.

Joining her on the floor, he reached out to pet the dog. Their hands knocked against one another and he reached for hers, clasping it warmly. Cady was finding it very difficult to hold onto her nasty mood.

"So, I bought a house."

"Yep. I heard."

"Of course you did. Word travels fast in a small town."

"New house. New dog. Did you get a new car yet? Gotta give back the rental sometime, right?" She frowned when Burke looked guiltily toward the big window. He had all his bases covered.

"I guess you're all settled into your new life then." She tried to tug her hand away and refused to meet his eyes when he tightened his grip.

"I promised to tell you about what happened when I met with my father in New York. That explanation is long overdue. I need to explain to you why I've been so anxious to start over here, to find my own place, my own way."

Cady paused. She honestly hadn't made the connection. All she'd thought about was that Burke was so eager to be accepted in Scallop Shores. It had never occurred to her that this gung-ho attitude was prompted by his visit to his father.

He'd been so upset that day. She'd tried to get him to talk about it and he'd refused. Clearly something had bothered him, but since they'd been back, she thought he was happier. Maybe not so much happy as—determined, she realized. And she'd completely dropped the ball, been so focused on herself and the fact that he wasn't asking her to stay in Scallop Shores. What kind of girlfriend did that make her?

Wait—girlfriend? Had she really just assigned herself that role? Cady peeked through long lashes. For the first time since they'd returned, she noticed the hard set to Burke's jaw, the way his hesitant smile didn't quite meet his eyes. He was hurting. If Bandit hadn't claimed the spot already, she would have curled into his lap, throwing her arms around his neck and kissing away his pain.

"Cady!" The bell over the door jangled harshly as Chase stuck his head in, still in uniform.

"Down here." She knew he couldn't see them there on the floor and scrambled up to meet her brother in the doorway.

"You weren't answering your phone." He frowned.

"I must have left it upstairs. What's the matter? Amanda's in labor?"

"No. It's Dad. Mom took him in with chest pains. They're at the ER. I'm headed over there now."

"Oh my God. What can I do?"

"Get the house ready. Swing by and pick up Amanda, so I know all my girls are taken care of."

"Chase. Tell him I love him." Cady wrung her hands.

"He knows that, baby. He knows." Chase gathered her against his broad chest, smooshing her cheek against the cold metal of his badge. He kissed the top of her head and set her aside gently. Nodding toward Burke, he ducked back out the door.

"You okay?" Burke was already behind her, squeezing her shoulder.

"Yeah, I'll be fine." She took a shuddering breath and swallowed hard to keep from losing it. Her eyelids stung where the tears hid behind them, trapped because she refused to let them fall.

"What did he mean, 'Get the house ready'?"

"He meant that we're about to be inundated with well-wishers, neighbors, and townsfolk. Someone needs to be there to receive them."

She twisted her fingers together, staring out the bakery window, though her brother had already driven away. She should be there too. Burke hooked an arm around her waist and drew her back against him.

"Amanda and I've got this. You go be with your dad. He needs you right now."

He slipped behind the counter and came up with a coffee urn. God, she loved this man! And if she wasn't such an emotional basket case right now, she'd tell him. But he didn't deserve to wonder if she was sincere, or if the stress of the moment led her to say something she didn't truly mean. He captured her lips in a brief kiss, ushered the dog out ahead of him, and slipped through the door.

•••

By the time Cady had spoken to someone in the ER, her father had been admitted to a private room upstairs. Her sneakers squeaked on the gleaming linoleum, sounding obnoxiously loud as she put more distance between herself and the crying babies, coughing, and general chaos that was the Emergency Room waiting area. Chase would be upset that she hadn't followed his orders. But Chase could stuff it, for all she cared.

She swore the elevator was moving in slow motion. It didn't help that nervous energy had her practically hopping in place. By the time the little ding sounded for the eighth floor, Cady stood with her nose to the doors, prying them open the very second she could get a finger hold. They didn't have any information for her downstairs, and no news was—well, it was no news. She wouldn't be happy until she saw her father with her own eyes.

"Wallace Eaton, please." She leaned over the counter at the nurses' station, not feeling the least bit guilty that she was interrupting what must have been a darned good romance novel.

"Are you family?" The nurse slipped a Post-It in her paperback and dropped it into a tote bag on the floor.

"I'm his daughter. Please, I need to see him."

"He's in room 819, about halfway down the hall, on the right."

"Thank you."

Pivoting on a squeaky heel, she headed in the direction the nurse had pointed. It was quiet up here, no commotion, no one running around or shouting orders for crash carts and "Get me 50 cc's of epi—stat!", whatever the jargon was they used on the medical dramas on TV. That had to be a good thing.

Cady pushed down her jitters and tried to present a calm front for her mother when she entered the room. She was uncomfortably close to throwing up, but her mom didn't need to know that. Taking one last, soothing breath, she tapped quietly on the door.

"Cady? Chase said you were headed to the house." Her mom patted the empty seat beside her.

"I know. I disobeyed a direct order. I was just too concerned about Dad. Burke and Amanda are at the house. They can handle things just as well as I could have." She scowled at her brother, instantly regretting it when she saw him gripping the windowsill while he avoided looking at the prone figure of his father in the bed.

"Mom, what happened?"

"He was in the garden, weeding. I brought him some water and found him massaging his shoulder. He tried to tell me it was nothing, but I've lived with the man for thirty-five years. I know when he's in pain. He wouldn't let me call an ambulance. Thank God he actually agreed to let me drive him to the ER."

Cady finally let her gaze fall on her father, lying so still. He was hooked up to machines, wires and IV tubing crisscrossing his bare chest. He looked—frail.

"He's sleeping?" She turned back to her mother.

"Not by choice, I'm afraid. He was quite insistent that nothing was wrong and he got a little worked up."

"Dad was always a lousy patient."

"Would you listen to yourself? You're already talking about him in the past tense! Dad's going to be fine. He just needs to take it easy." A tic in his left cheek and a bright sheen to his stormy eyes showed Cady just how close her brother was to crying.

"Of course he's going to be fine. Dad's a tough guy. He can weather anything."

Silently Cady stood and crossed the small room to Chase. Without speaking, the siblings reached out for each other, linking hands as they waited for the doctor who would give them news about Wallace's prognosis.

• • •

Hours later, Cady sat at her father's bedside alone. He was being kept overnight for observation. As far as heart attacks went, his had been relatively minor. Not that heart attacks were anything but serious. Still, they had been incredibly lucky. Tomorrow he'd be going home with a medicine cabinetful of meds he would need to take. And he'd have to follow doctor's orders and rest.

Her mother had asked for a cot to be brought in. She'd be spending the night. Chase had left momentarily to pick up Amanda. Once the doctor had assured them all that Wallace was going to make a full recovery, Chase was able to talk his mother into grabbing a late dinner at the hospital cafeteria before it closed. Cady opted to stay behind in case her dad woke up to find himself all alone.

Taking her father's beefy paw in her small hand, she traced the calluses and scars that marked a lifetime of hard work on the sea. Her dad had always been larger than life to her. She could still remember squealing in happy fright as he picked her up and pretended he'd toss her off the deck to the ground below. He scared away the monsters under her bed, and, later, the boys who came to pick her up on dates. He always had the best lap for cuddling during family movie nights.

This was a wake-up call, a bitter reminder that her dad wasn't always going to be around. He was getting older. Their roles were starting to reverse and sooner, rather than later, he was going to need help. *Only, she was going to be in New York.* Ah, good. Now that the fear had abated somewhat, she was free to wallow in guilt.

"Flutterby?" His voice was a gravely whisper.

"Dad? You haven't called me that since I was probably nine years old or so."

"You were eleven and you had a raging case of chicken pox. You were devastated that you had to miss the school field trip to the aquarium."

"Mom had already signed up to chaperone, so you stayed home and took care of me."

"We ate pancakes for lunch and watched *Tom and Jerry* in our pajamas."

"And I made you color in my Barbie coloring book with me."

"Hey, as long as I got the pages with Ken on them, I was happy."

"I love you, Daddy."

"Aw, don't go getting weepy on me, kiddo. Just had a little heart hiccup, was all. Your mom all right?"

"She's hanging in there. Chase and Amanda took her downstairs to eat."

"Good, good. Your fella, where's he?"

"Burke? He helped out at the house this afternoon. Amanda said he even mowed the lawn for you." She ducked her head, biting the inside of her cheek.

"City boy mowed *my* lawn? Hope Chase has time to stop by and fix it." This time their eyes met and they both laughed.

"Hey! It was my first time. Don't I get points for even getting the damned thing started?"

Cady spun around to find Burke pouting in the doorway. She jumped up and threw her arms around his waist, hugging him hard. She kissed his cheek with a loud smack.

"Yes, you get points for all of it. You rock."

"Damned right I do." He nodded at Wallace. "You look … good."

"I look like hell, but never mind that. Take my Cady out and make sure she eats."

"Yes, sir."

Returning to the bed, Cady gingerly kissed her father goodnight. She gave his hand one last squeeze, her smile too bright. Stupid tear ducts! She was not a crier. He gave her a reassuring nod and waved her out of his hospital room.

• • •

By the time they had left the hospital, there weren't any restaurants in town that were still open. So they'd ended up back at Logan's, raiding the glass case for day-old pastries and slightly fresher thumbprint cookies. Cady grabbed herself a Diet Coke and fixed Burke a latte before he could insist she not go to the trouble. Sitting side by side at the counter, he watched her scoop a cherry out of her cheese Danish with her finger and pop it into her mouth. Burke stared down into his steaming mug.

"You doing okay?" He sent her a sidelong glance, unsure of what to say.

"I was in the worst self-absorbed snit in the world before you came in to the bakery earlier. And then Chase comes flying in to tell us about Dad. Really puts things in perspective, you know?"

She hadn't answered his question. Not really. Burke slid a cookie from his plate onto hers, earning him a grin. He'd been worried about how he'd handle things if she broke down in a sobbing mess. He sensed the worst was past.

"My dad is going to be okay. So I'm going to be okay. Okay?" Her smile stretched a little wider.

Cady nibbled at the cookie, washing it down with a sip from her soda can. She nudged his foot with the side of her sneaker, peeking out at him from under her eyelashes.

"I shouldn't have interrupted your father/daughter time."

"You were checking up on him."

"Pretty pathetic that I care more about Wallace than I do about my own father, huh?"

"You tell me. Is your father deserving of your concern?" She pushed her plate aside and grasped one of his hands. "Maybe now would be a good time to catch me up on what happened when you met with him in New York."

Taking a deep breath, he blew it out and rehashed his meeting in his father's office. If he'd thought he had processed it, compartmentalized it, and stuffed it way down where it could no longer bother him, he was mistaken. Snakes roiled in the pit of his stomach and a simmering anger he hadn't realized was there began to boil to the surface. Even the soft touch of Cady's thumb rubbing his hand barely had the calming effect he knew she intended.

He told her about having to wait through the conference call. He told her how he'd started browsing through the knickknacks. He told her about the photos and how he'd slowly put two and two together and come up with a conclusion that was surprising at best, sickening at worst.

Gently, he pulled his hand away and pretended to focus on the latte that had long since cooled off. He studied a scratch in the worn Formica. *It was no big deal.* Still, he was scared to look at Cady. What would she think of a man who had essentially been tossed aside by his own father in favor of a younger, better version of himself?

"So, yeah, I won't be going back to New York any time soon."

He thought he saw her wince and he wanted like hell to apologize. But he couldn't. He meant it. Even if she moved there tomorrow, Cady would have to come back to Scallop Shores if she wanted to see him. Maybe he'd feel differently down the road—like *years* down the road. If he could let go of the hurt and the anger long enough to associate his old world with something besides the family he'd effectively written off.

"I don't blame you."

Bracing himself, he lifted his gaze to Cady's face. She looked like she was about to cry. But not *because* of him. For him. She swatted at an errant tear and tightened her jaw. She reached out a hand, as though giving him plenty of time to back away from the kind gesture, and cupped his cheek.

"Oh, Burke. This explains so much. The new house. The new car. Adopting a dog? I thought you were rushing into things. I didn't understand your compulsion to fit into Scallop Shores so badly."

"Yeah, the house, I might have rushed. The car, I needed. You said yourself that I'd have to give back the rental. And Bandit? The family that had rented the cottage nearest mine just left him. I wasn't planning to adopt a dog. But you have to admit that he came along at an eerily perfect time in my life."

They sat quietly for a moment. Burke unclenched the fist he hadn't realize he'd been holding onto, flexing his fingers a few times for good measure. His father's betrayal still stung. He felt embarrassed, humiliated, and belittled. But having someone else to share this shameful secret with made it easier to bear. Fate could be a cruel bitch, but fate had introduced him to Cady Eaton and her family, and for that, he'd be eternally grateful.

Chapter 17

If she could capture one perfect moment in time, it would be this one. Unwilling to open her eyes just yet, Cady pressed her face to Burke's chest, happy beyond words that he had agreed to stay the night. A light dusting of hair tickled her nose and she fought the urge to sneeze.

"Good morning." She could feel the deep rumble of his words vibrate through her skin.

"How did you know I was awake?"

"I felt you smile."

Cady lifted her head and peered up at him through what she could only assume was a raging case of bedhead.

"I'm happy you stayed."

"There isn't any other place I'd rather be." His tone was matter of fact. It wasn't a line and it didn't sound like something he felt obligated to say.

A glance at the clock showed Cady they had about an hour before she would have to get ready to open the bakery. She traced the outline of his ribs with her fingertips, enjoyed the rough texture of his leg as she moved her thigh up the length of it. She felt a rising panic at the passing of time. This moment they had together was fleeting. The time she had left to spend with him and her family, it would be over far too soon.

Burke rolled her onto her back, pressing her into the mattress as he covered her body with his own. His whiskers tripped nerve endings along the column of her sensitive neck. Filling her senses with his scent, Cady blocked out the insistent worrisome chatter that sounded more like a ticking clock.

"I need you ... now." His breathy declaration in her ear sent a shivery thrill straight to her center.

"Yes." She scraped her fingernails down the long expanse of his back, opening her thighs as she tilted up in invitation.

Cady gasped as he stretched her, seating himself fully in the first thrust. Yes. This. His hips moved quickly and she found herself having to grab his backside to keep up. He left a path of open-mouthed kisses everywhere he could find, whispering a litany of praises, of needs, of promises.

Arching her back, she tried to get even closer. Head thrashing on the pillow, she moaned, equal parts passion and frustration. Blessedly perceptive, Burke paused to lift her hip, hooking her leg over his shoulder. With a long intense stare, he drove into her again, stealing her breath and eliciting a shout that was sure to be heard by anyone on Main Street.

They raced to their finish together, encouraging each other with grunts and soft words. So close. She was so close. Staring sightlessly ahead, Cady strained every muscle she had. Searching for what, she wasn't sure. With a hoarse cry, Burke came apart. Again, as though he could read her thoughts, he changed his angle just right, pushing forward and guiding her into her own sweet ending. Together they crumpled to the mattress, replete.

The only sound in the room for several minutes was their combined panting. Cady actually saw stars as she gulped in lungfuls of air. Her muscles deliciously lax, she stared up at the ceiling. This was all she needed.

She'd written her letter of resignation to Mr. Logan yesterday. Today she was supposed to mail it to him but—where was he this week? It didn't matter. She wasn't going through with it. Everyone she loved, yes, she was including Burke in this blanket declaration, was in Scallop Shores. There was no choice. She had to stay.

"I'm not going."

"Of course you're going. You need to see this through."

What the hell? They'd just shared an incredible moment of passion and he was still pushing her to leave town? Cady sat up in bed, her expression a mixture of anger, hurt, and confusion.

"Everyone I … care for … is here. If I move to the city, I have no one."

"Nothing has changed, Cady. Before I came along, you were willing to strike out on your own. You had plans, dreams. You were willing to leave your loved ones behind to explore them. Don't let go of that now."

She drew her knees up to her chin and hugged them tightly. He was right. She was caving too easily. Her father's heart attack had scared them all, but he was going to be just fine.

Burke sat up, nudged her with his shoulder, and turned her to face him.

"Do you want to run the bakery for a dick like Logan for the rest of your life? A guy who can't appreciate your ideas to bring more money and customers into his business?"

"Well, when you put it that way." She sat up straighter. It felt good to have someone in her camp for once.

"Say money was not an issue. If you could do anything you wanted, what would you do? Would you want to work for someone else? And I'm not saying there is anything wrong with that, as long as your boss is someone you can like and respect and who treats you the way you deserve."

Cady chewed at her bottom lip, pondering the question. She'd been so focused on just getting to New York that she hadn't constructed a five-year or ten-year plan. What did she really want? A smile slowly spread across her face as she thought of those order catalogs downstairs.

"I want my own coffee shop. Dedicated first and foremost to coffee, but I'd still carry pastries, breakfast sandwiches, paninis." She was on a roll.

"There would be a cozy fireplace off to the side. You know how they used to have those big pot-bellied stoves in the old general stores? And they'd set up a checkerboard on an old whiskey barrel."

"Sounds like you're catering to Old Man Feeney and his buddies."

He wasn't supposed to have noticed that. Cady backpedaled quickly.

"Well, I've got to go with what I know, right? New York is a big place. It can't be completely populated with twentysomethings jetting off to their important jobs in the huge high rises. There have to be folks looking to slow down, take a load off.

"And not just retirees. Moms looking for a chance to decompress while their kids play." Her eyes lit up and she clamped her lips together to keep from squealing in excitement as her imaginary coffee shop began to take shape.

"Kids and a fireplace?" Burke's brow arced.

"It can be done. It can *so* be done." She bumped her shoulder into his. "Are you on my team or what?"

"I am *so* on your team." His grin was indulgent.

She stuck her tongue out at him and continued.

"There would be a basket of toys. Oh—maybe a play kitchen! How cute would that be?"

"And when you aren't working at your amazing new coffee shop? You are soaking up the city life? What is it you can't get in Scallop Shores that you know you'll get in the city?" He wasn't talking her out of this, she knew. He was merely curious.

"Here, every day is the same old, same old. I mean, there is only one streetlight in town. No one ever does anything exciting. People mark the passing of days by the changing of the seasons. Tourist season, foliage season, holiday season, and muddy season." She sighed.

She snuggled against him. "I'd seek out cultural experiences. I look forward to having more restaurant choices than deep-fried seafood or mom-and-pop American fare. I've never tried Indian or Thai. I'm curious about those dim sum places. And all those food trucks we saw when we were there? I'm going to be so busy!"

"And who will be joining you for these restaurant excursions?"

Was Burke jealous? She couldn't help the smile that question elicited, or the gentle squeeze on her heart.

"I thought part of the adventure would be learning to dine alone."

Cady's smile faltered when she realized it worked both ways. She thought of Burke staying in Scallop Shores and all the single women who would consider themselves lucky to snag such a gorgeous new member of the community. And if they ever learned that the man was part of the Sanders hotel dynasty, look out!

Seeming to sense her flagging enthusiasm, Burke squeezed her knee and brought one of her hands to his mouth for the sweetest kiss.

"There are some great little neighborhoods where I can totally picture your coffee shop. But where would you live? If you find an apartment above your shop, wouldn't that take away a lot of the adventure?"

"Yeah, I need a commute." She agreed, nodding.

"What if you had a move-in-ready place? Somewhere with a heated pool? You could do laps in the morning."

"Oh, I couldn't afford a place like that." Cady snorted. "I'll be lucky if I can afford a place with a basement laundry room."

"Well, say there's this place. And it's just sitting empty. With a rooftop pool ..." He let the description linger in the air.

Okay, she was a little slow on the uptake, but did he mean what she thought he meant? Her eyes widened and she grasped his face in both hands, turning him to look at her head on. His eyes danced with merriment and his toothy grin suggested he was enjoying this torture.

"You do *not* mean what I think you do!" She leaned even closer, pressing her nose to his.

"My apartment is yours if you want it."

She backed away as though he'd burned her. No freaking way! Would he laugh outright if she pinched herself?

"I thought your parents bought that penthouse. Isn't it in their name?"

"Actually the deed is now in your name. My dad thought he was buying me off with that trophy CEO position. Let's just say I negotiated a new deal."

"I can't ... I couldn't ..." She was feeling lightheaded.

"It's done. It's yours. And don't worry about taxes or anything. I made sure you would be living there free and clear."

"Burke."

He placed a finger to her lips, shaking his head to keep her from arguing.

"I told you I'm behind you on this. You have dreams. You have an agenda. This way you don't have to worry about finding a place to stay. You can put all your effort behind your coffee shop. Research locations. Figure out startup costs. Then come back to me with a financial plan. I want to be an investor."

"I ..."

"Yeah, I know. You love me." He winked.

"I was going to say I don't deserve you." But yes, she did love him. And as exciting as the idea of having her own coffee shop and living in a gorgeous penthouse in Central Park West was, a part of her was slowly dying.

• • •

Burke never claimed to be a saint. In fact he'd admit to buying a woman (or two, or three) an expensive piece of jewelry solely for the benefits he reaped when they expressed their—gratitude. But to give a woman an apartment? That was a first for him. And something he knew deserved more reflection, when he got up the nerve to explore that touchy-feely subject.

He'd intended to keep it a secret until Cady was all packed and ready to begin her search for a place to live. But during their morning "pillow talk" the other day, he could see her having second thoughts. She was scared and unsure, ready to take the easy way out and abandon her dreams to settle for small-town life. He'd fought the little devil on his shoulder who tempted him to play to Cady's insecurities and convince her to stay.

Pushing her to go after her dreams also meant having to admit that their days together were numbered. He wasn't ashamed to admit that he wanted to spend nearly every waking moment with her. With that in mind, Burke had suggested Cady call in sick to work and spend the day at the beach with him.

Ever since Wallace had been discharged from the hospital, Cady's routine was pretty predictable. Get up at an ungodly hour to bake fresh pastries for the bakery. Open the store at seven a.m. Close the bakery at two p.m. and then spend the rest of the afternoon at her parents' house—until her father kicked her out for being too "helpful."

Knowing how uber-responsible she was, he figured she'd turn him down for a day of beach bumming. So he was pleasantly surprised when she handed the reins over to her assistant, Sophie. She'd laughed and told him the place would be hers soon, anyway.

The smell of salty seawater and coconut sunscreen was calming. Cady lay on her belly, a huge pair of sunglasses covering her eyes and a scrap of a red bikini not covering the rest of her. Burke tried to concentrate on the paperback he'd brought with him, but knowing that Cady was reading the opening chapters of his first novel was tying his stomach up in knots. He sat up on the coarse blanket, scooting to the edge and planting his toes in the burning sand.

Rolling waves crashed against the shore in a muted roar. Seagulls shrieked overhead and children squealed and giggled all around him. A couple of teenage boys trudged by, kicking up sand as they puffed out their chests and strutted like peacocks. Burke felt his hackles rise when they nudged each other while making eyes at Cady, lying on the blanket. *Back off—she's mine!* He made like he was about to stand up, putting the fear of God into them with a fierce look. One kid slapped his buddy on the back and they ran off toward the water. *Yeah, you'd better run.*

Burke shaded his eyes with his hands and stared hard at the spot where the ocean met the sky. He was in unchartered territory here. If it weren't for his nanny growing up, he wouldn't have a clue what genuine love and affection even looked like.

He'd told his father he hadn't wanted to ever hear from him again. The man had backed off, apparently offering the CEO position to someone else. That was fine. But Burke was curious as to what explanation his mother was given. He'd expected to hear from her by now. Not because she missed the sound of his voice, but to give him a hard time about not taking over his familial duty.

It should bother him how little he cared whether he ever saw either of them again. Instead, it was the idea of saying goodbye to Cady that consumed his waking thoughts and rendered most nights sleepless. She'd wormed her way into a heart he hadn't realized he had. She made him feel things he didn't know he could feel.

"Oh my gosh, Burke. This is so good!"

Cady scrambled to a sitting position and gripped his bicep excitedly. Grunting, he turned to give her a skeptical look.

"I'm just glad I'm reading this in the bright light of day. Because if I were reading it before bed, I wouldn't be able to sleep for weeks." Her eyes were dancing with excitement.

"You're just saying that."

"I'm saying it because I mean it." She slapped lightly at his shoulder. "Stop being your own worst critic."

"Thank you. For reading what I've got down so far, and for giving me your honest opinion."

"You should have my dad read this. He loves the macabre. And he could use something to keep him busy so he doesn't try to overdo it."

"Whoa, no way! It was hard enough working up the nerve to let you read it. I don't think I'm ready for anyone else to see it just yet." He kissed her cheek to soften his words.

"You're going to have to let your baby out into the world someday. And I'm here to tell you that you are going to make some editor a very lucky person to have discovered you. When you're ready, show it to Bree … or Wynter. Oh! I bet Quinn might have contacts at her publishing house. Couldn't hurt to try." She bounced on the sand-covered blanket.

It was on the tip of his tongue to tell her he loved her. His chest tightened and he had to look away so Cady wouldn't catch the raw emotion he knew he wouldn't be able to hide right now. God, even his eyes stung. Unchartered territory indeed!

He'd already sent in his last article to Meredith. They'd parted on good terms and he was free to move on with his own writing. But the more he thought about it, the more he figured he owed to his old editor. An email wasn't enough. The assignment she'd begged him to take had changed his life. He made a note to send the woman roses and champagne. It was the least he could do.

They spent the entire day at the beach, sharing a slightly gritty turkey sub and salty potato chips, and washing it down with lukewarm lemonade. Playing in the surf like children, they also took a leisurely stroll from one end of the beach to the other, holding hands. They'd even napped on their blanket, Cady wrapped in his arms. Burke couldn't think of a day in recent memory where he'd had more fun. Well, there was the sightseeing in New York. Again, with Cady.

The weather had cooled significantly and they were now among the last to be packing up their belongings to leave. Burke shook the sand out of their blanket and they folded it together. Stuffing it into a giant L.L. Bean tote, Cady gasped and whirled around.

"Ooh, I keep forgetting to tell you."

Cady held up a finger and scanned their immediate surroundings, pouncing on a sturdy stick a few feet away and running after it. She motioned him over to the hard-packed wet sand. A working canvas.

"Okay, so I've been playing with floor plans. Here, let me show you."

When he had told her to research what she'd need, Burke hadn't expected her to be quite so thorough. She'd done her due diligence and her enthusiasm for this endeavor was contagious. He was happy that he'd encouraged her to expand her thinking because this bigger dream, owning her own business, was fleshing out as though it had been sitting in her mind, percolating for years. The fact that he got a special thrill out of seeing her so happy sure didn't hurt.

Yeah, it would kill him to see her go. But Burke knew he'd do anything to see her dreams come true. He slipped his hand into his little entrepreneur's and slung the huge tote bag onto his shoulder. Cady grabbed the cooler and they headed off for her truck.

The day wasn't over yet. He'd promised her a concert at the park. They swung by the rental cottage that wouldn't be his much longer, and picked up Bandit. Then they stopped at the bakery to switch out the beach cooler for a picnic basket. This one was packed more to his taste, containing a bottle of wine, assorted cheeses, fresh fruit, and some delicious rolls that Cady had made from scratch. She had let him choose whatever he liked from the bakery case for dessert, so tonight's delicacy were the cream cheese frosted brownies she told him she'd gotten up early to bake.

Clusters of families dotted the grass around the large gazebo overlooking the ocean. Cady and Burke found a spot near the middle, spreading their blanket for the second time that day. He smiled as she greeted folks around them, asking after relatives, their health, and general well being. There didn't seem to be a citizen in Scallop Shores that didn't know Cady. And she was well liked.

"Hey there, baby sis! Burke. Fancy running into you guys here." Chase loomed over them as he gently guided Amanda through the maze of blankets and lawn chairs assembled in front of the stage.

"Here, sit down." Cady got up on her knees and helped to ease Amanda down to the blanket.

"Good grief, it's going to take a crane to get me back on my feet once this is over." The pregnant woman groaned.

Burke watched Chase eyeing the picnic basket on the corner of the blanket.

"I'm not sharing my brownies with you."

"Too bad, bro. I was going to offer up Amanda's amazing lobster salad. It's so good."

Ugh. Okay, he had him there. Cady wasn't the only thing he'd developed an addiction to since moving to Maine. He had also discovered a great love of lobster. Steamed, in pasta, on a hot dog roll; just keep it coming.

"Fine. But you get the corner piece."

Chase slapped him on the back as he laughed.

"Come on. I need to go back to the SUV for our own basket. If you help me carry it I'll give you one of my beers."

"We brought wine."

"You can take the guy out of the city ..." Chase shook his head, still mumbling something under his breath as he headed off for the parking lot.

"Ladies." Burke tossed them a crooked grin before jogging to catch up with Cady's brother.

Chase raised the tailgate, hauling out a wicker basket the size of a television set and shoving it into Burke's arms.

"So I see some major congratulations are in order, bud. What did you say to her to get her to stay? I mean, whatever works, but we've been trying for years."

"Wait, no. You've got it all wrong. Cady isn't staying. Dude, she's already given her notice at the bakery. Labor Day weekend. Better get used to it."

"But you guys were all snuggly back there. Why would she leave that?"

Burke closed his eyes, releasing a sigh through his nostrils. His biceps burned with the weight of the basket in his arms. He shifted it into a more comfortable position and finally looked up at Chase.

"She deserves to be happy, Chase. Why can't you give her that? Let her go after her dreams. Let her find out who she wants to be."

They stared hard at one another for a brief moment before heading back to the activity.

"Have you talked to her about her ideas? Because I've got to tell you, they are pretty amazing. Your sister is so smart. She has a real head for business and she owes it to herself to give this a try."

"I thought you liked her. So why are you pushing her away?"

"I thought I liked her too. And I'm not pushing her away. I'm letting her go. Because I love her too much to trap her in a place she doesn't want to stay."

Chapter 18

Cady tried to follow the conversation going on around her, but it was hard to concentrate. The wind had really picked up in the last half hour and the sky was much too dark for mid-morning. The clouds were thick, pressing in against the bakery windows in an angry purple hue. A sense of foreboding had the tiny hairs on her skin standing up. It felt like a parade of ants marching across her body.

"Not long now and we get our town back." Earl Duffy lifted his coffee mug and nodded at the rest of the group seated at the counter.

"I was having fun calling the tow truck on any idiot who thought they could park in my driveway instead of plugging the parking meters at the beach like they're supposed to," snorted Old Man Feeney.

Cady grinned. She had to agree with him on that. Those folks got what they deserved. She rubbed her arms briskly and turned away from the windows.

"Mr. Feeney, what does your knee tell you today? This storm supposed to amount to anything?"

"Probably get a good downpour. We can use it, too. Could lose power for a bit. Too early for a hurricane." He rubbed his chin between his thumb and forefinger.

The next gust of wind tore at the awnings outside and had the lights in the bakery flickering, causing everyone inside to look around uneasily. Cady slapped a hand on the counter, making her customers jump.

"All right, I'm calling it. We're closing early today."

"Aw, it's just a boomer. It will blow over soon."

"Sorry, gentlemen. This one worries me. I want everyone to go home and wait it out in safety." She turned and gave them all a hard look.

"On second thought, most of you live alone. I think we should all head somewhere together. I'm going to make an urn of coffee and take it to Kittredge Manor. We can wait out the storm over there. You go on ahead. Tell them I sent you and to make you comfortable."

"I am not going to hide out from a silly storm with a bunch of old farts." Old Man Feeney puffed out his chest.

"You are an old fart, Feeney!" One of his cohorts chortled.

"I'm bringing the whoopie pies over there. And I happen to know a lot of folks who enjoy a hand or two of poker. Don't ask me where they get it, but the cash I've seen piled up on the table ..." Cady threw her hands up as she shrugged.

"Well, it's not like anyone would ever mistake me for someone who actually lived there. I could just be visiting, is all. Cash, you say?" Feeney was already putting his ball cap on his head as he made his way toward the door.

Her relief was palpable, knowing she'd be able to keep an eye on them over there. She got one of the giant urns out of the storage room and ran it out to her truck parked behind the bakery. When she got back inside, Burke was ushering the last of her customers out. He shut the door and turned the open sign to closed.

"What the hell is with those clouds? It's damned creepy, if you ask me."

"They were predicting high winds and intermittent thunder showers on the morning news. We've had some bad summer storms before, but nothing that has made my skin crawl like this. I'm worried, Burke. Something tells me it's going to be a lot rougher than the forecasters were expecting."

The wind whistled through the cracks in the old door, rattling it inside its frame. Cady stepped into Burke's arms, just for a moment, siphoning a bit of his rugged strength. To think that just a few months ago, he'd walked into her bakery, a *GQ* city guy to the core. Now he looked more like an advertisement for L.L. Bean.

"Didn't know you'd be signing up for this, did you?" She gave him a shaky grin.

"I'm on a mission to seek out adventure. Whatever I may have missed in my sheltered childhood."

"Well, speaking of shelter, I'm headed to Kittredge Manor. I need to make sure Auntie is okay. I've sent Feeney and the others on ahead." She slapped her forehead and spun on her heel.

"The rest of your family? Is Chase on duty?" Burke gripped her arm to hold her in place.

Her anxiety suddenly multiplied as she realized she couldn't be in two places at once.

"Chase asked me to stop by and check in on Amanda after work. With her due any day now he's so worried she's going to go into labor while he's at work. And my parents—"

"I'm on it. You go to Kittredge. Mr. Feeney told me to remind you that you promised to bring whoopie pies. I've got enough room in my car for Amanda and your parents. I'll go get them and bring them to you. Everyone can ride out the storm together."

"You'd do that? You'll go get them for me?"

Cady threw her arms around Burke's neck. She gripped him tightly, kissing him hard on the mouth.

"I love you."

"Good, because I love you too. I wish like hell that we had more time to discuss this. I'll see you at Kittredge." Burke headed for the front door, pointing toward the display case of whoopie pies, lest she forget her priorities.

Her cell phone jangled in her pocket and they both paused. She pulled it out and checked caller ID: Amanda.

"Hey, sweetie, what's up? Some storm coming, huh?" Her smile faltered when she heard the panic in Amanda's voice.

"I can't reach Chase. He's not answering his phone. Something's wrong, Cady. I know it."

"Okay, listen. You need to stay calm for the baby. Burke is on his way out to pick you and my parents up. We're bringing you all into town to wait out the storm. Burke has no medical training, so let's not force him to deliver a baby in the middle of a thunderstorm, all right?"

The poor man's eyes were wide as dinner plates as he listened in on her end of the conversation. Cady wasn't sure whether to laugh at his reaction or freak out along with her sister-in-law over Chase's safety. Her nerves were already completely shot.

"Tell him to hurry. We'll look for Chase together."

"Okay, sit tight, sweetie. He'll be there in a few minutes." She jabbed the end button and stuffed the phone back into the pocket of her denim skirt. Like hell were they driving all over Scallop Shores, putting their lives in danger to look for a police officer who was likely busy keeping the town safe. Chase would be furious enough when he learned she'd had Amanda moved into town, instead of keeping her safe at home like she'd promised.

"She's going to try to convince you to go looking for Chase. You take her directly to Kittredge. My brother can take care of himself." She closed her eyes and sent up a silent prayer that Amanda's worries were for naught.

Cady pressed her fingers to the cool glass of the bakery case. She gulped in a long, cleansing breath. Burke stood half in and half out of the doorway.

"I told you, I've got this. And Cady? I really do love you. Save one of those whoopie pies for me." He winked and was gone.

• • •

Great gusts of wind, malicious in their intent, tried to push Burke's car off into the trees. He gripped the steering wheel tightly, forcing himself to stay on his side of the road. Branches fell around him as he drove past, missiles launched from above. Though that was safer than the lawn chair that had come at him on Main Street. He'd been grateful the street was clear of traffic, as he'd had to veer into the other lane to avoid it.

He was nearly to Cady's parents' house when the rain started. One minute it was dark and forbidding, windy as hell but dry. The next thing he knew, a wall of torrential rain slammed down. Scrambling to get the wipers started, Burke cursed a blue streak. Mother Nature sure was pissed today!

The wipers going at full blast, it still wasn't enough to fully clear the windshield before the next pass. He had to slow down as he peered hard through the glass. The Eatons' long driveway was coming up on the left. A cluster of Oak leaves, still attached to a thin branch, thwacked against the windshield, making him jump in his seat. Heart pounding in his ears, he gritted his teeth and whipped his car hard to the left. The sooner they got back into town, the better.

Even though he parked as close to the porch steps as possible, he was still soaked to the bone by the time he raced up the stairs and pounded on the sliding glass door. May opened the door and practically yanked him inside. Burke stood dripping on the rug, catching his breath. Compared to the raging chaos of the storm outside, the quiet of the cozy house was almost eerie.

"Let me get you a towel."

"Don't bother. I'll just get soaked again on the way to the car. We need to hurry. It's friggin' nuts out there. Cady wants you guys all at Kittredge."

"She should have come here, instead. We could have waited it out here."

"Too many trees. She's afraid something is going to happen, being too far from town. And given that drive from hell to get here, I am inclined to agree with her."

"Let me just pack Wallace's medicine. Honey, get your shoes on. We need to leave." She hollered into the living room.

"'Bout damned time I get to leave my own house. That's some storm, ain't it, Burke?" Wallace shuffled into the dining room, a twinkle in his eye.

They all jumped at the resounding crack and subsequent crash, as a good-sized branch bounced off the roof of the storage shed. Burke steeled his spine and gave Cady's parents a grim smile.

"Grab what you need and let's go."

Buckling into the small car, the trio backed up the driveway until the fork that led to Chase's and Amanda's house. Fortunately, they still had power. But Burke imagined that was only temporary. It wasn't quite noon but the darkness made it feel like closer to twilight. Lights blazed in the downstairs as Amanda waited for them.

"I'm going to run in and get her. You wait here." Burke barked against the roar of the wind.

He was halfway to the door when he turned and went back to the car. His stomach churned and, though he couldn't say what exactly, something just didn't feel right about leaving them alone. He yanked open the door and reached a hand in to help them out.

"Change of plans. We all go together. Let's go!"

They hurried up to the covered porch, raindrops the size of plums pelting them as they ran.

"Thank God you're here. Chase hasn't answered his phone in hours. He knows to keep in touch because of the baby. Something's wrong."

Amanda didn't stop chattering as her in-laws and Burke pushed through the door. May slogged across the linoleum to the coat closet and took out Chase's long rain slicker and slipped it around her daughter-in-law. Burke gripped the young woman by her shoulders, nodding his head as he listened patiently, even as his brain was screaming at him to hurry.

A screech unlike anything he'd ever heard rent the air. His blood chilled in his veins when the unmistakable sound of breaking glass and wrenching metal met his ears. The house shook on its foundation just as the lights flickered out. Amanda screamed. Clutching at each other, they all moved as one, opening the door to take a peek outside.

Burke's car was crushed beneath a tall maple, ripped from the ground by its roots and now lay sideways across the driveway. Unashamed of the tears that flowed freely, he hugged May and then Wallace, kissing them both loudly on the forehead. They would have been sitting ducks out there.

"You saved us, Burke." May's trembling voice came out in a croak.

"We aren't out of danger yet."

"We're trapped. Chase is hurt somewhere and we can't get to him because we're trapped." Amanda was fast becoming hysterical.

He had to do something quickly.

"Does Chase have a chainsaw? I need to clear a path so we can get out of here."

"Son, I appreciate your enthusiasm, but have you ever used a chainsaw before?" Wallace frowned, arching a bushy grey brow.

"No, but I had never used a lawn mower before either. I can do this." Burke stepped out onto the porch, only to be stopped by Wallace's hand on his forearm.

"You've got balls, kid. I'll give you that. But Cady would kill me if I let you near a chainsaw, God help me."

"We've got to get the women out of here."

"And we will. Just have to go for a little walk through the woods, is all."

Huddled together, they left the house, descending the stairs and veering off for a path that Burke would have missed if Wallace hadn't been guiding him directly toward it. Amanda was muttering under her breath, with May chanting calm reassurances to counteract the hysteria. They ducked through wet branches, dodged a few broken ones and hurried as fast as they could through the trees back to the Eatons' house.

"I just need to go in and get my keys in the house," Wallace said.

"No need. I have a set right here." May patted the purse she held like a quarterback racing for a touchdown.

Had the situation not been so dire, Burke would have laughed. He held out his hand and waited while she rifled through the deep purse. Wallace hovered over the women like a gruff old bear, his arms extended as though that would protect them from the trees.

"Ah, here they are!" May pressed the key ring into Burke's fingers and rushed to help Amanda to the passenger side.

Everyone clambered into the car and Burke didn't even wait until they all had seatbelts on before gunning it up the driveway. Who knew how long they had before it, too, was blocked? The road was a barely passable mess. Wallace barked out instructions on how to turn on the wipers and where the lights were. Amanda curled toward the car door, crying softly.

Lightning flashed across the sky, backlighting the dark clouds. Burke wasn't sure if he was relieved or frightened when the deluge of rain quit as suddenly as it had begun, only to be replaced by hail. Now it was Wallace's turn to chant a litany of colorful words from the backseat.

"Hey, it could be worse. They could be the size of golf balls. These are kind of cool, actually," Burke ventured.

"Stop it! You're making it worse," Wallace snarled.

They settled into a tense silence. Burke navigated the road with a white-knuckled grip on the steering wheel. Amanda studied the scenery as they passed, as though she expected to see Chase at any moment. Apparently they were the only ones foolhardy enough to be on the road.

Pulling into the nursing home parking lot, Burke wasn't the only one to thank his maker for getting them there safely. The rain and hail forced them to hustle to the front door. Burke guided Amanda, while he couldn't decide who was helping whom as May and Wallace leaned on each other as they hurried up the walkway.

The hallways were teeming with residents and unexpected guests. Burke discovered Cady in the cafeteria, presiding over her precious coffee urn. He imagined that in another life, she had been an Italian mama, happiest when she was feeding her huge family. That scene led to one of Cady in his new home, sitting down to dinner with their own large brood.

She squealed once she'd spotted him, wiping her hands on her bakery apron that he doubted she even realized she still wore. She looked over his shoulder, trying to spot her family. He gave her a quick kiss and put an arm around her shoulders to lead her to the rec room.

"The good news is we're all here and in one piece."

"And Amanda isn't in labor."

"Not unless her water broke in the time it took me to settle her on the couch with a blanket."

"Bite your tongue!" Cady swatted his arm. "Wait. Then what's the bad news?"

"My brand-new car is sitting under a giant-ass tree in your brother's driveway. Flat as a pancake."

"No!"

"It was wicked cool." He grinned.

"Wait. Did you just say 'wicked'? Look at you, sounding more like a Mainer every day!"

They joined her family in the rec room and Burke smiled to see Cady hug and touch them, reassuring herself that they were all perfectly healthy. Auntie hurried in with a handmade afghan, which she wrapped around May, stroking her damp hair before she took a seat on the couch beside her.

"Cady, I'm not crazy. I feel it in my gut. Something is wrong with Chase. He would have checked in by now. Even just to text and let me know he's too busy to call."

Burke looked from Cady to Amanda. Both women look scared spitless. The problem was, they had no idea where Chase was. He could be anywhere in Scallop Shores. Cady wrapped her arms around her friend. His jaw rigid, Burke turned to Wallace.

"With your permission, I'd like to borrow your car and go look for Chase." He put a hand on Amanda's shoulder. "Do you know where he was the last time you spoke with him?"

"He said he was on duty in the harbor. That he had to make sure no tourists were stupid enough to take their boats out with a storm coming up."

"It's a start." Burke stepped toward the door, only to have Cady jump in front of him.

"Are you crazy? You can't go back out in that. I can't—"

"Lose me? I'm going to be just fine. And I'm going to find a way to make your pain-in-the-ass brother owe me big time."

"Oh, well, as long as your motives are noble." The half-smile she pasted on trembled slightly. She looked torn between wanting to keep him from leaving and needing him to rescue her brother.

"I'm going to be okay. And Chase is going to be okay. Let me bring him back so you and Amanda can smother him together."

"I'll call the station. Check again to see if they've heard from Chase yet. It's probably so crazy down there that they might have forgotten to let us know. I'll call you if I learn anything."

Her hands were fisted at her sides and he knew she was terrified, not just for her brother but for him. Burke had to do this. Because somewhere along the way, Chase had become his family too.

Chapter 19

Weren't thunderstorms supposed to be over relatively quickly? Burke tensed the muscles in his neck as another boom rumbled around him. If he wasn't careful, he'd end up a few inches shorter by the time he got out of the car. And this was just a summer squall. Who knew what he was in for when a hurricane decided to hit the coastal town? Or a blizzard. With a growing dread, he realized he'd really only seen Scallop Shores at its best.

Getting his bearings, Burke headed east, toward the harbor. Now that he was in town, the damage from the storm wasn't quite as devastating. Fewer trees meant fewer chances for downed power lines and broken branches. Lights glowed in the windows he passed, a sign that most residents were cozy and sheltered.

But where was Chase? The guy loved a good joke, and teased him incessantly, but he would never go so far as to worry his extremely pregnant wife into an early delivery. Okay, technically it wouldn't be early at this point. But Burke was damned sure that Chase intended to be there for every single moment of it.

Slowing to a crawl, since he wasn't going to aggravate anyone behind him with the road being empty, he scanned both sides. Chase's squad car wasn't along this stretch of beach. He hadn't seen it as he drove past the nicer boutique shops in this part of town. Following a hunch, Burke turned off on a residential street. He took note of each turn he made, so he could find his way back to the main road.

Burke was on his fourth right-hand turn. He was heading away from the water, uphill. How far was he from the middle of town? He blinked to refocus his gaze, as the windshield wipers were really starting to do a number on his vision. There! Parked in front of a little bungalow with a cobblestone walkway lined with rose bushes.

Granted, this could be anyone on the Scallop Shores police force. And if it wasn't Chase, then at least Burke had a new recruit to help him find Cady's brother. What the hell was he doing, having tea at someone's house? Burke sprinted from his borrowed car to the bungalow, rapping on the door and shuffling from one foot to the other as he shivered in the rain. Nothing. He pounded again, harder this time.

He heard movement inside, saw a shadow pass across the window. Still, it took this person ages to get to the door. Just as he was about to bang on the door again, it creaked open an inch. A rheumy eye peered suspiciously at him.

"Officer Eaton?"

"No, but I'm looking for him. Have you seen him? He's not answering his cell phone and his wife is scared to death."

The door opened a bit wider. An old woman in a ratty purple bathrobe held the doorknob in a tight grip. Her other hand was curled around one of those canes that had four prongs for more stability. She looked confused, and this immediately set off warning bells for Burke.

"He's here. Well, he came here. He was going to help me get LouLou Tomkins out of the tree." She looked around, as though trying to remember something more.

"Where's the tree, ma'am? In the backyard? How do I get there?"

"I must have dozed off. I'd forgotten he was here. Why hasn't he brought me my LouLou Tomkins yet? My precious little boy isn't used to scary storms. He's bound to be terrified."

"Ma'am? The tree? How do I find Officer Eaton?"

"Well, it's in the backyard, of course." She looked at him as though he were the one who was confused.

Burke closed his eyes, took a deep breath and tried again.

"Can I go around the house or will you need to let me in?"

"Boy, you're dripping wet. You can walk around the side of the house, same as Officer Eaton did. Don't come back without my cat." And with that, she slammed the door.

Feeling like he was in some sort of low-budget screwball comedy, Burke wiped the rainwater out of his eyes and jogged around the side of the bungalow.

"Chase! Dude, you'd better have a damned good reason for hauling my ass out into this crazy freaking weather!"

Where the hell was he? The yard was lined with mostly pine trees. Had he tried to climb one of those? No, wait, there was one on the other side of the house, lots of branches. Burke ran across the grass, slipping and sliding in the mud and the muck.

Shit! He'd spotted Chase, lying at the base of the old tree. His leg was bent at a scary angle and he wasn't moving. Shit. Shit. Shit. When he'd pictured this scenario, he'd figured Chase had run out of gas somewhere and his phone had died. Something they could laugh about later. He wasn't laughing now.

"Aw, buddy, what the hell did you do? Amanda is going to have my ass if I don't get you to her in one piece."

Burke dropped to the ground, shook his friend by the shoulder and grimaced when he didn't get a response. He slapped at Chase's face. Still nothing. What to do? He wasn't trained in first aid. Panic pushing bile up into his throat, Burke ripped open Chase's rain slicker. A startled hiss and a flash of fur had him flying backwards in surprise. He recovered quickly and leaned over the unconscious man.

"You try to give me mouth-to-mouth and I swear to God I will shoot you in the balls."

"Jesus, Chase, you scared the hell out of me!"

"Yeah, seeing your mug leaning over my face wasn't much of a picnic either." Chase's face was a nasty gray color and he looked as though he might pass out again at any moment.

"I'm no medic, but I think your leg is broken."

"No shit. Here. Take this damned cat and bring it to Mrs. Moulton." Chase moaned as he shifted so he could scoop the kitten out of the shelter of his coat and hand it to Burke.

"It's so tiny. Cute little furball."

"Don't be fooled. Damned thing has claws like meat hooks."

"I'll be right back." He couldn't resist adding, "Don't go anywhere."

"Bite me, jerk!"

In the time it had taken him to run around to the back of the house, find Chase and return with one LouLou Tomkins, the cat's owner had already forgotten he'd been on a rescue mission. She seemed startled to find her kitten being handed to her by a man she swore she'd never seen before. Burke made note of her address. The folks at Kittredge Manor needed to know about Mrs. Moulton.

Hurrying back to Chase, Burke was relieved to find that Mother Nature appeared to have worked off her temper tantrum. The wind had finally died down and the rain was little more than a drizzle. He slipped his phone from his pocket, intending to text Cady that he'd found her brother. But she'd want details and he didn't want to worry them further.

"Hey, I'm gonna call 911 and get you an ambulance. Why didn't you call earlier? You must have been lying out here for hours."

"We don't need 911. Save that for the emergencies. Just help me stand up and take me to the ER."

"This is an emergency, dummy! Your leg is ... aw, hell, that's a compound fracture isn't it?" Getting a better look at Chase's injury, Burke might have thrown up a little in his mouth. Sure tasted like it, going back down.

"Why the hell do you think I've been out here all day? Got knocked out when I fell. Then I may have passed out a time or two from the pain."

Chase gritted his teeth and pulled himself into a sitting position. He swayed a bit, and judging by the look on his face, Burke wouldn't have been surprised if he'd keel over one more time. The guy was seriously green around the gills.

"Where's your phone? Couldn't you call for help?"

"Landed on it. Pretty sure there are pieces of it stuck in my ass."

"Nice picture. I told Cady I'd find you and bring you back. You're on your own with that."

He reached a hand down and waited for Chase to grip it tightly. Together they got him upright, Burke widening his stance to keep Chase's weight off his injured leg. It felt like years before they reached the front yard and were within sight of the car.

"Why are you driving my dad's car?"

"Long story."

Helping his friend into the passenger side as gently as possible, Burke scrambled around and got behind the wheel. If he didn't call Cady and fill her in now, the hospital would have to make up a bed for him too, after she got done with him. He dug out his phone, spoke quickly and passed it off to Chase when Cady explained Amanda needed to hear her husband's voice.

He wouldn't be surprised if the guy had also broken a rib or two. He knew the fracture had to hurt like a sonofabitch, and Chase didn't seem to be able to draw a full breath. He was panting and his eyes were scrunched tight against the pain.

"You should try to get some rest." He suggested, after Chase hung up with his wife and handed his phone back to him.

"You seriously aren't going to go there." Chase coughed, his expression a mixture of pain and exhaustion.

"Go where?"

"I climbed a stupid tree to rescue a frickin' kitten and I fell. During a rainstorm. You owe me for the raccoon thing. Just get it over with. Let me have it."

"No way. You're in too much pain."

"Really? You feel too bad to razz me over this?"

"Didn't say that. I'm saying you're too distracted by the pain right now. I'm going to wait until you're feeling better and it'll bother you much worse."

"Dick."

"Yup."

Burke pulled up to the curb right outside the ER. They had a welcoming committee waiting for them. Cady and Amanda stood on the edge of the curb. Wallace, May, and Auntie waited just outside the doors to the ER.

As he watched, Cady directed two orderlies with a wheelchair toward the passenger side of the car. The men helped Chase into it, barely getting out of the way before Amanda flew at him, peppering his face with kisses.

"We owe you, you crazy, stubborn fool." Cady wrapped her arms around Burke's waist as soon as he stepped from the car, pressing her cheek to his chest.

Just stay in Scallop Shores and we'll call it even. Burke wished he could voice the words out loud. He palmed the top of her head as he held her close, breathing in the scent of her shampoo and thanking God that his woman had escaped harm today.

"Ma'am, we need to take your husband in for an X-ray, but you're welcome to have a seat in the waiting room." One orderly pushed Chase's wheelchair toward the lobby of the ER. The other paused to speak to Amanda.

"Tell you what, why don't you get me settled in a room in labor and delivery and when you're done fixing up my husband, you just park his bed next to mine?"

Everyone turned to stare at Amanda.

"My water just broke."

•••

Like any hardy New England town, Scallop Shores was business as usual the following morning. Folks helped each other clean up branches and other storm debris. Neighbors shored up fences and broken mailboxes. And Cady had made her father swear he wouldn't allow Burke to use his chainsaw to dig out that shiny new sedan from under the tree in Chase's drive.

And, as if it were any other day, and they hadn't just had a storm for the history books, Old Man Feeney and crew were seated along the counter. In between coffee refills, Cady forced them all to sit through another round of pictures on her phone. Her precious nephew, Willem Burke Eaton, had been born just before midnight, surrounded by family. She was the proudest auntie in the world.

She thought back to the previous night. While Chase and Amanda got some recuperative sleep, Cady had taken the opportunity to bond with baby Will. She nuzzled him close as she settled into the rocking chair, nudging it into a comfortable rhythm with the heel of one foot. There was nothing like the smell of a new baby. She could actually feel her ovaries squeezing.

She'd made a decision then. Burke would think she was settling, but she wasn't. There was no way she could leave Scallop Shores. Everything and everyone that mattered to her was right here. And if she was worried that life would be too dull, routine? This summer had given her just about all the excitement one lifetime could handle.

Sure, her pride would take a hit when she had to explain to Mr. Logan that she wouldn't be quitting after all. She'd have to work ten times as hard to prove she wasn't the ditz she seemed. But she'd have her espresso maker and her customers—who she also considered family—though she'd save them the embarrassment of actually admitting it out loud.

What would Burke say when she told him she was staying? Her stomach filled with butterflies at the notion. Last time he'd gently insisted she go. But she felt they'd been through so much since then. Surely he'd change his mind now? They could be together. They could have a future.

"I suppose you'll be wanting one of your own now?" Old Man Feeney's scratchy growl broke through her reverie.

"Why? You offering?" She sent him a saucy grin.

"You see that? Try to have a pleasant conversation with this sass and she has to go and ruin it." He scowled.

"For your information, Mr. Feeney, I am perfectly happy just being an auntie."

The bell over the bakery door tingled and Cady looked up. Burke stepped in, his sexy smile reaching in and giving those ovaries another good tug. Especially when she remembered the tears in his eyes when Chase had told him they'd given their son his name. Okay, perhaps the idea of motherhood wasn't completely out of the question. Cheeks heating, she dropped her gaze to the counter, attacking it with a wet rag.

"Care to change your answer, Missy?" Feeney elbowed the buddy on his right.

"That's enough out of you." She swatted him with the damp rag.

"Cady, we need to talk." Mr. Logan had come in through the back door and was standing right behind her.

How long had he been there, listening, watching? Was he upset over her treatment of his customers? Surely that couldn't have been construed as abusive? She bit her lip, looking at Burke in worry. His brief nod was reassuring. Head held high, she dropped the rag to the counter, wiped her hands on her apron, and led the way into the back office.

Nervous energy had her perching on the edge of the desk as she waited for Mr. Logan to close the door behind them. He pulled out the computer chair and sat down, pressing his fingertips together in a steeple. After a moment he gave Cady his full attention.

"If this is about Mr. Feeney—"

His forehead wrinkled in confusion.

"The fact that I closed up early yesterday—"

He raised his eyebrows at that. Guess he hadn't heard yet.

"No, Cady, this isn't about you. What do you think I'm going to do, fire you? You've got less than two weeks left here. What'd be the point?" He shook his head.

"I don't understand."

"I was hoping you wouldn't mind clearing out of the apartment a mite early. I promised Ernie he could repaint it however he liked. Your parents wouldn't mind putting you up for a week or so, right?"

"You're giving the apartment to Ernie?" She blinked in disbelief. Ernie was Mr. Logan's deadbeat son, who'd been kicked out of three different colleges so far.

"Yes, keep up. Ernie's not going back to USM in the fall and he needs a place to stay."

Okay, make that four colleges.

"I'll start packing as soon as I close up this afternoon." Cady's breath started to hitch in her chest. Something told her she wasn't going to be given the chance to ask for her job back.

"Perfect. And if you wouldn't mind letting Sophie and the others know we won't be needing them after Labor Day. They like you. It should come from you."

"Excuse me?" Halfway between a squeak and a shout, Cady launched herself off the desk and began to pace the small room.

"Yes, yes. I need you to let them go. I am closing the bakery. Well, converting it, I guess you could say. Ernie would like to turn it into one of those comic book/hobby type stores. I'm hoping I can convince him to just call it a toy store. But it's his idea. Don't want to cramp his style, you know."

Stunned, Cady could only stare at her boss. He had a good thing going here. He had regular customers that were already waiting outside when she came down to unlock the door each morning. Where would they go now? This wasn't fair!

"Do you really think this is a wise business decision? Are there enough people in town that will want to buy comic books on a regular basis?"

"I don't expect you to understand my *business decisions*, Ms. Eaton. This is about a father doing what he needs to do to keep his son out of trouble. When you have children of your own, you'll see that sacrifices have to be made. I know I'm losing money on this venture. I don't care."

He leaned back in the chair and peered up at her.

"Besides, you're moving to the big city. Getting out of this boring old town. What do you care what happens to the bakery?"

Though she could go on and on about how much she cared, she recognized the question as rhetorical and locked her jaw to keep from shooting her mouth off.

"Was there anything else, Mr. Logan?" She needed to get out of this office before she exploded.

"Yeah, you keep that espresso machine plugged in until the last second of the last day we're open. Got it? Get me one of those fancy sandwich boards and talk up your frou-frou drinks. Might as well earn as much as we can, while we can."

"Yes, sir." Without a backward glance, Cady yanked open the door and stalked out.

Unbelievable! Now he gives her the green light to make a big deal about her espresso drinks? She had half a mind to dump one of her *frou-frou drinks* in the odious man's lap! The nerve!

Taking a moment to compose herself, Cady ran a shaky hand through her hair. She blinked back frustrated tears and practiced a couple of fake smiles. She couldn't ask for her job back when her job no longer existed. She was being kicked out of her apartment.

She had no choice now. She had to move to the city. At least she knew she had a place to stay there.

"Everything okay?" Burke's voice was a gentle balm on her battered soul.

"Oh, just peachy."

On autopilot, Cady made her way to the espresso machine, grinding beans and heating milk for Burke's morning latte. The bottle of hazelnut syrup slipped from her hand and she caught it seconds before it smashed on the hard linoleum. *Don't cry. Don't cry.* She swallowed the tears, earning herself one hell of a stomachache in the process.

She started to hand his drink over and was forced to meet his eyes when he wouldn't immediately accept the cup. He looked concerned, but he also looked determined—and a little scared. She tore herself away and rang up the purchase. Making change, she forced a cheery smile and pushed the bills and coins into his hand.

"Walk me to the door?"

"Aw, shucks, boys. He's courtin' her." Old Man Feeney grinned wolfishly at the couple.

Cady rolled her eyes and made her way around the counter to stand in front of Burke.

"You afraid you're going to get lost on the way?" She managed to tease.

"I've been thinking a lot since yesterday. God, was that crazy or what?"

"Yup, crazy day."

"Anyway, I learned I'm a lot more selfish than I realized. And I'm not above begging."

She shook her head from side to side. No, he couldn't do this to her now. He had to be the strong one for both of them.

"Cady, stay in Scallop Shores." He set his coffee down on the nearest table and gripped her fingers in his. "I thought I had everything I wanted. All my dreams were coming true. But it's nothing unless you're here to share it with me."

"Please don't do this," she whispered.

"Don't go, Cady. Say you'll stay here ... with me."

"I can't." She slipped her fingers free and stepped back.

"I thought you loved me. I thought you wanted to stay." He didn't bother to hide the anguish, on his face and in his words.

Go away, Burke. I can't do this right now.

"You were right. I need to follow my dreams. I'll miss you." *More than you will ever know.*

He stayed there, staring at her as though willing her to change her mind. When she stood her ground, refusing to say another word, he let out a long sigh. Picking up his coffee, he left the bakery without a backward glance.

"Sophie, watch the front for me. Staff meeting at close. Make sure everyone stays until I get back down here."

Blindly, she pushed her way to the back stairs, stumbling up to the apartment that was no longer hers. The day had started out perfect, full of hope and new beginnings. And in the blink of an eye it had all changed. Sliding down against the door, Cady curled into a ball on the floor and gave in to the crippling sorrow that made it so hard to breathe. Sobs wracked her body, shaking her until her teeth rattled. Her head throbbed as if it would split open. Oh, if only it would.

Chapter 20

"Are you sure she's not going to think we're being just a tad manipulative?" Bree glanced out the window at the busy street for the umpteenth time.

Burke looked up from where he was checking an order of supplies that had just come in.

"This is her dream. We've just ... relocated it. It's all still hers." He opened a box of handmade mugs from a local artist that he knew Cady admired, pulling one out to examine it.

"She'll get her back up about the money you've put into it. Make no mistake about that." The elder Cadence pointed a gnarled finger at him.

"You mean the money *we* put into it, don't you?" He bit the inside of his cheek as he winked at her.

"I told her I was helping her out. I didn't tell her exactly how I'd planned to do so."

"Hey, where do you want these to-go cups?" Wallace held up a bulky box.

"I want you to set it down. You aren't supposed to be doing any of the heavy lifting, remember?"

"The damned thing can't weigh more than a few pounds. My new grandson weighs less than this box."

"Hands off, mister. Cady will have my hide if she knows you're overexerting yourself on her behalf. You can help Auntie fill the napkin dispensers."

"Yippee skippy! Who died and made you boss?" Wallace grumbled, but set the box on the floor and shuffled over to the counter to help his aunt-by-marriage.

"Here, sweetheart, you want to do something manly you can help me figure out how to put together this piece of sh—crap."

May put her hands on her hips and gave the toy kitchen set a little kick.

"No offense, my love, but putting things together has never been your strong suit." He chuckled, patting Auntie on the arm before heading over to remove the screwdriver from his frustrated wife's clenched fist.

Burke smiled. Good. The man had something to occupy him that wouldn't tax him physically but still made him feel that he was contributing.

The place was coming together quickly. They'd had to work fast to make sure they were done before Logan's closed their doors. Cady was busy getting her apartment packed up, as well as the bakery, so that kept her focus away from what the rest of them had been doing. Everyone took turns helping out Burke when they could get away from their other jobs.

Not that Cady would have noticed what Burke, in particular, had been up to. She'd made it a point to avoid him ever since she'd gotten the news about the bakery closing—news that he'd had to hear from everyone else but her. Stubborn woman had put on the blinders, assuming she had no choice but to move to New York now. There was always more than one choice.

Leasing this space and outfitting it to meet Cady's business needs didn't come without some sacrifices on his part, as well. He had the money and the means to pull strings—if he used his father's connections. It meant letting Cady's family and friends in on his secret.

No longer was he just plain old Burke Sanders. Now they understood that he was the heir to a hotel dynasty. Or he had been. Either way, Burke was pleased to learn that no one treated him any differently from when they had known him as the wannabe writer from the city.

Fortunately, throwing his name around did not have to involve interaction with his father. His name alone opened doors that made it possible to get paperwork pushed through quickly. It helped get furniture delivered faster. It ensured carpenters, plumbers, and any other workers hired would put in long hours, in exchange for a sizeable bonus once the work was complete.

He'd been willing to do it all himself, with the help of local contractors. It shouldn't have come as any surprise that Cady's friends and family would drop everything to lend a hand. She did so much for everyone else. For once, they had a way to return the favor.

Bree was right, no doubt, that Cady would be upset at first. After all, he'd been the one to encourage her to follow through with her dream and move to the city when she'd wanted to give up and stay in Scallop Shores. He knew in his heart that she'd be happier staying, but if she felt she was giving up her independence or in any way settling—

He chewed on his lower lip as he worried that one over in his brain.

The idea was that she'd take one look at her new coffee shop and fall head over heels in love. Then it wouldn't matter where it was actually located. It was hers, her baby, her dream come to life.

Short of breaking into the bakery and stealing her old espresso machine, he couldn't think of a way to get it in place before they opened. The whole thing needed to be a surprise. In the end, he hoped she'd be just as excited to use the brand-new, state-of-the-art machine he'd bought for her.

"Feeney's complaining that they let the Breakfast Blend run out the day before closing." Chase hobbled into the coffee shop-to-be, holding the door open as he awkwardly hauled his crutches in behind him.

"Here, take a load off. You tell him about the plan?" Burke signed for another delivery and gestured for the UPS guy to unload the boxes in the corner before he carried a chair over for Chase.

"Yeah, we're all set for tomorrow morning. Cady's gonna be ripshit." Receiving a pointed stare from his mother, Chase offered her a reproachful grin. "Fine. She's gonna be pissed. What? I cleaned it up … some."

A loud thumping on the door sent Burke's heart lurching into his throat. Everyone froze, turning with matching guilty faces. Shoulders slumping in relief, he sent up a silent "thank you" when he saw that it was Cady's friend, Shannon. She held a large cardboard box and appeared to have kicked at the door to get their attention. He hurried to let her in.

"Oh my gosh, you guys. This place looks amazing! Cady is going to be so excited." Shannon set the big box down on the newly installed counter and gave Burke a big hug.

"Hey, thanks so much for helping us out like this. I know it's an awful lot to ask you to spend so much time in a hot kitchen, what with the weather being so miserable lately."

"Oh, don't be silly. I love to bake. I don't get to do it enough when school's in session."

"Thanks, too, for keeping an eye on Bandit for me. Between getting this coffee shop ready to open and moving into the new house, I feel like I've hardly seen the poor mutt." Bree had really come through for him when he'd worried about what to do with the dog while they were getting this place prepped. She knew Shannon's triplets had been begging for a dog for some time now. A total win-win situation.

"Well, the kids are thrilled to spend time with him. It was so nice of you to give us this chance to see if we're cut out for having a dog of our own."

"I know I'm not exactly an expert on dog ownership, but I really can't recommend it enough." Burke peeked into the box on the counter and briefly considered swiping a cookie.

"Go ahead. There's an extra batch of snickerdoodles in there for you."

"Really? But you've already done so much."

"Consider it an apology." Shannon grimaced.

"Do I dare ask?"

"How do you feel about Bandit receiving a little makeover?"

"My previous question bears repeating."

"This morning I discovered that Brenna had painted the poor dog's nails a bright red. Scared the heck out of me. I thought he was bleeding at first. She was so proud, I didn't have the heart to get angry."

Laughter bubbled up from his chest and he slapped his palms on his thighs. He couldn't wait to see his new-and-improved furry companion. Maybe he could even talk Brenna and her brothers into giving Bandit a bath. He'd have to broach that one when he picked him up later.

"Okay, let it not be said that this slave driver didn't offer his workers refreshments. Snickerdoodles for everyone!"

Shannon nudged him aside and drew out the cookies and ripped the lid off with a flourish. A cheer went up through the coffee shop.

"I made a pitcher of iced tea earlier. I'll get it out of the fridge." Bree headed behind the counter.

Tomorrow was the day of reckoning. They were unveiling the store to the entire town. It had been easier than he'd thought to get the word out without alerting Cady. His new buddy, Mr. Feeney, had insisted on taking point on that part. Turns out the old gossip had a sneaky side too. And he was having way too much fun with his role.

Burke wouldn't get any sleep tonight. He had half a mind to spend the night at the coffee shop. Rubbing the knot at the back of his neck, he looked around at everyone who had helped make this happen. He couldn't have done it without them.

At first, Scallop Shores was just a place to hang his hat while he wrote his Great American Novel. His dream had been to write—for himself, not on assignment. Somewhere along the line, his dream had morphed into something fuller, better than he could have ever imagined. He'd become a part of something, and it felt so good to belong. But without Cady, it was a mere shadow of what it could be. It was a dream in black and white. Cady—she was color, rich and vibrant. She was his everything.

•••

This was it. The last day of business for Logan's Bakery. Cady had spent a fitful night on the futon in what used to be her old bedroom. Giving up at about four a.m., she searched the kitchen cupboards as quietly as possible, not wanting to disturb her parents' sleep. Her mother had enough ingredients for a batch or two of muffins. Slipping out into the cool morning, and switching on the old flashlight she'd dug out of the utility drawer, Cady headed for the tree line on the edge of the property.

It was a little late in the season, but she knew of a spot where the blueberries hadn't been picked bare. Carrying a bucket and forgoing her shoes, she trudged on. Goosebumps rose on her arms as the wet grass chilled her bare feet. She welcomed the discomfort. Ever since Mr. Logan had told her he was closing the bakery, she'd felt as though she were slowly losing all sense of feeling.

She'd been such a coward, hiding from Burke these last couple of weeks. It wasn't his fault things hadn't worked out. And they could have spent what little time they had left together. What was that saying? It was better to have loved and lost than never to have loved at all. Bullshit. It would have been far better if she had hung onto her heart. Leaving her family was hard enough. Leaving Burke was like leaving a necessary body part behind. She needed him in order to live.

Only now she was too late. She'd pushed him away because it was going to be too hard to say goodbye. She just hadn't realized how far she'd pushed until the night before, when she'd swallowed her pride and went to see him at his rental cottage.

The driveway was empty, but she got out and knocked on the door anyway. When there was no answer, she peered in the window. One bare bulb in the hallway was on, illuminating a cottage stripped of any sign of habitation. Burke's personal items were all gone. The couch and chair had been draped in white sheets. He'd moved into his new house. She'd laughed out loud then, a sharp bark of a laugh that was directed more at herself than at the situation. Until that moment she had completely forgotten—she had no idea where his new house was.

She could have called him then. Her fingers itched to grab her cell phone and dial his number. But he'd actually made things easier on her. It was for the best. A clean break.

The light was on in the dining room when Cady returned from her hunt for fresh blueberries. Damn it. She'd woken someone up after all. Swiping at the last of the tears she'd allowed herself, she hung her head as she pulled open the sliding glass door, ready to make her apologies.

"Need I remind you of the critters that like to roam around at this hour, young lady? They think they're safe and if you startle them you'll only have yourself to blame." May frowned down at her daughter's muddy feet. "And barefoot, to boot. You're lucky that a porcupine didn't shoot you full of quills."

"Wouldn't be the worst thing to happen to me today." Cady shrugged. She was going to miss her mother's well-meaning lectures.

"Oh, sweetheart. It's going to be rough, but you'll make it through stronger than ever. Sit down and let me make you some eggs. You'll need your strength today."

Cady dutifully ate the meal put in front of her. She baked two dozen blueberry muffins and took a long, indulgent shower. Packing up the muffins, she gave each parent a kiss and a big hug.

Odd that her father couldn't seem to wipe the foolish grin off his face. The poor man. It was probably all that was preventing him from crying like a baby.

"I'm going to swing by the truck rental place on my way home. I'll see you about three o'clock?" Her things were boxed and sitting on the deck, ready to be packed into the rental truck for her journey to New York. She started her day in Scallop Shores, but she'd be ending it in New York.

"Certainly, dear."

"We'll be here." Again with the smile that was wholly inappropriate, given what she was going through today.

She reached the bakery with about half an hour to spare. Though it didn't need it, she wiped down the glass display case until it shone. She'd let the coffee supply dwindle, and oh, how Old Man Feeney howled when his precious Breakfast Blend had run out three days ago. God, she was going to miss the old coot!

A pot of decaf sat on one burner, while a pot of Sumatran, the only full-on caffeine flavor she had left, sat on the other. Cady ran her fingertips over her little-used espresso machine. She couldn't help but wonder if she'd been able to draw in more of a crowd with her *frou-frou* drinks, perhaps Mr. Logan would have thought twice about closing the bakery.

Cady blinked herself out of her woolgathering. Looking up at the clock above the door, she gasped at the time! Seven fifteen a.m.! She'd never opened late—not in the entire time she'd worked at Logan's. Feeney and the others should have been banging the door down by now. Tripping over her own feet to get to the front door, she yanked it open, sticking her head out and looking this way and that.

No one. Old Man Feeney wasn't there. Burt and Toby, Earl Duffy, and the retired fishermen and school bus drivers that made up her regular morning crowd. None of them. Surely they knew she was open one more day? They had discussed it yesterday. She was sure of it.

Stepping back inside, Cady slowly made her way behind the counter. With a heavy sigh, she turned off the coffee burners. If the bulk of her business, the regulars she could always count on, weren't going to show up, it was pointless to wait around for any stragglers. She wouldn't be serving any coffee today. Apparently they were closing a day early. Let Mr. Logan fire her for that!

She could get the rental truck early. Only they weren't open yet. Not many places were open this early, even in the summer. Her feet pushed her forward, out the door and down the street. She didn't know where she was headed, and she didn't particularly care.

Turning the corner, Cady tried to smile over the profusion of flowers everywhere. The window boxes in front of Tiny Tots held, appropriately enough, baby's breath. Whiskey barrels set up at regular intervals overflowed with bright red petunias and sharply contrasting yellow marigolds. The Book Nook was going with a pink-on-pink theme. It was so cheerful it hurt her eyes.

Lungs burning with unshed tears, she was about ready to turn and run for the safety of her old pickup truck when Cady spotted the balloons. Someone had leased the old restaurant. Curiosity pulled her forward. It was a regular beehive of activity. When had this happened? Had she been so focused on packing and closing down Logan's that she'd been blind to what amounted to a fairly big deal in a town as small as Scallop Shores?

A bell tinkled above the door as she stepped inside. Bistro tables filled the center of the space. Some tall, some regular height, all occupied with chatting customers. To the left were cozy armchairs, little tables perched beside them to set drinks down. To her right was the most adorable play area, bins full of puzzles, Legos, and toys. And in the corner a fancy toy kitchen. The entire area had been sectioned off with a low wall made of a thick, clear plastic.

It was high enough to keep kids safe, but low enough for parents to be able to see inside. It was just like the idea she'd had for her coffee shop—only better. There was even a gorgeous fireplace in the back corner.

The loud chuff of milk steaming in an espresso maker had Cady locking her jaw and turning toward the back wall, where a long, gleaming counter was installed. Someone had stolen her idea! But she'd only told Burke. It was her dream. She didn't understand. Nostrils flaring, she stormed toward whoever was working that machine.

"You're late."

Stumbling to a halt, Cady registered the occupants of the counter stools. Here was her morning crowd. *Her* regulars. This crook had stolen her customers too!

"I opened for you. You weren't there. We had one more day." She shut her mouth before she started blubbering in front of these men who had known her since she was a baby.

"Nah, we've got all the time in the world. But you're still late." Old Man Feeney nodded at Cady, as though gesturing for her to get behind the counter.

Was he nuts? This wasn't her place.

"Hey, there you are! We're swamped. I was just about to send Feeney to get you."

Burke appeared at her side, slipping a pink apron over her head and spinning her around so he could tie it behind her. She barely had time to register the fact that he wore a matching one before she was shoved behind the counter.

"How did you—" She pointed at the espresso machine that looked even more impressive than hers.

"Learn to make coffee drinks? Sophie and I have been studying the instruction manual and all the YouTube videos we could find. But this is your territory. Get in there, sister!"

She wanted to stamp her foot like a child. She wanted to fold her arms across her chest until he acknowledged her. But Burke had disappeared into the crowd and she lost sight of him. A line of customers reached clear to the door. Each one of them made it a point to congratulate her on *her* new business. Did they not realize this wasn't hers? Burke had stolen her idea.

"We're running a little low on pastries. Should I call Shannon and see if she has more?"

"Foster?" Amanda's brother looked ridiculous, outfitted in another pink apron.

He stood at her elbow, awaiting orders. This was the craziest day she'd ever experienced.

"Go to Logan's. You'll find the door unlocked. Oh, God, the door's unlocked." Cady's giggle turned into a snort and she had to rein it in before she totally lost it.

"I brought in some fresh muffins this morning. There are bagels and bread for toasting. Just bring it all."

"I'll come with you, Foster."

"Bree?" Could this day get any more bizarre?

"Hey, sweetie. I'm snagging any milk and creamer you've got left over there, okay?"

"Raid it all. Logan's is done."

She'd spotted Burke here and there, but had never been able to catch him before he disappeared again. The rat! Customers kept her busy until they were able to flip the closed sign at two o'clock. Cady hadn't been this tired in a long time.

Untying the apron and tossing it on the nearest table, she slapped her hands on her hips and glared at the man exiting the back storage room.

"You! I want an explanation and I want it now!" Her chest rose and fell as she pointed a finger at the man she'd thought she was in love with.

"And you'll get it. But let the others go free. They were only acting under my orders." Burke nodded at Foster, Bree, and Sophie, waving them toward the door, and their supposed safety.

Fine. She'd deal with their betrayal later.

...

"I don't understand."

She slumped into a chair, absently wrapping her hand around an artisan-crafted mug. It was a blue glazed stone earthenware. Beautiful. Just what she would have chosen for her own coffee shop.

"You didn't want this. You wanted to write. *That* was your dream."

"And it still is. Nothing has changed for me, Cady."

"Nothing except stealing *my* dream and making it your own!" She didn't care if the rest of the town could hear her shouting.

"Listen to yourself. Why would I want to steal your dream? I'm a writer. What the hell do I know about coffee? This is your passion, not mine."

"Then why did you open this coffee shop? Why did you steal my customers?"

"I didn't steal them. They're yours. They are loyal to you. It was actually Mr. Feeney's idea to deliberately open on Logan's Bakery's last day. One last 'screw you, Logan!' were his exact words, I believe."

"But I'm leaving. I was planning on packing up the truck and being on the road in a couple of hours."

"I know. And I was hoping we ... I could change your mind. This place is yours. Well, technically I'm a silent partner, but the money that paid for the lease and all the work, supplies and furniture was yours."

"What are you talking about? I don't have that kind of money." Even as the words slipped past her lips, Cady was recalling a conversation she'd had with Auntie. A conversation that had taken place not too far from this new coffee shop.

Sometime, shortly after she'd arrived at the shop and been corralled into work, Cady had spotted her parents come in with Auntie. The foolish smile was still on her father's face, and this time it started to make sense. Chase, Amanda, and the baby managed a visit closer to lunch time.

Standing up, she began to wander the store's interior. The stonework on the fireplace was incredible. It was rigged for gas and operated by the flip of a switch. It would be pleasantly cozy in the winter months. The stools at the counter had backs and thicker cushions. Just like she'd wanted for her older customers. He'd done it. He had listened to everything she'd ticked off on her wish list and fulfilled them all.

"How on earth did you manage to get all this done so quickly?" The look on Burke's face was contrite.

"I may have used a little familial influence." He buffed the counter with an elbow, scrubbing at it with a corner of his apron while studiously avoiding her eyes.

"You'd have had to let my family and the folks in town know who you are."

"I did. And I also let them know that this was a one-time deal. After this, Sanders is just a surname. You know I wouldn't have used my father's connections for just any reason. It had to be special, worth the trouble."

"Was it? Worth the trouble?"

"That's something only you can decide." He eyed her from the counter, watching as she made her way slowly around the coffee shop, stopping to run a hand over the butter-soft leather of the armchairs.

"This was supposed to be my dream, something that I made happen. Something that I worked my ass off for."

"You did make this happen. This, all of this"—he threw his arms wide—"came out of your dreams. None of this would be here if it weren't for you and all the hard work you put into planning it."

"But it wasn't supposed to be *here*." She pressed her lips together, turning to face him from the opposite end of the shop.

"Baby, you really want to get technical, *I'm* not supposed to be here. If it weren't for you having encouraged me to follow my own dreams, I'd probably be packing up my own things and heading out to start my tediously boring new life as CEO of Sanders Resorts."

"But you fell in love with Scallop Shores." The smile on her lips was tremulous.

"I fell in love with you. Scallop Shores and all the crazy, loveable people that come with it were all a package deal.

"When I hoped we could convince you to stay if we opened up your coffee shop here, I swear to God there wasn't a single person who didn't come ask me how they could help. Do you even know how much you're loved here?"

Dammit, that did it. Fat tears rolled down her cheeks. Cady liked to think that she was so much different than everyone else in town. She didn't need them. She needed adventure, new places to see, new people to meet. But she was so wrong. Everything she could possibly want, everyone she loved, was right here in Scallop Shores.

"The morning after the storm, before Mr. Logan came in, I couldn't wait to tell you that I'd decided to stay. I thought I was going to have to fight to get you to understand that my heart was here. That I couldn't leave.

"Then he told me the bakery was closing. I thought I didn't have a choice. It was killing me to have to say goodbye."

"You always had a choice. But you were panicking and I get that."

Closing the distance, she ran into his arms, sobbing. He held her tightly against his hard chest rocking her until she could breathe again without sniveling. Reaching across the counter for a napkin from a nearby dispenser, she blew her nose and took a few calming breaths before kissing Burke lingeringly on the mouth.

"I love you. I didn't want to leave you. I want to stay here. I ... Wait, I have no place to stay!"

Burke laughed at that.

"You're staying with me, silly. Bandit misses you."

"And that's another thing. I have no idea where you even live now." Cady pushed against his chest, finally getting a good look at the words embroidered on the apron.

"Oh." She breathed.

Cady's Dream. He'd named the coffee shop Cady's Dream.

Burke looked down at the apron, then back at her.

"We can always change it. But we needed something."

"It's perfect. You came up with it?"

"Nope. The name is all Mr. Feeney's idea."

"God, I love that man!"

"Should I worry?"

"Nope. Love you more."

"And don't forget, we can always visit New York any time you want ... if you'll let us stay in *your* apartment." Burke gave her a wink before swooping in to claim her lips in a scorching kiss.

About the Author

Jennifer DeCuir is a busy writer mom, raising two kids and a husband. She mutters to herself, drinks way too much coffee, and can't help whining about all the rain in Western Washington. But her family loves her anyway.

She'd love to hear from you. Her favorite haunts are her website: *www.jenniferdecuir.com*, Facebook: *www.facebook.com/JenniferDeCuirauthor* and Twitter: @JenniferDeCuir.

More from This Author
(From *Wynter's Journey* by Jennifer DeCuir)

She was in Hell—and it had well and truly frozen over. Already exhausted from her cross-country flight, Wynter slumped from the weight of her misery as she stared at the two-story farmhouse. White clapboard and white wraparound front porch with tall white columns acted as sentries guarding the gates of Hell. And all of it blending in quite hideously with the snow that blanketed every blessed surface of the postage-stamp sized dot on the map that was Braeden, VT.

The only color breaking up the monotonous white was the bright stain of red that served as the front door. Under other circumstances, it might have been considered cheerful, bright even. But Wynter was tired and more than a little nervous. In her current state, all she could think of was blood. She shivered, thinking to herself that she should not have come.

A cough alerted her to the cab driver, waiting to be paid. Wynter closed her eyes, her trembling fingers reaching for the small fold of bills in her coat pocket—the last of her money. By stiffing the man his tip, she could keep the last precious twenty-dollar bill. Quickly, she handed the entire amount across the front seat to the driver, unable to meet his eyes for that uncharitable thought.

Cold air sucked away what little warmth the old car's heater had generated when the driver opened his door. He whistled an off-key tune, pulling her meager possessions from the trunk before he came back into view, setting her bags beside the neatly plowed walkway. He disappeared again, slammed the trunk closed and came around to help her exit the vehicle.

"Careful, it's slipperier than it looks." The older man gripped her gloved hands, steadying her when her travel weary knees and top-heavy frame made her pinwheel first toward the snowbank on her left and then toward the one on her right.

"You sure you ought to be travelin' by yourself at this point?" He looked down at her very round belly.

"Got the all-clear from the doctor just yesterday." Wynter smiled brightly through the bald-faced lie.

The airline had tried to give her a hard time. However, they didn't have an actual rule that she couldn't fly at 36 weeks. When Wynter had pointed out that it was a one-way flight and she promised to check in with her OB (another lie, as she didn't have a doctor lined up in Vermont), they let her on her flight.

"Well, good luck then. You go on in and sit down. Tell them to fix you up something warm to drink." He tipped his hat, sparing a final glance at her protruding middle and got back into the cab.

He'd driven away before Wynter could remember to ask if he'd carry her bags up to the front door. Gritting her teeth and cursing her own brash decision-making, she slung her duffel bag over her shoulder and picked the other two up by their handles. The driveway wasn't long, but in her current condition, she was panting by the time she reached the covered porch.

Now came the hard part. Sam wasn't expecting her. More to the point, he'd been avoiding her for the last twelve years. She knew the reception she'd get wouldn't be a welcome one. But that was okay. She had her trump card—a promise Sam had made years ago. Her baby's future depended on him honoring that promise. Her means of escape having driven away, Wynter took a deep breath and knocked at the big red door.

She shuffled her feet, wishing she'd had enough money to purchase a thick pair of winter boots for her impromptu cross-country adventure. Okay, to be fair, there really hadn't been much time. One minute she held a one-way ticket to Florida, purchased by her parents, the next she had changed her destination, and hopefully, the overall direction of her life.

At one time, too long ago for her taste, Sam had been her rock, one of her closest friends and someone she could go to in a moment of crisis. Now Wynter was newly widowed, about to raise a baby on her own. She could no longer afford the apartment she had shared with her husband in California. And, at thirty years old, she was forced to consider moving back in with her parents—an option she'd desperately like to avoid. If ever there was a moment of crisis, this was it.

Why wasn't Sam answering the door? Wynter's eyes flew to the curtain-covered window beside the door, looking for movement. Did he know who was out there? Had he seen the ugly green and orange cab pull up and dump out the last person on Earth that he expected to see? Was he hiding on the other side of the door, willing her to turn around and walk the five miles or so to town?

Well, it wasn't going to happen. Wynter swallowed hard, past the lump forming in her throat. Her Sam wouldn't leave her out on his doorstep to freeze. His mom had raised him right. Even if he didn't want her there, he'd invite her in to warm up and rest. She rubbed her arms and stamped her sneakered feet. He wasn't here. She hadn't even considered that option.

A little bit wildly now, she paid closer attention to her surroundings. The next house over was barely visible through the spindly winter-bare trees on the other side of the road. Sam's covered porch offered little in the way of protection from the wind. Fear clawing at her throat, Wynter eyed the glass windows and pondered how she might break in. But any rocks were buried beneath at least a foot of snow, and the only furniture on the porch was a swing, attached to the shingled roof with thick chains.

She crumpled onto the swing, defeat sapping the rest of her strength. Making herself as small as possible, she huddled against the cold wood, tears stinging the backs of her eyelids. Her idea had been to ask Sam for a place to stay, temporarily. She knew, through his sister, that he lived alone. She'd intended to look for a job, something she could walk to until she saved up enough for a beater car. Choking on a sob, Wynter realized the futility of her hastily made plans.

She hadn't counted on Sam living in the boonies. She wasn't sure where the actual town was, or if there was even the possibility of a job. Wynter was so desperate to stay independent, to keep her domineering parents from taking over her life and the raising of her child that she'd run to the one person she could think of.

"Where are you, Sam? I need you." And the tears that had threatened from the moment the cab started to creep deeper and deeper into no-man's land finally caught up with her.

Hunching into her thick parka and pulling her knees up as best she could, Wynter tucked herself into the swing and gave in to the hopelessness that she could no longer hold at bay. Wrapping her arms protectively around the life that grew inside her, she started to cry.

• • •

He heard her long before he saw her. The biting wind carried the great, wrenching sobs over the tall snowbanks and across the road. Sam had been shoveling out the driveway for Riley, his only neighbor, so the woman's cries had to be coming from his place. Quickening his pace, his eyes narrowed, searching. Was this person hurt? How had she gotten there? He didn't think to ask himself who it might be. It didn't matter. She was upset. She needed help.

Tossing the shovel in the general direction of his mailbox, Sam hurried up the driveway, casting a glance this way and that. He spotted the woman on his porch swing, curled up against the cold. Her face was hidden; he couldn't tell her age. It was then he noticed the pile of luggage at her feet. Okay, now he'd ask: who on Earth was she? He certainly wasn't expecting any guests.

He stepped closer and leaned down. He was about to speak when a lock of hair, bold, fiery red, slipped from beneath her knit cap. His heart clutched and the comforting smile on his face slid away as she lifted her tear-soaked face, her lower lip trembling. Dear God, no. Please, anyone but her.

"Wynter," he managed to croak out.

"Sam. Oh, my God, I'm sorry you found me like this." She shook her head back and forth, cringing. "I'm sorry I just showed up like this."

"How did you find me?" He spun on his heel and lifted his face to the bracing Vermont morning.

It didn't matter. It was the twenty-first century. Anyone with a working knowledge of technology could locate just about anyone on the planet. If she really wanted to find him, she would have eventually. He just hadn't expected her to try.

"Pauline. Please don't be mad at her, Sam. Blame me. I ... I need you."

He thanked God he wasn't facing her when she'd uttered that. He closed his eyes, emotions boiling to the surface. Guilt pulled at his gut. He'd left her. He hadn't expected to ever see her again. And damned if it didn't feel good to see her again. A long time ago he'd have given anything to hear those words. Now they scored fresh abrasions on an already battered heart.

"Where's Holt?" He spat out the name of his one-time best friend.

"He's dead, Sam. That's mostly why I'm here."

Well, that cleared up why she was crying her heart out. Sam straightened his spine, grief squeezing his heart in a tight fist, so that even drawing a breath was difficult. Wynter had found him. There was nothing he could do now but invite her in. He'd figure out a polite way to get rid of her later.

"Come on, it's cold out here. Let's get inside before you lose your toes to frostbite."

He turned his back quickly. If Wynter was looking for a cozy chat over coffee, catching up on ten plus years of life's milestones, she would be sorely disappointed.

Sam snatched up the suitcases and muscled his way through the front door. Dropping her bags in the corner and trusting she'd follow, he ducked into the kitchen on the left. He took down a couple of mugs.

"You still take cream and sugar in your coffee?" He dug in the silverware drawer for spoons.

"Yes, thank you." Her voice was soft, throaty, and still had the power to kick him in the gut.

"I've got some Oreos around if you're hungry. I wasn't expecting company." He paused to let that sink in. Hey, if she was going to make him uncomfortable with just her presence, then he needed some way of leveling the playing field.

"Double Stuffed?" Okay. She wasn't going to let him get under her skin so easily.

Sam finally turned around, a plastic bottle of coffee creamer in his hand. She'd removed her coat, hat, and gloves. Her hair was short now, sticking up in crazy orange tufts. Lucille Ball's ragamuffin cousin. Gray eyes, the color of the storm clouds outside, were red-rimmed and swollen.

"Holy Mary, Mother-of-God! You're pregnant." His eyes had reached her distended belly. How the hell had he missed that? He unsteadily set the creamer on the counter.

Wynter wrapped her arms around her big stomach, rubbing gently. "She's my whole world, Sam. She's all I have left."

Just when he thought he could get through this visit, another reminder of what he'd lost slapped him upside the head. Wynter had built a life with Holt. She was having his baby. Holt, however briefly, had enjoyed the life Sam had wanted with all his heart and soul. And Sam only had himself to blame.

Torn between wanting to take her in his arms and comfort her, and needing to push her back into a cab headed to where she'd come from, Sam shook his head and kept his distance. He'd get through this. They'd have a cup of coffee, he'd let her rest for a bit and then he'd drive her to the airport.

It started to snow. Big fat flakes drifted down from the sky, thick with low, nasty-looking clouds. Sam glared out at the steely sky and silently railed at Mother Nature with every foul expletive he could think of.

How could he have forgotten the storm? It was why he'd shoveled Riley out before he'd even had a cup of coffee. It was a break in the weather, and he hadn't known just how much time he had before they got dumped on again. Of all the miserable, rotten luck!

"Oh, look, it's snowing," crooned Wynter. "It's so beautiful." Her statement was punctuated with a huge grin.

At least she wasn't crying anymore. Sam plowed a hand through his hair and sighed.

"Snow's a four letter word around here. It was great, the first time or two, back in November. But it's only January and you know we've got at least two more months of this crap." He gestured toward the dining room, off the kitchen, pulling out a chair for Wynter when she paused in the doorway to look around.

"Well, if you've lived in Southern California at Christmastime, like I have, you learn to appreciate the white stuff."

Yeah, back to the chatty, catching-up thing. Sam didn't want chatty. He didn't want catching up. He wanted his privacy back. He forgot his manners.

"Listen, Wynnie." He knew the nickname irked her. "I'm not sure what dragged you all the way out here from sunny SoCal, but you can't stay here. As soon as the roads are passable, I'll take you back to the airport."

"No, you can't!" Her eyes widened and she closed the distance between them to grip his hands, her fingers ice cold. "You were my last hope, Sam." She stood up taller, closer, her belly brushing against him. After all this time, he still wanted to pull her to him, and it took all his willpower not to recoil from her touch.

"What do you want from me, Wynter? Can't you see how hard it is to see you again? Why are you doing this to me?" He couldn't look away from her charcoal eyes, welling up with tears.

"You promised me, Sam. You promised." The last word was nearly unintelligible as the tears spilled out and down her cheeks.

The desperation in her terrified stare, the desolation in her voice. Coming here had not been an easy decision for her. Suddenly it came rushing back to him, memories from a time he'd locked away. Sitting on the window bench together in Wynter's bedroom, the window he'd climbed through many times. Holding her hands much like she was holding his now. He'd promised her that if she ever needed him, no matter what, he'd be there for her. She'd come to collect on that promise.

Also by Jennifer DeCuir:

Five of Hearts

Praise for Five of Hearts:

". . . a light romance with enough tension to entertain readers."—Anna *Fitzgerald, InD Tale Magazine*

Drawn to Jonah

Praise for Drawn to Jonah:

"The characters in DeCuir's book have drawn me in, enveloped me in a hug, served me something warm and gooey to eat, and invited me to be part of their family. Heartwarming, sexy, and a dash of magical realism makes this book a must buy."—Brooke Moss, author of *Baby Bump*

"Jennifer DeCuir's writing is as warm and cozy as snuggling up to a crackling fire on a cold winter's day!"—Laura Marie Altom, author of *The SEAL's Christmas Twins*

"This book was absolutely amazing . . . I loved the ending and I highly recommend this book to anyone who wants to read about love, taking chances and family."—Night Owl Romance

In the mood for more Crimson Romance?
Check out *Love's Replay* by Synithia Williams at
CrimsonRomance.com.